ECHOES
OF MEMORY

Books by Sara Driscoll

FBI K-9s

Lone Wolf

Before It's Too Late

Storm Rising

No Man's Land

Leave No Trace

Under Pressure

Still Waters

That Others May Live

NYPD Negotiators

Exit Strategy

Shot Caller

Lockdown

Standalones

Echoes of Memory

ECHOES
OF MEMORY

Sara Driscoll

KENSINGTON
PUBLISHING CORP.

www.kensingtonbooks.com

KENSINGTON BOOKS are published by

Kensington Publishing Corp.
900 Third Avenue
New York, NY 10022

All Kensington titles, imprints and distributed lines are available at special quantity discounts for bulk purchases for sales promotion, premiums, fund-raising, educational or institutional use.

Special book excerpts or customized printings can also be created to fit specific needs. For details, write or phone the office of the Kensington Special Sales Manager, Kensington Publishing Corp., 900 Third Avenue, New York, NY, 10022. Attn. Special Sales Department. Phone: 1-800-221-2647.

Library of Congress Card Catalogue Number: 2024934883

The K with book logo Reg. U.S. Pat. & TM. Off.

ISBN: 978-1-4967-4870-6

First Kensington Hardcover Edition: August 2024

ISBN: 978-1-4967-4871-3 (ebook)

10 9 8 7 6 5 4 3 2 1

Printed in the United States of America

ECHOES
OF MEMORY

CHAPTER 1

L ife can change in the blink of an eye.
For Quinn Fleming, the attack took not only months
of her life as she recovered, but also her memories. Those
from the time of the assault, but also her ability to form
and retain new memories. New snapshots of a life well
lived, of family and friends. Of a lover and a career, of
goals and plans.

All gone. Leaving only a terrifying blankness.

Taking the words of Robert Frost to heart—*the only
way out is through*—Quinn learned to put one foot in
front of the other, finding ways to compensate and falling
back on skills retained from before the day the life she
knew ended. Because to surrender to the darkness was
more terrifying than trying to force her way through it.

Quinn checked the wall clock, a large wooden panel
overlaid with a watercolor vase of garishly bright flowers.
Her boss, Jacinta, had bought the clock when she opened
her florist shop, Gaslamp Blooms, saying she liked the rus-
tic charm of the whitewashed boards, the simple flowers,
and the swirl detail on the wrought-iron hands.

Quinn frowned as she studied the timepiece. Not because of the time—though it was getting late . . . again—
but because of the arrangement of daisies, tulips, petunias,

and pansies. The perfection of the design set her teeth on edge. Too symmetrical, too pastel, too predictable.

Boring.

She had considerable artistic skills herself—pastels and colored pencils being her media of choice—but liked to dabble occasionally in oil paints, and knew she would have captured a more vibrant and lifelike scene.

Where was the panache of nature and the lack of man-made symmetry to complement the colors and textures? The silk of petals against the slick sheen of greenery? The surprising pop of color hiding among quieter tones? Not to mention no painting could ever convey the complex perfume of the blooms.

Closing her eyes, she drew in a slow breath through her nose, her lips curving with pleasure at the combined scents. Opening her eyes, she looked down at the hand-tied bridal bouquet cradled in her hands. Anchored by the gorgeous silvery-lavender blush of amnesia roses, offset by bright bursts of lilac freesia and spikes of lavender, threaded through with clusters of white spray roses and branches of willow eucalyptus, and cradled in the wide, waxy leaves of Italian Ruscus, the bouquet had the kind of life and beauty that hadn't been accurately captured behind plodding clock hands.

Unable to help what was now an ingrained habit of self-defense, she glanced down again, scanning the floral order, laid out in precise detail, and then at the open notebook beside it, its pages sprawled open, marked by a narrow brown ribbon.

Write it all down. Check it. Then check it again.

Her mantra. When you couldn't trust yourself, you found ways to compensate.

She no longer trusted herself.

Picking up a set of clippers, she made quick work of the ragged stems, trimming them to an even, scant few inches below where the bottom of the ribbon would lie when she added it the next morning. Then Jacinta would deliver the full shipment to the church well before the morning's eleven o'clock wedding mass.

Bouquet complete, she moved to the walk-in cooler, yanking open the heavy door inset with a twelve-by-twelve-inch window to reveal the rainbow contents within. She stepped inside, cold air washing over her, raising goose-flesh on her forearms as she lowered the bouquet into the waiting vase of water. Now all the bouquet needed the next morning was a quick wrap of smoky silver satin ribbon, secured with a line of pearl straight pins, before being placed into the bride's hands.

Perfect.

A quick scan of the cold room confirmed the arrangements she'd already checked and rechecked—bouton-nieres for the groom and ushers, corsages for the mothers nestled in clear plastic containers to protect the fragile blooms, the smaller hand-tied bouquets for the brides-maids, twin altar arrangements and a dozen pew arrange-ments for the church, and another container of loose amnesia and white roses for the wedding cake.

She cast a disparaging glance in the direction of the am-nesia roses. Gorgeous, but lately they were a nagging re-minder of what she'd lost and a physical representation of her shortcomings. Still, she wouldn't allow those failings to ruin a couple's special day. She would do what was re-quired to make sure everything was perfect.

She left the cooler, firmly latching the door behind her, as if she could similarly lock those same shortcomings away.

At the counter, she couldn't refrain from a quick check of the order one more time before she slipped it into the file folder.

Another glance at the clock as it ticked past nine o'clock

told her this job had taken far too long. All her fault, but it was why she preferred to work the late shift in the shop, closing up at seven o'clock and then working until the job was finished. Jacinta didn't know how many overtime hours she'd worked since coming back. She wouldn't force her boss, who had been nothing but understanding and endlessly flexible following her release from the hospital, to pay for the work that used to come as naturally as breathing, and now was a marathon of uncertainty and triple-checking. She'd yet to make an error, but her self-confidence remained in tatters, nonetheless.

She'd never meant to stay this long. Now the light had long faded away, meaning a wait for the bus in the dark, an idea that sent a shiver of terror down her spine. She'd meant to still have the safety of the last of the day's light for the return trip but had lost track of the time.

Get it done. Then figure out your next step.

She splayed fingers over the open notebook on the counter, reviewing the list outlining everything that needed to be done to close the shop for the night—securing the small amount of cash, reviewing the receipts, making sure the live plants had been watered and the cut blooms in the cold cabinet up front had sufficient volume, taking out the trash, shutting off the lights, locking up.

All steps she knew by heart from *before*, but she wouldn't allow herself to make a mistake and didn't trust herself not to. She was well aware of how far she'd fallen, of how low her confidence ebbed. Even when she knew what to do because that knowledge was cemented in memories formed before her world turned upside down.

She closed the notebook and slipped it into a back pocket of jeans that carried the pale outline of its constant presence. Then she gathered the trash into a black garbage bag and dragged it to the rear of the shop. Jacinta had told her repeatedly to leave the garbage for her to do first thing the next morning in the light, but Quinn felt guilty leaving extra work for her. Though she appreciated her boss's care and concern for her well-being, especially when it came to working alone at night following her attack, the alley was behind a locked, barred gate and the trip there and back would only take sixty seconds at most.

She unlocked the deadbolt and stepped out into summer humidity so thick it flowed over her skin. She stood at the end of the narrow, dead-end alley that cut between the buildings on this block, with only a pair of dingy security lights to fractionally lighten the gloom. In the distance, live music from one of the clubs spilled into the streets, and laughter echoed from down the alley.

Gaslamp Blooms was located in the heart of San Diego's chic and historic Gaslamp Quarter. An eclectic mix of boutique shops, art galleries, restaurants, and clubs, the Gaslamp, as it was known locally, was a national historic site and still bore the footprint of its early builder, Alonzo Horton—Horton Plaza Park, sold to the city in the late 1800s, lay only a handful of blocks to the north, not to mention a hotel and apartment block also bearing his name. The Gaslamp was a popular hot spot, considered chic by locals and visitors alike. The district was busy during the day, but after the shops and galleries closed every evening, the area really came alive. And on a Friday or Saturday night, only more so.

The music and laughter should have lifted her spirits. Instead, it twisted her stomach and caught at her breath.

It had been a social evening, just like the one she could hear now, that had sealed her fate. She only knew what she'd been told; she had no actual memory of the incident herself. The attack had taken that from her.

Maybe that was a blessing.

Instead, she'd learned repetition could, with time, start to rebuild knowledge instead of a true memory. She'd reviewed the account in her copy of the police report—an account derived from interviews with everyone she'd had contact with that evening, as well as evidence at the scene—enough so she now had a basic understanding of the night her life had changed forever.

She'd been on her way home, not from work, but from a night out with friends a few blocks north of where she now stood. It had been a Friday night similar to this one, an evening of drinks and dancing just down the street, blowing off steam at the end of a long work week. She'd stayed out late, having sweet-talked Jacinta into giving her a rare Saturday off. There'd been no wedding on the books for that Saturday, and Jacinta had told her she'd cover the shift solo and to party for both of them—she had a date that night with her cat and the latest steamy, streaming period drama. Quinn had enjoyed dinner and then danced for hours. Yes, alcohol had been involved, but she hadn't overindulged. Maybe she was a tiny bit tipsy, but that had been the extent of it. She'd watched the time and had promptly bid her friends goodbye in time to catch the last Route 3 bus of the night just before midnight to take her home to her rented apartment on Ocean View Boulevard, south of the sprawling Mount Hope Cemetery.

That's when everything went wrong.

Already at the north end of the Gaslamp, she'd apparently decided the bus stop at Fourth Avenue and B Street was closer than the one at Fourth and G. She'd left the more populated area of downtown and headed north, leaving the restaurants and clubs behind to enter a quieter area flanked by a shuttered drugstore on one side and a darkened office building on the other. Ahead, a boarded-up hotel was being renovated, and a tarp-covered pedestrian tunnel ran the entire length of the facade, protecting those on the sidewalk from the external work going on overhead during the workday. The construction site had been deserted, but the safety feature remained.

It was unknown if the attacker surprised Quinn from inside the tunnel, or if he'd been drawn by a pretty blonde with an artistically messy updo, followed her up the deserted street, and struck once away from the prying eyes of anyone driving by. What was known was she was beaten unconscious and then robbed of her phone, her credit cards, some cash, her dead mother's sapphire ring, and the life she knew.

A bartender walking home after the end of his shift had found her body rolled into a corner of the scaffolding. He nearly hadn't seen her in the dark, walking with his eyes fixed on his phone, and would have missed her entirely if he hadn't tripped over an uneven raised lip on a section of sidewalk and madly juggled his phone in an effort not to let it smash onto the concrete. But as the light from the screen flashed around the enclosed space, it caught the rhinestone detailing on her platform stiletto sandals. He'd likely saved Quinn's life that night, calling 911 and staying with her until help arrived. She'd regained consciousness in a hospital bed the next day, alone, confused, and terrified at the blankness where the attack should have been.

She only grew more terrified when it became clear that blankness might dog her steps for the rest of her life.

Doctors told her about the amazing recuperative power of the brain—"neuroplasticity" as they called it, having the ability to literally rewire itself in response to trauma or stroke. The first six months were crucial and her recovery might be bumpy and uneven, something she could attest to—how could she remember the word "neuroplasticity" when she couldn't remember what she'd eaten for lunch that day without looking at her notebook? Now, almost three months later, she was beginning to dread that the majority of her healing and rewiring was complete, and this was going to be her life forever—an almost entirely blank page, punctuated by only the most mundane and repetitive acts, creating, essentially, a single collective memory.

A crash of dishes drew her attention to the restaurant across the alley. A plastic dairy crate jammed between the door and the frame left an eighteen-inch gap to allow hot kitchen air to escape. Considering the unusual heat of this August evening, the temperature inside must have been truly unbearable if the stagnant alley air was considered cooler. Raised voices followed the crash—one accusatory, the other full of derogatory humor—but then subsided. It wouldn't do to have the restaurant patrons think there were hot, sweaty, exhausted chefs behind the kitchen door of one of the area's swankiest restaurants. Facing out onto Fifth Avenue, the street that traversed the heart of the Gaslamp, Casa Morales was a local success story, lauded by restaurant critics and patrons alike, and was typically swarmed on a Friday evening. Quinn could picture Fifth right now: the thick foot traffic, the outdoor patios lining the sidewalk and spilling out into the outer lane, a popular holdover from the pandemic loved by restaurant owners because it let them expand their virtual floor space. But here on Fourth Avenue, it was quieter at this time of night, with almost all the foot traffic a full city block over, separated by the bulk of the packed one- and two-story buildings.

She dragged the garbage bag to the dumpster, grasped it with both hands, and heaved it over the tall lip. The thump of a door closing made her spin around in surprise to face the alley, now even darker with Casa Morales's kitchen door closed, its energetic spill of light and activity gone, leaving the alley quiet and somehow colder despite the thick heat.

She turned to head back to lock up the flower shop when a flash of movement caught her attention at the end of the alley—a lone man, dressed in dark clothes, slipping into the skinny driveway only half the width of the alley. Someone had left the narrow-barred gate open again, allowing him into the private lane. For only the briefest of moments, he was silhouetted against the backdrop of the streetlight-flooded sidewalk, giving her a fleeting view of long pants and sleeves despite the heat, either close-cropped hair or a bald head, and a tall, wiry build, before he pressed against the side of the building well inside the gate, and probably fifteen or twenty feet into the lane.

Something about his furtive movements telegraphed danger to Quinn. Or, at the very least, illicit action.

Was he coming for her?

Cold sweat prickled as her heart started to hammer, and she shrank back into the shadows, squeezing into the scant space between the bulk of the garbage and the organic waste dumpsters, suddenly feeling her isolation in the alley with a stranger blocking the only unobstructed exit to the outside world. Her heel landed in something soft and squishy, and she began to slip sideways, catching herself with a hand on the dumpster, clamping her jaw shut hard to keep from crying out in surprise. Behind her, quiet scrabbling told her she wasn't the only living creature hiding in the shadows, and a shudder ran through her at the thought of sheltering with vermin who might consider her their freshest meal ever.

Better the rats than what might be out in the alley.

Her gaze shot to the door of the flower shop, just visible from where she sheltered, dark under the security light that had stopped working more than a year ago. If she was in jeopardy, how fast could she pull out the correct key, jam it into the dimly lit lock, shoot back the latch bolt, slide inside, and shut the door behind her? If she could latch it, the door would lock automatically, but that gave entirely too much time for an attacker to block the door, or slide into the deserted shop behind her. She could only imagine what he could do to her then. Alternatively, if she ran to the restaurant, even if she pounded on the door, would her cries for help be heard over the din of the busy kitchen?

Stay out of sight.

Quinn sank deeper into the shadows, wincing as the rough, rusted steel of the garbage dumpster rasped along her bare arm below her cap sleeve, scraping the soft flesh. She slapped one hand over it, the wound burning under her grip. A putrid stench rose around her, mostly from the food rotting in the heat inside the organic waste dumpster, though she couldn't be sure it wasn't joined by the smell of decomposing rat. It made her stomach rise into her gorge, but sheer terror helped her beat it down again. If she lost control of her stomach, there would be no doubt as to her position. Saliva pooled sourly under her tongue, and she concentrated on inhaling shallow breaths through her mouth to keep the stench out of her nose.

She kept her eyes fixed on the mouth of the alley where the man nearly disappeared in the dimness, his body flat against the wall. Had she not seen him move into place, she'd have never spotted him. She might have strolled out into the dark alley to be jumped just as she had been only months before.

A whimper rose in the back of her throat, and she pressed a shaking hand to her lips to ensure no trace of sound whispered through. There was safety in the quiet darkness; she just needed to stay in it. Surely, he'd go away soon. But in the meantime, she'd be prepared just in case. She pulled her store keys out of her pocket, clutching her fingers around them tight so they could make no noise, and then rearranged them to lie in her clenched fist with two of the keys sticking out between her fingers.

A jab to the throat or eyes could do major damage. She might be terrified, but she wasn't going down without a fight. It might be a fearful and pathetic life, but it was hers.

Likely only sixty or ninety seconds had ticked by, but it already felt like she'd been hunkered in the stinking dark for fifteen minutes. And still the man remained motionless against the wall.

Slowly, realization sank in that she wasn't his target, that his attention was solely focused out onto the street, not into the alley. Then it dawned that what she initially saw as danger, might be desperation.

The thought barely had time to coalesce when a second figure appeared in the mouth of the alley, moving fast. He headed for the man sheltering inside the gate, his steps sure with single-minded purpose and aggression; there was no doubt in Quinn's mind that violence was his intent. Quinn had the briefest impression of height and bulk before the two men collided. Their struggle sent them reeling into the alley proper, around the corner toward one of the shop doors, and out of sight of the street. Nearer now, and in a direct line to her hiding place, Quinn tried to track the fight as the two men grappled in and out of the murky light, the one clearly at an advantage because of his stature.

It happened so fast Quinn could barely follow their movements, but the larger man got behind the smaller, wrapped one arm around his neck and gave it a brutal jerk. The wiry man went limp, and might have tumbled to the ground had his attacker's arm not stayed around his neck.

He hung there unmoving, and it took seconds for

Quinn's stunned brain to compute what she was actually seeing.

He's dead.

The words ricocheted around her brain as she pushed even farther into the shadows. Her back hit rough brick and her heel rammed into something solid, sending it spinning. There was a muffled metallic clang as the object hit the dumpster, and she had to clamp both hands over her mouth to keep a startled cry of fear from breaking loose.

The tall man whipped around to face the rear of the alley, the limp body dangling from his choke hold flopping awkwardly and then falling still. He was only a dark form, mostly hidden by shadows, but she could feel his eyes on her, penetrating the darkness. Seeing into her soul.

He'd just killed a man; what did he have to lose in killing the only witness to his crime?

She clamped her teeth tight to hold in the scream fighting to break free, catching the soft skin of her inner lip, and tasting a metallic tang as blood spurted onto her tongue. Her breath rasped hard and fast, and her head spun as she fought for calm.

The man took a step toward her, the lower extremities of his burden dragging behind him along the filthy alley.

The kitchen door to Casa Morales abruptly opened, the milk crate sliding back into place as light spilled into the darkness. The tableau at the end of the courtyard—one man standing tall, the other limp in his hold—was spotlit by the light cascading into the alley for a second before the living melted with the dead into the shadows.

With a grinding of brakes, a white panel van pulled up to the mouth of the alley, the side door sliding open by seemingly invisible hands. There was only a moment's hesitation—Quinn could imagine the battle going on in the man's mind, to fight or escape—before a dark form ran into the light at the end of the alley, a mass over his shoulder. He jumped into the van's cargo hold, dropping his bundle carelessly. For a moment, he paused in the open doorway, staring into the darkness at the end of the alley.

Looking for her.

His head whipped sideways as if someone spoke to him, and then he grabbed the door and slammed it shut. The van took off down F Street, quickly, but not so fast as to attract attention.

Then Quinn was alone in the alley, her heart pounding so loudly in her ears it blocked out all other sound.

CHAPTER 2

Quinn hunched in the shadows for long seconds, one hand still plastered over her mouth, paralyzed with fear. Her breath jerking in her chest, she stared at the now empty laneway, jarred by the cheerful music drifting overhead from one of the clubs when her world had just been turned on its axis. Dare she leave and risk being caught in the open, the only moving creature in the deserted alley? Should she make a break for the shop doorway and get inside, so they'd never know who'd been outside to witness that horror?

Logic finally pushed through the fog of terror on a single insistent note. Move. *Now.* Before anyone changed their mind and they circled back to clear up the inconvenience of a pesky witness. If she was gone, they'd never know if someone had truly been there, or if only the scurrying rats had witnessed their crime. Or if they found traces of a human, they'd never know from which shop they'd come.

Bracing her free hand against the filthy wall, Quinn pushed off hard and fast, slipping out from between the dumpsters and sprinting for the back door of the flower shop. She took extra seconds to stay near the wall, in the murkier shadows, rather than taking the shorter route straight across the alley, just in case. Reaching the door, she raised her shaking hand, the keys still protruding from between her fingers as she aimed for the lock. Her hands shook so violently she fumbled the keys, the key ring tumbling to the dirty concrete at her feet with a metallic jangle that struck her ears like the earthshaking clang of a gong. With a muttered curse, she picked it up, willing her hands to steady as she selected the correct key and tried again to line it up with the lock. The key vibrated in her white-knuckled grip, bouncing off the edge of the lock twice before it finally shot home. She opened the door, slipped inside, and pulled it closed behind her.

She leaned against the door and slid down to sit with her knees pressed against her chest. And rocked.

Holy Mother of God, she'd witnessed a murder.

She had to call it in. But first she had to get her heart out of her throat.

Write it down. Check it. Then check it again.

As her mantra sounded in her head, she knew there was something else she had to do first, and thrust her hand into her back pocket to pull out the notebook. She knew herself—if she didn't write down what she'd witnessed in exacting detail this minute, chances were good it would be gone the next. And then someone would have died and the only person who could have helped the police find his killer would have willfully left him without justice.

The world was unfair, had been brutally unfair to her. She knew the pain of it. She could never be intentionally cruel to someone else in that same way, even if they weren't alive to experience it themselves.

Her hands still trembled as she opened the book to the second ribbon—not the regular tasks she had to do as part of daily life, marked by the first strip of brown satin, but her daily updates, where she noted the details of her everyday life, so what her brain wouldn't retain, her journal would. Still not trusting her legs to hold her, she stretched them out in front of her, pressed the open book to one thigh, pulled the pen out of its elastic loop, and began to write.

Experience had taught her to include every last detail, because you were never sure what was important. So she wrote down what still played in her head like a Technicolor cinema classic, then went back and added more, scribbling in the margin and circling key points. A third time, to make sure she got it all down, while her heart rate finally slowed when no one pounded on the door at her back.

Finished, having expelled every sight and nuance she could recall before it trickled away, she let the pen drop from her lax fingers as the book slid from her lap to tip onto the floor. She needed to call the cops, but had to take a moment to breathe. Now she'd written it down, and now what she needed to tell them was safe, she felt limp and drained, as if placing the call would require more energy than she possessed.

Part of her recognized the call wasn't the real problem. It was holding it together for the cops.

Better to call now while the ticking time bomb that was her brain still had a hope of retaining the memories.

She pulled her cell phone from her pocket, lay her notebook open in her lap, and dialed 911 before she could change her mind.

"Nine-one-one. Police, fire, or ambulance?" The voice was tinny, with the slight edge of bored repetition.

Quinn could imagine even a job keeping victims calm following an attack or helping fathers deliver their own children at the side of the road could lose its thrill given enough time. "Police."

"You have the police. Where is the location of your emergency?"

Quinn rattled off the address of the flower shop, then backtracked. "Well, in the alley just behind this row of shops, but I don't think it has an actual address."

"You're at that street address?"

"Yes."

"What is the nature of your emergency?"

Quinn took a breath, closed her eyes, and blew it out, centering herself. Calming herself. "I just witnessed a murder."

"Are you safe?" Any trace of boredom was gone, replaced by a practical briskness overlaid with concern.

"Yes, ma'am. I locked myself into my workplace."

"What did you see?"

Quinn described taking out the trash, and the man entering the alley, furtively, as if hiding. The second man entering, the murder. The getaway.

"What is the description of the victim, starting at his head?"

Quinn's eyes dropped to the open pages of her book. A quick scan, just to double-check. "Tall, thin, wearing pants and, I think, a long-sleeved shirt. Either really short hair or he was bald."

"What color was his clothing?"

"I think black, but he kept to the shadows." Panic rose for a moment; she hadn't written down that particular detail. Then she had a flash of memory, of light falling across a limp form, an arm swinging loose. "No, wait. The shirt was dark burgundy. And the pants were black or really dark-wash jeans. He was too far away, and the light wasn't good." Picking up her pen, she added that detail into the margin.

"That's good. Now the second man. What did he look like?"

A shiver ran through her at the thought of the killer. This would be a memory she wouldn't miss. "Tall, broad, muscular." As the kill replayed in her head, she could hear the crunch of bone shattering as tissues shred. It was a sound she hadn't heard in real life, but one her imagination conjured for her in stereo sound. "Powerful."

"What was he wearing?"

"Dark clothes." She closed her eyes, not bothering to scan her notes for information she knew wasn't there. "I don't know what specifically, it was just dark."

"Can you describe the vehicle?

"A white panel van. It had a door that opened on the side, but no windows in the rear compartment. That's about it."

"Did you see the license plate?"

"No."

"Officers have been dispatched," the operator said. "But I'm going to ask you a few more questions while I have you on the line. Can you confirm the phone number you're calling from in case we get disconnected?" She waited while Quinn repeated the phone number she'd memorized long before her attack. "Good. Can I get your last name?"

"Quinn."

"And your first name, Ms. Quinn?"

"It's . . ." Embarrassed heat warmed Quinn's cheeks. She needed to get it together before they thought she couldn't get her story straight. "I'm sorry. I'm a little flustered. Quinn is my first name. Fleming is my last name. Quinn Fleming."

"That's okay, Ms. Fleming. Help is on the way. When the van left, which direction did it go?"

"West. Toward Fourth. They were moving fast, but not so fast they cut into traffic and attracted attention."

"And there was only the one vehicle?"

"Yes." In the distance, the wail of a siren rose. "I think I hear them coming."

"Two officers have been dispatched. Would you like me to stay on the line with you until they arrive?"

"I . . . I think I'd like that."

It was less than a minute before a black-and-white SUV pulled up to the door, AMERICA'S FINEST and TO PROTECT AND SERVE stamped above and below the familiar gold logo of the City of San Diego on its door. Quinn said goodbye to the 911 operator with her thanks, and hurried to the locked front door where a police officer stood, peering in.

Just before she unlocked the door, she ran a hand over the back pocket of her jeans, searching for the familiar contours of her notebook. *You can do this.*

She took a deep breath, pasted on what she hoped was a smile projecting confidence, unlocked the door, and stepped back as the officer entered. Dressed all in black, he was tall and lean, clean-shaven with strawberry-blond hair and deep blue eyes. Quinn's first thought was he must have been every girl's burning crush in high school. Her second was that his eyes were flat, without a trace of warmth.

"Ma'am, I'm Officer Clark."

"Thank you for coming so quickly." Quinn relocked the door as he stepped farther into the shop, his eyes roaming over every shelf and corner, assessing the potential for threats. As his gaze focused on the back room, visible through both the open doorway and the cut-out window behind the counter, she said, "Feel free to look everywhere, but I was just back there. There's no one here."

"The report says the incident took place in the alley behind the shop. You're unharmed?"

"Yes."

"I need to contain the crime scene, but I need to confirm your safety first." He quickly moved through the store, checking in the cold room, the rear workspace, the cramped office and lunchroom in the back, and the washroom. His movements were quick and efficient, and he kept his right hand near his holstered weapon on his hip, in case of attack. But he realized in less than a minute the shop was indeed empty. "I need to see the crime scene. It's through the door marked emergency exit?"

"Yes. Near the mouth of the alley that opens out on F Street."

"Stay here, please, until I can assess the situation. Only open the door when I knock four times and identify myself." Pulling his service weapon from its holster, he opened the door just enough to slip through, and stepped out into the alley, letting the door close behind him with a soft whump.

Which left Quinn alone in the quiet shop with only her pounding heart for company. She closed her eyes, concentrating on bringing back the sight of what she'd seen, her heart rate kicking as only a vague image filled her mind. *Not yet, it's too soon.* Her memories had faded in a relatively short time period immediately following the attack, but as she recovered, her memories often lasted an hour or slightly more before they started to drift away. Yet now, when she needed every detail of the incident, they were slipping away too soon.

The attacker was taller, broader than his victim . . . wasn't he?

She reached for her notebook with a shaking, clammy hand, opening its pages and skimming to the description of the attacker. Taller, broader, yes.

Four sharp raps came through the door along with Clark calling out his designation, and Quinn jumped, nearly dropping the notebook. She slapped it closed, slid it into her pocket, and opened the door.

Clark stood in the alley, his weapon again in its holster. "Please come outside, Ms. Fleming."

Quinn ensured the store key was still in her front pocket and then stepped out into the muggy heat. The alley looked like nothing had changed in the mere short minutes since she'd stepped out with the trash; why did it feel so different? Dark, sinister, as if an unseen threat was lurking just out of sight in the depths of the shadows. She sidled closer to Clark.

A second siren grew louder as another car closed in on their location.

Clark unsnapped the flap on a pouch on his utility belt and pulled out a notebook with a black leather cover. He flipped open the cover and extracted a pen. "I'd like you to walk me through what happened this evening."

Quinn took him through her steps in taking out the trash, and then showed him where she'd hidden between the two dumpsters. When she would have slipped between them to demonstrate, he caught her arm. "We'll stay out here. I'd like the crime scene techs to be able to access the site untouched."

That's part of the crime scene? Didn't he understand the murder took place seventy-five feet away? "Of course. I'm sorry. I've never done this before."

"Please show me exactly where the incident occurred. Let's get closer, but not enter the area."

Quinn led him down to the far end of the alley, taking care to stay far away from the site of the murder. "He came from the east, around the corner, and hid there, against the wall." She pointed to a spot on the wall leading through the narrowest part of the alley, about fifteen feet inside the open gate. "He pressed himself against the wall, so from where I stood, I could only barely see him once he stopped moving."

"And what did he look like? What was he wearing?"

"He was . . . he . . ." Panic rose into her throat as the picture she'd been trying to hold in her mind wavered. She pulled her notebook from her pocket. "I made notes." She opened the book, the spine cracking ominously with her excessive force.

"We don't need notes. I need you to tell me your impressions, not have a prepared statement. What did he look like? Tall, short, skinny, fat? Just talk to me."

"Ummm . . . he . . ." Her breath was coming fast, and Quinn worried she'd start to hyperventilate. No help for it. She skimmed the page. "He was tall, lean. I think he may have been bald."

"Not from your notes," Clark said again, his voice taking on a harder edge. "Anyone can read from notes; I need to know what you saw. I don't want a set story. You just lived it, so tell me."

"I'm . . . I'm a little nervous. And I wrote everything down because I was worried I'd forget. I—" She stumbled to a halt as the approaching siren drowned out her words.

A second SDPD car pulled up to the mouth of the alley, lights flashing, as the siren cut off sharply. A man climbed out of the vehicle, spotted Clark and Quinn—and Clark's signal of all clear—and jogged down the narrow driveway. He was young, slightly shorter and thicker than Clark, with short-cropped dark hair. "Clark."

"Lugo. Ms. Fleming was walking me through the incident."

Officer Lugo scanned the alley where they stood. "Where did the murder occur?"

Quinn felt two sets of eyes focus on her expectantly as Lugo impatiently cut to the chase. She pointed to the location where the alley opened up, but fell into shadows. "There."

Lugo pulled his flashlight off his belt and flipped it on. Clenching it in a fist raised to his shoulder, he shone the light over grimy concrete, scattered garbage, and graffitied walls. He made a second pass more carefully over the wall—which was filthy but bore no obvious signs of violence—and then the concrete. "Got some piss here. But that could have come from any homeless guy passing through." He turned back to Quinn. "Tell us what happened."

"The victim entered the alley and pressed against the wall there."

"A man?" Lugo asked.

"Yes." A quick glance at her notes. "He was tall. Slender. Kind of a wiry build." She looked up to find Clark frowning down at her notebook but pushed onward. "Short hair or bald. Seemed nervous."

"Did he speak?"

"No. When I saw him come into the alley, I thought he was coming for me and I hid over there"—she indicated the dumpsters at the far end—"but then I realized he hadn't seen me. He was watching for someone else."

"What makes you say that?"

"His body language. He moved . . . furtively. And then pressed against the wall like he was trying to disappear."

Clark paused his writing, his pen suspended over his notepad. "How long until the second person appeared?"

"Maybe a minute? Or only slightly longer?"

"A man?"

That one she was sure of. "Yes."

"And what did he look like?"

Another furtive notebook check, this one taking longer as she lost her place and had to find that exact piece of information. "He was bigger. Dressed all in black. Moved very—"

"Look at me."

Quinn froze and then forced herself to peer up at Clark.

"Keep your eyes on me. How did he move?"

"Aggressively."

"What happened next? *No.* Don't look at your notes. What happened next?"

"He attacked the man in the alley."

"How?"

"He . . . uh . . ." She closed her eyes and concentrated. It was like the memory was trapped behind frosted glass, indistinct, and rapidly dissolving. It was terrifying to feel it sifting through her fingers like sand. She'd never tried to retain a single specific memory for any length of time. Usually, she moved through her day and then when she tried to think back, it was gone.

This was like watching someone die by inches as the last seconds of a man's life disintegrated in real time.

But the more she pushed, the harder panic clawed along her spine, catching her breath and freezing her blood, the more the memory slipped out of reach.

There was no choice but to tell them. "Look, after I witnessed the murder, I went inside and wrote everything down. Sometimes my memory isn't good, especially when I'm under stress, so I wanted to make sure I captured everything."

"The incident just happened. I want you to tell me what you saw. Not what you have in your little script—"

"It's not a script!"

"—you possibly wrote a couple of hours ago, or someone wrote for you—"

"That's not it at all!"

"Prove it to us. Put the book away and tell us what happened. In your own words."

"These *are* my words." She looked from one man to the other, read suspicion in both expressions. "Let me walk you through it." She barreled on, openly reading from her notes, describing the scene she'd witnessed in all the detail she could include. A knot tangled in her stomach at the growing unfamiliarity of the tale she told, and she stumbled several times in the telling as she looked up and caught the eye of one of the officers.

She was losing their attention. Losing their trust.

She trailed off at the end of her description and for a moment silence hung heavy between them, broken only by the ambient sounds around them of the city at play on a weekend evening. Finally, Clark slid his notebook into its pouch on his utility belt and grabbed his own flashlight. Standing well back from one end of the area Quinn had indicated, he carefully examined every inch of ground. Lugo started at the far end, and they slowly worked toward each other.

Quinn stood behind them, silent, her arms wrapped around herself, her notebook still clasped in her white-knuckled fist. She'd finished her tale, but wasn't yet ready to let go of her single support system.

Finally, only feet apart, they stopped. Quinn caught the glance that passed between the two men and interpreted what it communicated—no blood, no bullet holes, no clear signs of a scuffle. Essentially no crime scene. Was there really a crime? When they turned to stare at her, she saw the rest of their conclusion. Not only was there no trace of a crime, but they had a single witness who couldn't tell them what happened without referring to a "script."

They didn't believe her.

It was Clark who finally broke the silence. "We'd like you to go back into the flower shop. Make sure the doors are locked, and please wait there for us. We're going to wait for crime scene techs to arrive to go over this alley with a fine-toothed comb. Then we'll come find you. Can you do that for us?" His tone wasn't cruel or derogatory, simply detached as he dealt with someone who was doing nothing more than wasting the department's precious time.

"Yes." Her voice sounded small and defeated, even to her own ears. Which in turn only fed the shame roiling inside her.

"Thanks." Turning away from her, the men walked toward the SUV at the end of the alley, and into the wash of flashing red and blue lights illuminating the growing crowd on the far side of the car.

Quinn returned to the rear door of the shop and let herself into the quiet, fragrant space. Then simply hung her head and blinked back the tears burning her eyes and blurring her vision.

The man who died had one person who could have given law enforcement some clue as to what happened to him, one person who could have helped bring justice—to him, to his family, to those he'd loved, and who'd loved him in return.

One person. Her.

She'd failed.

CHAPTER 3

Quinn's steps dragged as she pushed up the stairs leading to her apartment. Exhaustion weighed heavily as the adrenaline reaction that had started hours ago and pumped until well after she'd quit the shop finally drained away, leaving her hollowed out and weak.

All she wanted was the peace and quiet of her own space, where no one would ask her questions, look at her suspiciously, or speak in subdued tones just out of earshot, all while sending surreptitious glances her way. She wanted to retreat, to curl into a ball, and beat back the humiliation that crawled through her.

They'd made her feel small and stupid. Perhaps that hadn't been their overt intention, but it had certainly been the result.

The officers had finally let her go. Returning to the shop, Clark and Lugo had run through the entire incident with her again, but in reading through the same notes a second time, no new information was revealed. They'd asked more questions, pressed for details, but her own recollections of the ordeal were gone, evaporated as if they'd never been. All she had were the details in her notebook, and she'd already gone over that. Twice.

She'd seen the sidelong glances they'd exchanged before they'd told her to go home. Seen the resignation, the disgust, the annoyance that she'd wasted their time. Perhaps even thought the whole thing had just been a cry for attention.

She'd done everything she could to convince them of her sincere desire to help, but it was clear she'd been unsuccessful.

Her apartment was located at the top of an external flight of steps. The modest, two-story complex held six apartments, three on each floor, with two flights of stairs flanking the second-floor balcony that ran the length of the side of the building, stretching across a series of doors. Quinn stopped in front of her black door, where a large brass 6 hung under a lantern-styled wall sconce on the white stuccoed wall. For a moment, she stared at the deadbolt, as if the effort required to dig in her cross-body bag for her key was simply more than she could manage. *Do this last thing. Then you can hide away and lick your wounds.* Taking a fortifying breath, she squared her shoulders, opened the zipper, and found her key in its usual place in a small inner pocket.

She opened her door and stepped into darkness. She hadn't left any lights on, thinking she'd be home before dusk, but she'd been so very delayed at the store—hours late because of the floral arrangement and then hours more because of the murder. Luckily, she'd lived in this apartment for years, and her hand unerringly found the light switch. As light flooded the space, she blinked against the brightness before casting her gaze around the apartment as if seeing it for the first time.

The apartment was compact, neat, and clean. Organized with everything in its place. Ordinary builder's beige walls throughout, but with warm touches of color to brighten the plain space. Her grandmother's jewel-tone quilt lay draped over the back of the couch, holding throw pillows that carried the punch of rich burgundy to match the curtains, which were drawn back to the night beyond. A long, unframed canvas landscape hung above the quilt, a forest glade in browns and greens, sunlight slanting in long, brilliant rays to fall across ground cover, moss, and a winding path beckoning her to step into the scene. A small flat-screen TV sat on a short console on the wall opposite the window.

Her only framed photo sat on the console. In it, her mother smiled out at her from where she sat on a towel spread over pale sand. Quinn had taken the photo herself as a teenager, and it was one of her most precious possessions. It was an image of motherly love, taken on a day when Lyla Fleming should have been working, but she'd taken her daughter to the beach for some "girl time." It was just the two of them against the world back then, her father long and forever out of the picture, and her mother had been everything to Quinn. Gone much too soon following a cancer diagnosis with little left to remember her by. And the most precious keepsake—her sapphire ring—gone in the attack.

To her right, her two-seater table—all that was needed for someone living alone—sat at the end of the L-shaped kitchen, while the drafting table she used for her sketching was tucked into the corner under a wide window for natural light. A framed oil painting of two blush-pink peonies in a glass vase half-filled with water hung on the wall above the table; the initials in the corner marked it as one of Quinn's own creations. Down the dark hallway lay her bedroom, bathroom, the narrow linen closet she also used for her art supplies, and a second closet containing a stacked, compact washer and dryer. The posting for the rental had described the apartment as "efficient"; everyone else would call it minuscule. But for Quinn, in her solitary life, it suited her needs. Only more so now when additional things would necessitate more compensation.

That compensation stood out in the bright pops of color that defined her living space as different from anyone else's. That separated her life *before* from the one that came *after*. The one that needed daily reminders in the form of notes seemingly covering almost every surface.

She looked down at the narrow console table tucked against the wall beside the door. A small woven basket sat at one end of the table, a bright green note in front of it reading *KEYS*. A blue note centered in the empty space beside it read *PURSE*. She dropped the keys in the basket and bowed her head to pull off her bag, leaving it on the table.

Wandering over to the living room, she pulled the drapes closed, shutting out the world and insulating her own private space. Sometimes the solitary isolation of her life tore at Quinn; tonight wasn't one of those nights.

She scanned the living room, over reminders she'd added in desperation shortly after coming back from the hospital, so scared that with all she'd lost, she'd lose even more in time—the cabinet storing her DVDs and the drawers in her coffee table holding her remote controls, both labeled with their contents; the paper under her laptop listing her various passwords and commonly used websites for prescriptions, banking, and shopping; the coil-ringed book emblazoned with *Sketchbook* sitting beside a pair of 6B and 9B pencils. All had been in place *before*, and those memories blessedly remained intact. Still, she couldn't bring herself to remove the security of those notes, afraid to face the blankness of uncertainty. But the living room only held a few reminders.

She turned toward the kitchen, where her most obvious crutch was displayed.

She hadn't let anyone into her apartment since she'd returned from the hospital because she hadn't wanted anyone to see what it took for her to move through life now. All people saw outwardly was the book she carried everywhere, which could be deployed with little notice and an offhanded joke about life being too busy with too many things to remember, so she liked lists to keep herself organized.

Organized. Hell, *sane*.

But her kitchen . . . Every cupboard door, every drawer was marked with a neon sticky note. As in the living room, memories formed before the attack still rang true, but she no longer trusted them. The Post-it notes were the physical manifestation of that distrust.

Cutlery. Dish towels. Pens. Baking pans. Plates. Glasses. The sign above the stove, in huge block black capital letters on a full-size piece of paper: DON'T WALK AWAY. A sign of the terror she worried she might burn the building to the ground if she wandered off, forgetting the pot boiling on the stove. Beside the stove, the portable timer she took with her whenever anything was in the oven, with a row of sticky notes nearby to label the reason for the timer: *Dinner. Baking. Cleaning.* And others.

The notepad on the counter listed what she had in the fridge and freezer. A big desk-style calendar with a bound upper border and triangular corner protectors to keep pages flat outlined what meal was scheduled on which specific day, including when to defrost it, because she'd learned detailed planning saved moments of confusion later. That same calendar listed her work schedule for the week so there was no chance she'd miss a shift. The San Diego Metropolitan Transit System—known by the locals as the MTS—schedule was also at hand, so she could look up each day what time to begin her commute. She knew it was Route 3—as it had been long before the attack—but a recent schedule change meant each morning she had no idea what time to meet the bus.

She rose every morning at six thirty, sometimes too early for that day's shift at the shop, but that meant she never had to rely on messages to herself to change the alarm on her bedside clock. Because she'd learned when each day began as an utterly blank page, giving herself time to cover for the mistakes that inevitably happened meant no one but her realized them.

And she wouldn't remember those errors by the next day. She'd once noted those mistakes in her notebook, but when reviewing them left her feeling inadequate, she'd left herself a note carefully inked on one of her ribbons— *Good and necessary things only*—to remind herself to practice some self-care, to treat herself gently on this road to recovery.

When she'd left this morning, her apartment had felt like a refuge, a place of safety where she could lean on any needed accommodations as she simply tried to put one foot in front of the other as she fought her way back to "normal." Now it seemed the rooms taunted her from every surface.

She'd thought she was improving. It was a two-steps-forward, one-step-back kind of progress, but it was forward motion.

Now it simply felt like she was back to square one.

CHAPTER 4

"These are lovely, Mr. Sharpton. Mrs. Sharpton will love them. You always pick such pretty flowers for her."

The older man smiled at Quinn, his watery blue eyes twinkling with pleasure in his pale, heavily lined face. "I couldn't do it without you."

"I'm sure you could. But I'm always happy to assist. Let me wrap those for you. You're going straight home to get them in water?"

At his nod, Quinn carried the armful of mixed blooms—peach roses, deep pink Peruvian lilies, cream carnations, and white snapdragon—into the back room where she trimmed the stems, added greenery, and then carefully wrapped the bouquet in colorful florist's paper. When she carried the bouquet out to the front counter, she found Mr. Sharpton bent over a small white card with a spray of summer flowers and *Especially for you* stamped across the top in a flowing script. He filled the space below with a shaky hand.

Mr. Sharpton had been a regular for years, so even though Quinn didn't remember his specific visit last week, she remembered his visits from months before and Mrs. Sharpton's preferences. Part of his Saturday errands included a stop at Gaslamp Blooms for a bouquet for his wife, stuck at home with a bad hip . . . bad back, bad knees, aching feet, or a migraine. Quinn always thought Mrs. Sharpton just wanted a morning of peace to herself and sent Mr. Sharpton off on a weekly round of errands to make sure she had a little alone time. As was his habit, he made this the last stop on his list of tasks, to buy flowers for his wife of fifty-two years.

It was adorable—*he* was adorable—and Quinn thought there was a lesson in the longevity of a marriage to be learned in time apart as well as gifts from the heart. Maybe someday she'd be lucky enough to find her own Mr. Sharpton.

"All ready for you, Mr. Sharpton." She rang up the sale, and then waited patiently as he counted out his purchase in actual cash; no new-fangled credit cards for this customer.

The bell on the front door jangled, and Quinn glanced up, expecting Jacinta back from delivering the wedding flowers Quinn had prepared last night. But, instead, it was an unfamiliar woman. Tall, with an easy muscular grace that spoke of physical fitness, her dark hair was styled into a simple knot at the nape of her neck. She wore a white, scoop-neck shirt under a tailored navy blazer with matching slacks.

"That should be all of it." Mr. Sharpton pushed a stack of bills topped by coins across the counter toward her. "Double-check it for me, please?"

"Of course." Quinn quickly counted the money—exact, as always—and handed Mr. Sharpton his bouquet. "Enjoy the rest of your weekend. Please say hi to Mrs. Sharpton for me."

"I will, indeed." With a cheerful smile, he scooped up his prize, and with a nod at the newcomer who now approached the counter, whistled his way out the door.

"Someone's going to be extremely happy tonight," the woman commented.

"Every Saturday without fail. His wife is a lucky woman. Can I assist you? Are you looking for anything specific?"

"I'm looking for Quinn Fleming."

"That's me."

The woman pulled a black flip case from her pocket and opened it to reveal a gold badge, overlaid with SAN DIEGO POLICE in blue enamel, paired with an ID card printed with her picture. "Detective Nura Reyes, SDPD." She closed the case with an efficient snap.

Quinn felt the first stirrings of foreboding. "You're looking for me?"

"Yes." Reyes simply stared at her, but didn't continue.

"About?"

"Last night."

Her heart rate spiking and a cold sweat breaking out across the back of her neck, Quinn fought to keep her expression calm and serene. "If you'll excuse me for a moment, let me see if the owner has returned through the back so I can give you a couple of minutes." With what she hoped was a steady smile, Quinn slowly—*don't rush!*—walked into the back room, turning left, away from the open workspace and the refrigerated storage, and into the small lunchroom, out of sight of the public area of the store. Letting out a shaky breath, she jammed her hand into her pocket and dragged out her notebook.

She imagined if she could remember each time this happened, being caught trying to cover for a memory lost to her, she'd be used to this feeling of panic. Though she doubted it often happened in relation to the police. Then again, maybe it did happen regularly. She wouldn't remember.

She opened the book to the second ribbon, her eyes falling on her notes from her morning routine, one finally familiar with repetition, to the night before, realizing with shock she'd written several pages of notes. She started scanning desperately, feelings of terror, shock, and fear for her own life washing over her as if she was experiencing the murder for the first time.

"You don't remember what happened, do you?"

Quinn jerked at the sound of Reyes's voice from the doorway, the notebook tumbling from her shaking fingers to fall to the floor. Before she could retrieve it, Reyes swooped in, picked up the book, and flipped through it.

"This area isn't for customers," Quinn protested weakly.

"I'm not a customer. I'm here to investigate last night's crime." Dark eyes rose to meet Quinn's. "Answer the question, please. You don't remember what happened last night, do you?" She flipped back several more pages. "Or the day before, or the day before that, apparently." She looked up again, waiting expectantly.

Shame coursed hot through Quinn, but she forced herself to raise her chin and meet Reyes's eyes. "No."

Reyes considered her for a few seconds, rhythmically tapping the cover of the notebook with her index finger.

No nail polish, Quinn noticed, with neat, short nails. No-nonsense, like the woman, she suspected.

"I thought not." Reyes closed the notebook and extended it to Quinn. "You didn't panic when I introduced myself. It was like you couldn't see any reason for a visit from a cop . . . because you didn't. Not until I referred to last night. That's when you panicked. Tried to cover it, and nearly did, but I was watching for a reaction. I needed to test a theory."

"What theory?"

"That you were the Quinn Fleming who was assaulted only a few blocks from here and left for dead. Who woke in the hospital with amnesia. Are you still having memory problems?" When Quinn was surprised into silence, Reyes coaxed, "You might as well tell me. It'll make this whole process easier. And will let me work with you, instead of you working against me."

Quinn walked over to drop into one of the two chairs by the small table. "I don't remember what happened last night."

"How long do memories last for you?"

"I remember everything that happened before my attack. Right afterward, I couldn't form any new memories that lasted more than about ten minutes. Now, it's more like an hour, though repetition is helping."

"Going over the memory again?"

"Yes, but it takes more repetition. Actually doing the thing again and again, that reinforcement is better for building a memory. For instance, I have two cups of coffee, double cream, double sugar, and a bagel with cream cheese in the morning for breakfast. Each morning."

"How many weeks did it take to remember that?"

"Two or three, but that was early on and I'd probably do better now. I still write it down every morning which also helps me remember. But a onetime incident..." Quinn bowed her head, focused on the notebook loosely clasped in her hands. "As I said, maybe an hour, give or take on either side."

Reyes pulled out the other chair. "That's why you wrote it all down last night."

"Yes. I can't remember specific memories, but whether that fact itself is a memory or not, it's at least something I'm aware of. I know how to read and write, how to take a bus to get to work, how to arrange flowers."

"All things you knew before."

Quinn nodded. "As I said, with repetition, some memories are beginning to form. I don't know if it's of a particular event or a consolidation of multiple events, but something is beginning to stick. Last night, I knew to make notes, knew to make them before I even called nine-one-one. According to additional notes I made afterward, the memory was dissolving even faster than usual."

"Probably due to stress. It must have been terrifying."

Quinn's laugh had a sharp edge. "I'll take your word for it. I only had time to skim part of it before you came back here and found me." The front door jingled, and Quinn shot to her feet. "I'm the only one in the store. I have to get that." She hurried out to the front room, sensing Reyes following her. Her cheerful words of greeting for a customer died unspoken as she came face-to-face with her boss.

Jacinta, in her mid-fifties, her long black hair tied into a ponytail and wearing a flowing white tunic top over navy leggings, stopped dead in the aisle, still carrying the plastic crates used for transporting smaller arrangements. She glanced from Quinn, to the strange woman appearing out of her back rooms, to Quinn again. "Quinn? Is everything all right?"

How could she possibly sum up the fear, the uncertainty, and the feelings of inadequacy surging through her? Not sure how to answer, Quinn settled for a half-hearted shrug.

"What does that mean?"

Reyes extended her flip case as Jacinta's eyes went wide. "I'm Detective Reyes with the SDPD. Do you know about the incident last night?"

"Where? *Here?*" Jacinta set down the crates and quickly moved to Quinn, running her hand down Quinn's back as she searched her face. "You closed last night. You're okay?"

"Yes."

"There was an incident last night in the alley behind your store," Reyes cut in smoothly. "Ms. Fleming was a witness. I'd like to go over the statement she gave the responding officers last night, if you can spare her for a little while."

Jacinta's eyes reflected a mixture of concern and alarm. "What kind of incident?"

Quinn shifted her weight restlessly on her feet. She'd been able to scan enough of her notes to know the crime. "A murder."

Color drained from Jacinta's face. "*What?*"

"Ms. Fleming reported seeing a man killed. I need to speak with her in private."

"You can use my office. Close the door and take all the time you need. I'm here for the rest of the day."

"The arrangement for the O'Donnell anniversary party is in the cold room." Quinn's words came fast, a mixture of nerves at the upcoming interview and guilt at leaving Jacinta alone out front on a busy Saturday. "And I've started the casket spray for the Escarra funeral—"

Jacinta's hand closed over Quinn's where they were twisted together at her waist and squeezed gently. "Don't worry, I have it. When you're free, come and give me a hand."

"I'll take this as my lunch break."

"You'll do no such thing. Go do what you have to do now, and we'll work out the rest later."

Quinn turned her hands, gripped back, as a little of the burden of stress lifted from her shoulders. "Thank you."

"You know no thanks are required. Go on. If you need me, I'm here."

Quinn squeezed a little tighter, then let go of the older woman's hands and led Reyes into Jacinta's office. At the rear of the shop, the windowless office was only big enough for a desk, two chairs—one behind the desk, one in front— and three filing cabinets. The top of the cabinets was loaded with stacks of florist catalogs, mismatched vases, rounds of ribbon, and a box of jumbled cubes of floral foam. Jacinta's desk held a desktop computer surrounded by a flurry of order forms and invoices, an open binder of current orders, three paper coffee cups, all with varying levels of cold black coffee, a ceramic mug filled with a rainbow of pens and pencils, and a desk sign that decreed BLOOM WHERE YOU'RE PLANTED.

"Is this okay?"

"It's fine." Reyes closed the door behind her and then rolled the desk chair out so the two chairs sat side by side. She pulled a notebook and pen out of her jacket pocket, sat down, and looked up at Quinn when she didn't move. "Have a seat."

"Oh. Right, of course." Quinn sat and neatly folded her arms in her lap, trying to appear casual.

"I want you to relax. You haven't done anything wrong."

Clearly, casual wasn't working. "I don't know if I can help you."

"Because of your memory?"

"Yes."

Reyes studied her for a moment before speaking. "Do you have any idea how unpredictable witnesses can be?"

"You mean witnesses like me?"

"No, I mean witnesses with normal memory capabilities. You think you're an unreliable witness, but you've done something most witnesses will never do. You wrote down every detail concerning what you saw when it was fresh in your mind. And you've drawn a line there. That's it, that's all you remember."

"I won't be able to help more."

"You also won't be able to help less."

Frustrated, confused, Quinn surged to her feet, paced to the far side of the desk and back, wishing there was more room to work off some of the energy prickling up her spine and jangling her nerves. "I don't know what that means."

"I'll explain. *Sit down.* Please."

Quinn sank into her chair.

"Normal witnesses mean to do their best," Reyes stated, "but often in trying to be helpful, they end up being less helpful. We call it the misinformation effect. Ever heard of it before your assault?"

Quinn shook her head.

"It's a fancy term that means a person's memory of an event can change over time." She paused, as if considering. "According to the records you didn't remember your assault right after it happened. Do you, now?"

"Only from the copy of the police report someone gave me. I've read it over enough times that I know what happened. But I don't remember the incident itself."

"Good to know. But let's look at that incident as an example. Even with normal memory abilities, after something like that, you wouldn't remember every detail of it. That kind of stress inhibits memory formation. Not to mention, you wouldn't have been able to note every detail about your attacker because you were too busy fighting for your life. People tend to recall traumatic events more like a series of snapshots, not a moving picture. There are gaps. And people naturally try to fill in those gaps so the whole story makes sense for them. They do this by reviewing the event in their minds, by retelling it to family and friends. And cops. In doing so, their story can change. The witness doesn't mean to embroider, doesn't even realize they are, but they do, and their testimony becomes unreliable. The longer it is between the event and the court case, the more unreliable the witness can get. Memory isn't only a reproduction of an event, but also a reconstruction."

"But I can't do that."

"*Exactly.* This file came across my desk this morning and it caught my eye for a couple of reasons. Part of it was the report from the responding officers that you had a written 'script,' as they described it, outlining what happened. They had zero proof it was actually your story, but they couldn't get you to tell them what had happened without going back to your notebook."

"They didn't believe me."

"They didn't, for a couple of reasons. But primarily it was your reporting of the event. They didn't think to look you up in our system. Once I did that, and read through the information including your medical reports, I had a better idea of what was really going on."

"You have my medical files?"

"As part of the investigation into your assault, yes. Do you remember Detective Barrow?"

"No."

"Barrow was the detective assigned to your case. Which is still open, by the way. But as part of his investigation, he included some of your medical records, especially pertaining to the extent of your head injury. A series of blows so severe they damaged your memory centers. Which informed me on your part in this investigation. You knew you'd forget what had happened, so you wrote down everything you could. Can I see your notebook for a second?"

Quinn pulled it out of her pocket and handed it over.

Reyes opened it to the first page. "As I thought." She turned the book around to where the entire first page was filled with block letters: *WRITE IT ALL DOWN. CHECK IT. THEN CHECK IT AGAIN.* "You carry a book in your back pocket. You assumed you would question why you carried a book, so you left yourself a note on the first page, a natural place any curious person would look. You said your memory is improving with repetition. Do you remember now to write in the notebook? To look for help in it?"

"Yes." Something was gnawing at Quinn, and she suspected she wouldn't like the answer, but was compelled to ask anyway. "You said the responding officers didn't believe me for a couple of reasons, but only mentioned my notebook. What else made them not believe me?"

"Crime scene services went over the alley and came out of it with essentially zero useful evidence. You described a bloodless killing. There's no body. There's no evidence of a specific vehicle among all the other cars, trucks, and vans on F Street. There are no security cameras pointed at the alley to capture the event. The alley is full of trace evidence, but nothing necessarily specific to the crime that stands out. There was some fresh urine, but whether that was from the dead man or a live one isn't clear, and urine isn't a great source of DNA. Still, they'll do a comparison if a body shows up. Also, lots of fingerprints and fibers, but how many businesses use that alley?"

Quinn did a quick count of the businesses around the block. "About a dozen."

"Assuming it wasn't actually someone who normally would use the alley, then we're talking about an exclusion list of every employee in every business, many of which are restaurants with large staffs. We'd need that list to narrow down the trace evidence they collected last night in hope of finding someone who shouldn't have been there. And you said last night that someone had left the gate open, so who knows who might have wandered in from outside that pool of people? All for a crime we have no proof actually happened"—she raised the notebook into the air, shook it twice—"except for this. When they handed off the case to me, they thought it was already closed, at least until a body shows up to substantiate the crime."

"If it shows up," Quinn muttered.

"If it shows up," Reyes agreed. "But I saw the bigger picture. And maybe there won't be any leads to follow due to the lack of evidence, but I wanted to meet with you to go over your written report, line by line, to make sure I understand your comments and to see if anything shakes loose."

"It won't."

"Dotting the i's, crossing the t's. I want to make sure we've covered everything there is." She opened Quinn's notebook and slid the pen free. Flipping to the most recent pages and finding the beginning of the notes on the incident, she wrote in the margin at the top of the page, *Remember anything new? Call Det. Nura Reyes*, and followed it with a phone number. "I have no expectations you'll remember anything else. But if you do, I want you to know you can call me anytime, day or night. That's my cell phone and it's always with me."

"What if it's not real? What if it's . . . what did you call it? The misinformation effect?"

"I always take subsequent memory reports with a grain of salt, knowing that can happen. You let me know, and then let me make the call about whether I think it's a real memory or not. Sound good? Will what I've written there remind you?"

"It should."

"Good. I'd like to walk through this with you a line at a time. We may not add anything to your report, which I'm going to photograph and add verbatim to the record, but maybe going over it again will bump something in your memory. Let's start at the beginning."

For the next half hour, they went through Quinn's notes, one line at a time. Quinn didn't feel she'd added anything to the case, but Reyes seemed pleased and left the shop with a reminder to Quinn to call if she ever needed anything.

As Reyes left, Quinn heard her talking to Jacinta, leaving her card and contact information, and reassuring her if she or Quinn had any questions or concerns, all they had to do was call. Then the jingle of the door announcing new customers, followed by a second, marking Reyes's exit.

Quinn sagged back in her chair, totally drained.

She needed to return to work; she'd already taken so much time away from Jacinta. She was so generous with her time and understanding, and Quinn didn't want to take advantage of her. But first, she needed to make notes on her meeting with Reyes. Opening the notebook, she began to write.

Five minutes later, she tucked the pen into its loop, then flipped to the beginning of her statement about the murder, directly under Reyes's contact info. With great care, she turned down the corner of that page and then closed the book. She knew herself, knew by tomorrow morning she'd have forgotten what happened today. Would forget again the story of what happened last night and the part she played in it. Wouldn't know an important phone number resided there. But the tiny gap left by that dog-eared page would catch her attention. One page defaced in another otherwise perfect book. She would recognize it as a message to herself.

Pay attention. Look at me.

Let me remember for you.

Because there was more here than met the eye.

CHAPTER 5

Quinn rolled over in bed to stare up at the ceiling in the near total dark. She tossed off the light sheet and rubbed her fingers over the sheen of sweat forming on her chest above the low neck of her sleep tank.

Maybe it was the heat that wouldn't let her rest. August in San Diego was usually in the high seventies or low eighties, but this past week had been unusually hot and humid. Like many residences in Southern California, air-conditioning wasn't installed in her unit because of the frequent cooling ocean breezes.

She glared in the direction of her curtains, half-open to allow airflow through her second-story window, and dimly visible through the scant moonlight. They were motionless as the still, suffocating air mass blanketing her city remained stubbornly in place. Until those cooling breezes returned, Quinn feared her sleep would suffer.

It wasn't like her to toss and turn, unable to settle before bed. With a groan of frustration, she had to admit she didn't know if that was true. She knew it was true before the attack, but what did she know about after? Each newly formed memory was a hard-fought struggle of repetition, and maybe her bedtime routine wasn't constant enough for her to remember. Maybe, like tonight, on most other nights, she was simply too tired to rise from her bed to make notes about her sleep troubles.

She was exhausted in body and soul. Was this normal and she was worn down all the time now?

How long could she go on if that was true?

It was like her brain simply couldn't turn off, but without a coherent image of the day she'd just experienced behind her, she didn't know why. She should be able to sleep the slumber of someone with a clear conscience and no worries.

So why couldn't she settle?

She turned onto her side, her back to the minimal light coming through her open window, and worked to clear her mind the only way she knew how as slowly, one stem at a time, she built a magnificent bridal bouquet in her imagination. She picked a theme color—lavender—and selected blooms one at a time, starting with fresh lilac. Normally, this was a selection she'd never place in a bouquet as it wouldn't last, but tonight any bloom was available to her with unending longevity for her fantasy bouquet. She added creamy roses, gorgeously full pink ranunculus blooms, tiny hot-pink ombre sweet pea clusters, the subtle checkerboard of draping fritillaria cups, and the graceful curl of jasmine vine, all set off with a waterfall of trailing lavender ribbons.

She rearranged the bouquet three times before she finally dozed off.

The menace stole stealthily into her dreams.

Darkness dripping with heat, the sulfurous scent of rot hanging damp in the thick air. A rapid click echoing through an enclosed space. Tiny rat feet scuttling through trash. The flap of material snapping like a boom of thunder. A column of light, slashing through the gloom.

The knowledge something was out there. Something followed.

Her skin clammy and cold, sweat turning to tracks of ice as her pulse skyrocketed. Her breath rasping between gritted teeth, her movements jerky and uncoordinated as she burst into a run.

A rush of footfalls closing behind her.

Pain. A struggle for survival.

Images tumbling one over another in a flurry of mere glimpses.

A flash of feral teeth in the shadows. The splash of graffiti on brick. Cries echoing in an enclosed space. Dark eyes, glinting with calculation. The splatter of blood on cement.

Terror. Helplessness . . .

She sat bolt upright in bed with a gasp carrying the thread of an alarmed cry. Braced on both hands, her sweaty palms pressed to damp, tangled sheets, all she could do was hang her head and try to catch her sawing breath as her heart punched repeatedly against her breastbone. As her chest rose and fell, she tried to concentrate on the face that had come to her only in partial snatches, but she couldn't tie it all together as a single image.

But she knew how to try.

Her breath still ragged, she rolled over toward the bedside table, her hand flailing until it finally found the lamp. A sharp jerk of the dangling chain flooded the room with light; she shrank away from it, her eyes screwed shut against the glare. She forced her lids open, blinking rapidly against light bordering on painful as she reached for the sketchbook, HB pencil, and eraser stacked beside the lamp. This had been her habit since before the assault—on rare evenings when she was struggling to wind down, she'd curl up in bed and sketch whatever came to mind: animals, people she'd seen that day, a scene at the shop, a particular arrangement she liked. Had she used it since then? As she flipped the book open, she realized she had no idea as none of the images were dated. She quickly flipped past sketches of a pod of seals, Mr. Sharpton cradling an armful of roses, and a couple standing at the bus stop at First and Broadway, a stand of palms rising from the boulevard behind them to frame them as they stood gazing at each other, mindless of everyone around them.

Finding a blank page, she gripped the pencil and began to sketch. The graphite line started smoothly, but then jerked uncontrollably in her shaking hand, skittering upward, leaving a lightning bolt to mark its passing. She dropped the pencil, balled her fist, and pressed it to her lips. She closed her eyes, sucked in a breath, and held it for a moment as she let the images wash over her.

You can do this.

She opened her eyes, set her jaw, picked up her discarded pencil, and put it to paper.

She had no idea how long she drew, but when she raised her head, she had pages of sketches. Without a full face to draw, she'd taken what she could remember, and, instead of trying to embroider a complete image, she'd concentrated on what she'd seen, instinctively falling back on her artistic skills. All those classes she'd taken through her teen years as she'd learned how to take the image before her and translate it into carbon and pastel. All those artistic studies. Normally, if she was at her drafting table, she'd have used a variety of pencils of different hardness and blackness to get it just right, but even with just her HB pencil, the images held pinpoint accuracy to what she remembered.

One page was covered with eyes, some wide, some narrowed, some with drawn brows, one partly hidden under a fringe of ragged hair. Then there was the page of mouths, some open as if in speech, some with gritted teeth, some in a grimly set flat line, and one in a twisted smile.

Every image conveyed a furious anger, though one hinted

at a perverse enjoyment. It made her put her pencil down to wipe her palm off on her sleep shorts.

She flipped to the next page. This one held a few sketches of ears. She considered those for a moment. She'd heard ears were as different as fingerprints and a person could be identified by their ears.

The next need pressed close—she had to write down her impressions, odd and vague as they were, before they disappeared.

She grabbed her notepad off the bedside table, pulling the pen free, and let the book fall open to the page with the second ribbon. But as she angled the notebook to a more comfortable position, about to set pen to paper, the tiny gap in the pages caught her eye.

She froze. *What is that?*

She flipped to the dog-eared page to find a message scrawled across the top—*Remember anything new? Call Det. Nura Reyes*, followed by a local phone number.

She stared in confusion at the single line of handwriting. She didn't recognize the script or the name. And remember? Remember what?

There was the rub. She couldn't remember anything.

Or had she? Her gaze slid sideways to the sketchbook.

She glanced at the clock to find the glowing green numbers reading 3:24 AM, feeling the seconds tick away. It was so late; who called a stranger in the middle of the night to wake them from a sound sleep?

To hell with consideration. Something's wrong. The police left you a contact number. Use it.

She reached for her phone and dialed the number on the page.

It rang four times before Quinn heard a muttered curse, then, "Hello?" The voice was husky and soft, as if not wanting to wake a slumbering partner.

"Detective Reyes?"

"Yes." The voice was already sharper.

"I . . . I don't know why I'm calling you except I have your name in my book."

"Quinn?"

"Yes."

"Hang on."

Quinn heard a mattress creak, the soft pad of footfalls, and a door closing. There was a pause followed by a muffled exclamation and then the sound of a chair being pulled across a tile floor. "I'm here." The last word carried the edge of a yawn. "Do you remember who I am?"

"I don't. We've met?"

"We have. We'll probably have to do this every time you call me until it becomes so rote you remember on your own, but let me explain." She quickly took Quinn through the events of the last two days. "Do you remember any of that?"

"No."

"But something made you call me. At . . ." Reyes broke off for a moment. "Coming up on three thirty in the morning."

"I found a note in my book with your name and phone number. Did you write that?"

"I did. Why were you up and looking at your notebook this early in the morning?"

"I had a dream. A nightmare, really."

"Did you remember something in this nightmare?"

"I . . . I don't know."

A sigh came over the line. "Yet you still called. Something happened to make you call. What?"

"It wasn't anything coherent, more like a bunch of scattershot images. And not even full images, it was more like I was peering through a spyglass and could only see part of the scene."

"What were the images of?"

Quinn took a minute, closing her eyes, trying to bring it

all into focus. "Violence. A struggle. Darkness." She took in a breath. "Fury. But pleasure in the kill."

There was another screech of chair legs. "Hang on, I need to write this all down. Have you done that?"

"Not yet. I was going to, but I saw your number and took a chance. I know how this goes. I know I won't be able to hang on to this for long. I didn't know why the police left me a phone number, but I thought I'd better call. I'm sorry it's so early."

"It's not a problem. You did the right thing, Quinn. I know you have trouble remembering things, but you know at this point it's a problem. Do me a favor and write something else in your book? Under my name, make a note to call anytime, day or night. I don't want you second-guessing next time. I just want you to call."

Quinn did as directed.

"It sounds to me like your subconscious is trying to send you a message," Reyes continued. "You say you can't remember things without repetition. I know the last few months are a blur, but you remember things normally from before your assault?"

"Yes."

"Do you usually dream? I mean, we all dream, but do you tend to remember your dreams?"

"At least before the attack, I'd usually sleep like the dead. I mean, occasionally I'd remember a dream on waking, but not often. And never something like this. Since the attack, I know from my notes I sometimes wake and get out of bed in the middle of the night, but I don't know it was because of dreams. I just may not have been able to sleep."

"I'm no psychologist, but this sounds to me like you retained more than you thought. I mean, aren't retention and recall two different memory functions? Who's to say it's not recall you struggle with versus retention?"

"I don't know I've ever thought of it that way. I mean, I may have discussed it in group therapy, but I don't remember it."

"You remember group therapy? What kind?"

"A group for people like me who've suffered traumatic brain injury. I only remember some of it. I see it in my calendar, so I know it's something I do. I know where it is, because that's in my calendar, too. I remember the man who leads it and what he looks like. His name is Will, and I must have gone to a bunch of sessions to remember that. I don't remember who else is in the session, which makes me think it's not necessarily always the same people as they heal and move on with their lives."

"I'm impressed, Quinn. Life has handed you a short stick, but you have the courage to do everything you can to manage it as best you can."

Embarrassed, Quinn didn't know how to answer as she stared down at her sheet, plucking at it relentlessly with her thumb and index finger.

Reyes didn't seem to notice. "What can you tell me about what you remember? And while you're telling me, I want you to write down what you remember."

"I can do that, but the sketches are probably more important."

"The sketches?"

"I drew what I could remember."

Silence for a moment, then, "You can do that? Accurately?"

"I think so. It's a hobby, but I took drawing classes for years as a teenager. Am I calling your cell?"

"Yes."

"Hang on. Let me text you some pictures." She put the phone on speaker, and flipped over to her camera, taking a shot of each page. Then she texted those photos to Reyes. "You should have them now." She put the phone down on the bed beside her and picked up her sketchbook, staring at the page filled with eyes.

"Well, I'll be damned," Reyes murmured. "You *can* draw. These are terrific. And accurate, you think?"

"Yes." She frowned down at the page. "But it's all so jumbled. Just flashes. And not of a coherent face, just pieces."

"Do you think it's just one face?"

Quinn stared down at the eyes. *Are they all from one person?* "I don't actually know."

"Let's keep in mind this could be both killer and victim. What else do you remember? Tell me everything, even if it seems unimportant or indistinct. And write it down as you're telling me, no matter what it is. We don't know what will be important later. Too much information is better than not enough."

"As I said, it was mostly a jumble." Quinn checked the date on her clock, jotted it down, and then started a bullet point list. "It was dark, everything was in shadows."

"But you could still see something?"

"Flashes. A brick wall with graffiti, dark silhouettes. Some light. Eyes. Staring at me. *Seeing me.*"

"In your original story about the murder, you said you were afraid the killer saw you in the shadows. That he was looking right at you."

Quinn's gaze dropped to the sketchbook. "If those were the eyes, that would have been terrifying."

"Especially after what you saw." When silence stretched between the women for ongoing seconds, Reyes asked, "What's wrong?"

"It's not wrong . . . exactly. But you believe me. You said those other two cops thought I was making it all up, but you believe me."

"Yes."

"Why?"

"Because I trust my gut. You work this job long enough, you get a feel for people. The feeling I get from you is you're trying to the best of your ability to give me the whole story. Anyone who reports a murder can be considered for the crime. Did you report it to look like a bystander when the death was at your hands? We have to consider any witness, to see if there's a connection. But I don't get that from you. What I get from you is you'd prefer to stay out of the limelight. Staying in the background allows you to compensate for your current challenges without anyone seeing the struggle. But in reporting the murder, you had to know your current handicap would be revealed. Studied and dissected. But you did it anyway. More than that, you reported a crime that has very little, if any, evidence we can track. Not that you necessarily would have known how bad that would be, but you did know there was no body to find. And yet, you still reported it. You're still talking to me now."

"Maybe I just can't remember I hated that man and had a reason to kill him?" Quinn's voice cracked on the last word.

A chuckle came down the line to her. "I have to admit most of my witnesses don't play devil's advocate to make sure they're considered for the crime. You're too much of a straight shooter for that. And I don't think you're stupid. Furthermore, I can hear the fear in your voice that you're afraid it might be true. I don't think it is. I think you're testing me to see how much you can trust me, to see if I might turn on you. Quinn, I want you to trust me. I don't see anything in this case to connect you to the murder. I'd like any help you can provide, and will do whatever I can to get your truth from you. So take a breath. You're in safe hands."

"You must think I'm an idiot."

"No. I think you're scared, and understandably con-

fused. And will be again by morning. Let's set you up for
success. Walk me through every image you can remember.
Write it all down. Write down that I'm someone you can
trust. Remember every part of this is a message to yourself. You trust what you write in your notebook?"

"Always."

"Then add in whatever you need so in the morning,
when it's all strange and new, you'll know you can at least
come to me if you need help. Okay?"

The kindness in Reyes's voice comforted like a soft blanket. "Yes. You're so nice. How do you manage murderers
and street thugs?"

A laugh burst from Reyes, one immediately stifled,
likely to avoid waking anyone asleep nearby. "Oh, don't
you worry about that." Her voice had a sharp edge to it
now. "Those who deserve a kick-ass cop, get one. Rough
handling isn't what's going to help you, and, for me, what
I want to do is find out more about this crime. Let's go
through it again before it's gone. Start at the beginning,
make your own notes as you go, and I'll make mine. We're
going to do all five senses. Let's start with sight."

"Okay." Quinn took a deep breath and closed her eyes
to concentrate on the memory before it evaporated. "There
was a dirty brick wall, vandalized with spray paint, with
trash on the ground beside it. I recognized it because I've
worked with Jacinta for a few years now. It was the alley
behind the shop. But I could only see a sliver of it."

She took Reyes into her dream.

CHAPTER 6

The buzz invaded her sleep like an angry bee. Rolling over, Quinn slapped the top of her alarm clock, punting the alarm nine minutes into the future. She sagged onto her back, her arm curving over her head to fall to the pillow.

She let out a long sigh, laden with fatigue. Why was she so exhausted? In the *before* times, she always rose with a spring in her step, ready to meet the day. Today, her limbs were leaden, her eyelids weighed down, and all she wanted to do was curl up for another half hour.

What shift are you working today? Maybe you don't have that half hour.

That thought jolted her a little more awake. When the golden rule in your existence was to carry on as if your life was perfectly normal, you couldn't afford mistakes like being late. Other people got to sleep in, to dally over a second cup of coffee, to fight with their kids about an incomplete assignment as they were shepherded out the door, or to get stuck in traffic. She could not.

A little bubble hitched in her chest, making her wonder if she felt this way every morning. *Existence.* Surely there was more to life than just getting by, just putting one foot in front of the other and trying to bravado your way through every day. She knew her life had once been joyful, and so, so easy. Nothing required advance strategy or excessive note-taking. She just . . . was. Now she was nothing more than a shadow of that former self.

If memories represented your identity, who you were and where you came from, then who were you when you couldn't make new ones, and when you couldn't even remember who you were last week?

It was also lonely not being able to lean on anyone. She couldn't remember much, but apparently there had been enough repetition the emotion stuck with her, along with the certainty it had to be this way. So far, Jacinta had been beyond supportive, but if she knew all, her patience might eventually wear thin, and Quinn desperately needed both Jacinta's support and her employment. The sharper sting was the loss of most of her friends, the buddies she'd partied with on that last night of the *before* times. Had they tried to make themselves part of her new life? She wasn't sure now; those memories, if they ever existed, were lost in the fog of her damaged brain. All she knew is, it hadn't happened enough times for her to have painstakingly formed a new memory of most of them.

She thought of the person she'd been six months ago. If any of them had been attacked and left for dead, and had suffered a debilitating injury, would she have stuck around for them, or would she have been too busy with working, dating, just having fun? With an uncomfortable gnawing in the pit of her stomach, she had to admit she wasn't sure that version of herself would have stepped up. This version would, because this version bore the scars of a difficult recovery. Both mental and physical pain informed empathy.

Enough of this wallowing. It does no one any good, least of all you.

Bracing both hands on the bedsheets, she levered herself

to a sitting position. She turned to shut off her alarm, but froze when her gaze fell upon her sketchbook, sitting on the far corner of her bedside table, her notebook perched atop it. The sketchbook itself wasn't an abnormality, but it was open and covered with . . . eyes?

Had she had trouble sleeping last night?

She reached for both sketchbook and notebook, knowing if anything had happened last night, she'd have left herself a reminder. Setting the sketchbook in her lap, she picked up the notebook, but found herself drawn instead to the images. Like an exercise from her youth, but with a precision she wouldn't have been able to match back then. She flipped the page, only to find more drawings, this time of mouths.

So much anger flowed from the images, overlaid with a shimmer of pleasure.

A shiver ran down her spine, and she wasn't sure why.

One more page flip brought her to a scatter of ears.

What on earth happened last night? If she couldn't sleep, she would have drawn something happy, something that would bring her relaxation, satisfaction, and joy, not the images she sensed that conveyed hate and pain.

She reached for her notepad. As she went to open it, she noticed the dog-eared corner, and flipped to that page instead of the ribbon to stare down at her own handwriting.

I witnessed a murder tonight.

She jerked, the book falling from suddenly nerveless fingers to tumble to the sketchbook and then roll onto the sheets. For a long moment, she stared at the notebook as if it were a venomous snake instead of leather, paper, and fabric.

If there was one thing she'd learned since the attack, it was, she was always more sure of herself if she knew as much as possible. And that constant need for reinforcement eventually led to a memory staying with her if she put enough effort into it. If she'd left herself a message, written it down in detail, and then defaced the book to attract her attention, she was clearly communicating it was important for her to read. To start that commitment to a memory, no matter how horrible.

A murder?

What did she do to deserve this extra burden?

She picked up the book, forced herself to open it again, and then noticed the extra note at the top of the page. A strange hand with a detective's name and phone number. But more than that, one more line in her own hand. *Call anytime, day or night. She's a helper.*

She's a helper. It was something Quinn's mother had often repeated to her, words of comfort and trust for moments when she was scared. *Look for the helpers.* When there was scary news on the television, or if something bad happened at school, she was to look for the helpers. Look for those who assisted the hurt, lost, cold, or hungry.

Reyes was a helper.

Quinn still knew herself at her core, and that woman would recognize the traits of a helper. Kind, trustworthy, someone to depend on.

Something so awful had happened that Quinn needed a helper, and she'd sent herself a message that someone had come into her life to assist.

She wasn't alone after all.

Using that thought to bolster her, she opened the book again, turning to the dog-eared page, and read. Read about murder, about the cops who didn't believe her, about the one who did. About the dream she had last night.

She sagged against the pillows. She had to hand it to herself—she made such thorough notes, that it was like experiencing it all over again, from the cold horror that set her hands to trembling, to the burning humiliation at the hands of officers who talked down to her and discounted her experience, to the relief of someone actually believing her, even when the evidence didn't clearly support her tale, to the confusion of the jumbled dream images and the need for clarity.

But the emotion that remained was determination. Someone had died, and if she could help, she needed to do so with everything in her power.

That bartender walking home had done the same for her. Had found her, called 911, and stayed with her until more helpers arrived.

It was time for her to be a helper. She'd been powerless only months ago and she'd struggled every day since to make her way in the world. Perhaps she could find her power by helping others.

She tossed off the covers and swung her feet off the bed as she reached for her cell phone where it charged under the lamp. She usually carried it in one back pocket with her notebook in the other, so she could use it as a memory aid. She called up the alarm function, selected vibrate only, and set herself a series of alarms with instructions through the day for when she knew she could take the time to review her notebook—on the bus on the way in, on her lunch, on her way home, after dinner.

Repetition eventually formed a memory, so she was going to review everything pertaining to this again and again. And if anything new was added, she'd review that, too. And, eventually, she wouldn't have to, because the information would be there for her to recall. She may not remember the event itself, but she would remember the details. That would have to do.

With knowledge came power. With purpose came power. She was going to take that power back starting now.

CHAPTER 7

Quinn pushed through the doors of the First Unitarian
Universalist Church, stepping out of the noise and
bustle of the front entrance of UC San Diego Medical Center across the street and into the hush of hallowed spaces.
She scanned the hallway, reflexively looking for the sign at
the end of the corridor to guide her way, even though the
church was becoming a familiar location. The cardboard
placard read UCSD HEALTH TRAUMATIC BRAIN INJURY SUP-
PORT GROUP in block letters above an arrow pointing to a
side corridor leading to the left.

You know where you're going. Time to trust yourself.

But the self–pep talk only grated on her this evening.
She'd spent the entire bus ride here reviewing her notes on
the murder and now felt jumpy and skittish. She'd actually
paused outside the doors, hesitating, questioning if she
should attend tonight, if she'd be useful to anyone else, or
if they'd be useful to her.

This is one way to be a helper. You can do this.

She squared her shoulders and strode down the hall-
ways, taking the turn to the left to find a door propped
open and an identical sign directing attendees inside. She
stepped into what was now becoming a recognized sight. She
wasn't sure how many sessions she'd attended, but guessed

by this point it had to be six or eight times for the circle of chairs, the pair of couches in the corner against perpendicular walls, and the sun-drenched table bearing a pair of thermal coffee carafes under the bank of windows to feel comfortably familiar instead of jarringly strange.

She scanned the room. Four other people were there so far—three men and a woman—but only one of them was familiar.

Will.

As if hearing her thoughts, he shifted his gaze to where she stood in the doorway. He said a quiet word to the two men and came toward her.

She placed him in his early thirties, but gray already threaded through the chestnut hair at his temples. His close-cropped beard was neatly trimmed, and his brown eyes were warm as he opened his arms in greeting. "Quinn, good to see you. Do you remember me?"

"You're Will. You lead the sessions."

His smile lit his eyes. "Excellent. Last week was the first week you remembered me, and I was hoping it stuck. Do you remember last week's session?" Quinn automatically reached for the notebook in her back pocket, but Will touched his fingers to her forearm, staying the motion. "No, you don't need your book. Baby steps, right? You remember me, which is amazing. You don't have to remember each individual session. I know you've been making notes on helpful strategies in the front part of your book, so you're taking good information out of each meeting you can access whenever you need." His gaze shot over her shoulder. "We have more arrivals. Grab a cup of coffee and we'll get started in a few minutes." He flashed her a smile of encouragement and stepped aside to greet the newcomer. "Cliff, good to see you."

Quinn moved to the coffee table where the only other woman stood, mixing cream into a paper cup of coffee.

She gave the woman a brief smile of greeting before turning to the coffee carafe.

"Don't remember me yet?"

Quinn froze in the act of pulling a cup from the stack before turning to the woman. She looked to be about Quinn's age, with her long red hair caught up in a messy bun, stylish in a lacy peasant blouse, colorful boho skirt, and strappy sandals. Panic shot through Quinn as her brain came up empty.

The woman must have sensed Quinn's reaction because she stepped forward with an understanding smile. "It's okay. You told me it could take you a few weeks, if not more, for my face to become familiar. I'm Vivian, but everyone calls me Viv."

"We've met before."

"A few times. This is my fourth session." She raised two fingers to press against her temple. "Car accident. Been out of the hospital now for six weeks, but I'm having trouble managing." Her gaze darted back toward Will. "Will's been great. The whole group is. Sometimes it just helps to know you're not alone."

Quinn scanned toward the circle of chairs. She couldn't remember any specific conversations, but was filled with a sense of camaraderie. Of belonging.

Sometimes when the memories weren't there, the emotional impact could linger.

This was a good place.

"Grab your coffee." Viv picked up hers. "Then come join me."

"Be right there." Quinn poured and fixed her coffee, and then followed Viv over to the circle of chairs as people took their places.

She scanned the faces, with a couple of them ringing the bell of recognition, some even with a few details filtering through. These were the people who must have been to all the sessions she'd attended, so she'd sat through their introductions numerous times. There was Doris, who looked to be in her seventies, who was recovering from a stroke. Peter sat across from her in his INVISIBLE ILLNESS WARRIOR T-shirt, a young man in his twenties with post-concussion syndrome from too many hits on the football field. And Ted, a forty-something cancer survivor, who'd lost a good chunk of his frontal lobe to surgery.

Others drifted in to fill the chairs, but Quinn didn't recognize them, or, if she thought their faces might have seemed familiar, couldn't remember their stories.

Will let everyone settle before he called the session to order. "Good evening, and thank you all for coming." His gaze traveled the circle. "Great turnout tonight. This is what I love about weekly sessions—it keeps everyone motivated to come back." He paused on a middle-aged woman three chairs over from him who sat clutching her handbag in her lap. "And it's wonderful to see a new face. We're a very open group here. You can discuss anything with us."

"Thank you," the woman said, with a small, hopeful smile.

"At the beginning of every meeting," Will continued, "we like to do introductions. Sometimes we're new, sometimes we have trouble remembering, and sometimes we get overwhelmed by too many new faces. We go around the circle at the beginning of each session. We'll start with me. I'm Will Dawsey and I'm a Certified Brain Injury Specialist. I entered the field because as a child and teenager, I played a lot of hockey and took too many hits. So many, I had to stop before permanent damage was done. I'm not just a medical professional; I'm one of you. That being said, I know my stuff. To be certified, I had to spend over five hundred hours helping people like you recover from serious injuries. I'm based out of UC San Diego Medical across the street, working with patients recovering from traumatic brain injury. I started this group because it was a group just like this that got me through some of my worst times, that showed me I wasn't alone, and that the hive mind can be the best support out there. There are some great groups on the internet, but the personal touch is better when it comes to everything we have to deal with.

"As we'll hear tonight, the term TBI covers a lot of ground, with its basis in many different causes. Each of you are unique, with your own unique situation, be it from stroke, accident, or assault, and there will be differences between you in both injury and recovery, but the important thing for us this evening is the commonalities we share. We can help each other out by sharing our struggles, letting each other know we're not alone, and in helping each other find ways to manage the challenges we face." He turned to the man on his left. "Ron, let's start with you."

"Sure." In his fifties, Ron looked like he was about to stroll out onto the links in his khaki trousers and polo shirt. He held the hand of the woman who sat beside him in a sleeveless collared blouse and knee-length skirt. "Hi, I'm Ron. I suffered a brain injury four years ago when I fell off my roof putting up Christmas lights and a bunch of landscaping rocks broke my fall. And me. I was in a coma for over a month with critical brain swelling. When I came to, I suffered from mood swings and irritability. Still do, though I'm learning to manage it better. I also have trouble focusing." He raised the hand joined with that of the woman beside him. "But my Cindy is with me every step of the way, even to coming out to these sessions so she can air her concerns and learn techniques to help me." He squeezed Cindy's hand and smiled into her eyes. "Together, we're going to figure this out."

"We sure are." Cindy took that as her cue. "As Ron said, I'm Cindy, Ron's wife. When Ron fell off the roof, I thought I'd lost him. What we lost was the life we had before the accident. But we're building a new life now. It's a little different than we thought it would be, but it's ours, and we're together. That's what counts."

There was a smattering of applause and then the introductions moved to the new woman. She seemed to force herself to set her purse on the ground and fold her hands in her lap in an appearance of ease, but the slight twitch of her left eye gave away her nervousness. "Hi, I'm Marilyn and this is my first time joining you. I'm here because my eighty-two-year-old mother had a stroke a few months ago. It's really changed her. She's anxious, unmotivated, and forgetful, even if it's something as inconsequential as what drawer holds the spoons. I'm hoping to learn some strategies to help her. Her doctors are great for the medical aspects, but when it comes to just . . . living, it's not their specialty. One of the nurses at her residence recommended finding a group like this. She's not strong enough right now to come, but maybe, someday, she'll be able to."

Doris, across the circle, nodded her agreement.

"I think you'll find some good experience here," said Will. "Many of us have been through a lot already and are happy to share what's worked for us. Doris is managing a similar situation herself and has made some amazing improvements. Right, Doris?"

"Absolutely. I can talk to you after the session as well if you want a little more of what's worked for me."

As the introductions came around to Quinn, the tangled ball of stress that never seemed to dislodge from her gut tightened further. Her memory lapses made her never want to be the center of attention, to never be put in a spot where it would be obvious she might not recall something she should. The less she talked, the less obvious her challenges appeared. Or at least that was the hope. "Hi, all, I'm Quinn. I was assaulted almost three months ago and sustained a head injury during the attack. I'm getting better, but I have some memory issues as a result." She knew it was ridiculous that even in this company she had trouble opening up about how debilitating her memory lapses were; this was the safest she'd be with the most understanding of confidants, but she quickly passed the baton. "Viv?"

"Hi, I'm Vivian. I was in a car accident eight weeks ago. T-boned at El Cajon and Thirty-Sixth. The fatigue and dizziness are kicking my ass. And the muscle spasticity isn't easing off yet. It's better; it's not all the time—it comes and goes—but it still can be an issue, especially if I need to react to something quickly. Stress locks me up. But I'm learning to manage it and am hopeful I can learn a few more coping mechanisms to get me through." She grinned into the circle. "And now you know if I stagger, I'm not drunk." She winked at Will. "Gotta keep that sense of humor."

"Absolutely." Will gave her a thumbs-up and a matching grin. "Peter, you're up."

After introductions, Will opened the floor. "Who wants to start?"

"I will," Luis said. In his forties, he was still recovering more than a year later after he was struck by a pickup truck while he was crossing the street at a pedestrian crosswalk. "I've been really struggling with motivation. I put stuff off. If I don't want to do the dishes, they just pile up. And since I live alone, there's no one to clean up after me. It's even affecting tasks I need to do as part of my job, because I just don't want to do them. I'm worried it's going to affect my job performance. I mean, everyone has stuff in their job that's at the bottom of their list because they hate doing it, but if I keep this up, I could get fired."

"Thanks, Luis." Will scanned around the circle. "I'm willing to bet this isn't something Luis suffers from alone.

Anyone else?" There were affirmative murmurs from several people around the circle. "I have a medical suggestion for him, but I'd like to hear your strategies first. What worked for you?" He turned to Peter, who leaned forward in his chair, his hands balled on his knees. "Peter, you have a suggestion?"

"Oh yeah." Peter scooped a hank of blond hair out of his eyes. "This is me for sure. Do you like games?"

Luis looked confounded at the quick change in topic. "Games?"

"Yeah, games. Video games in particular."

Luis actually flushed. "I have a fishing simulator I like. And the PGA Tour game."

"Nice! So, gamify the tasks."

"Gamify?"

"That's what I do. I give myself rewards for tasks as motivation. My easiest one is coffee. I *love* coffee. But I don't get my next cup until this or that gets done. Just don't stack the deck too high against yourself, at least at first. And pick what works for you."

"That's kind of what I do," Doris said. "But my reward is a break. I set a timer. Started at one minute, now I do five minutes. Work for that time period at whatever you're doing. For me, it's dishes or laundry. Timer goes off and I can take a break. Then do it again. It's more manageable for me when it happens in short chunks. And some days, when the timer goes off, I've not quite finished the job, so I keep going until it's done. That's just a bonus."

"Maybe I couldn't do my whole job that way, but I could use it to complete some of it." Some of the strain etched into Luis's face eased. "Thanks!"

"I can add what might be another angle on the root of your problem," said Will. "See how gamification works for you. If that rings the bell, then you're making strides. If you feel it's not enough, you might want to consider talking to your doctor about an Adderall trial. Have you heard of it?"

"Heard the name. Don't know what it does."

"Adderall increases dopamine and norepinephrine levels in the brain, but what you'd see is an increase in focus and calm which might help you keep with tasks longer. You could even combine it with gamification if that works for you but only gets you so far. Maybe instead of five minutes on task, you could do ten or fifteen before needing a break or reward." Will turned to the new member of the group. "Marilyn, what are the challenges your mother is facing? You said she's unmotivated, so maybe the timer trick could help for her. The anxiety may need a doctor's care, or, if it's not too bad, bringing her with you to these sessions may be helpful to her. Just hearing how other people are managing, or hearing about their difficulties, might make her realize others are walking the same path. And that there are people she can lean on." He looked to the group at large. "But Marilyn said her mother can't find the spoons. I know this is something some of you have dealt with. Can you give Marilyn some advice?" His gaze slid to Quinn.

She shrank back in her chair, her gaze dropping to the scarred tile floor at her feet. She could talk about what she did, but she heard the original solution here. Surely Ted would—

"I can tell you what worked for me."

Relief washed through Quinn at the sound of Ted's voice. As Ted launched into an explanation of labeled drawers and closets, checklists, a big calendar in a prominent spot, and a daily planner, Quinn kept her head down and her eyes on the floor.

She'd been wrong to come tonight. The notes in the front of her book said she'd picked up useful management skills from these sessions, but she was simply too unsettled to absorb anything useful or to contribute to the conversation. All she wanted to do was go home, back to her sanctuary, back to her pencils and pastels, where she could get some of this emotion down on paper. That would be more worthwhile than this, by a long shot.

The conversation turned to how acupuncture could improve muscle spasticity, and then how to deal with panic attacks, including long descriptions of how they felt, something that only left Quinn's heart pounding as if one was actually happening to her.

Spending an hour discussing everyone's problems usually left Quinn feeling comforted she wasn't alone. That others shared her issues or needed her help to solve theirs. It was give-and-take, and a matter of misery loving company.

But tonight, the room felt suffocating, and the talk of struggles and feelings of inadequacy simply left her feeling vulnerable. It wasn't just about her now, it was about the life of a man she couldn't remember.

A man who would remain in the shadows because of her shortcomings.

CHAPTER 8

It was a relief when Will called the meeting to a close. "You're coming next week?" asked Viv as she stood and stretched, her body gracefully catlike.

It was clear the hour had energized Viv. Quinn couldn't contain the spurt of envy, which left her feeling even lower because it was entirely undeserved. "That's the plan." She gathered her bag and empty coffee cup, rose from her chair, and glanced at her watch. "You go ahead. I need to check the bus schedule and I don't want to hold you up." She reached for her notebook, which would inform her of which bus to take.

"If it's like last time, you need the Route Three bus. Me too, because I'm not driving again, yet. The next one's at 9:08, out on Front Street. We'll just make it."

Quinn's smile was full of gratitude for someone who assisted and left her feeling like it wasn't a big deal.

They said good night to Ron and Cindy and were making their way toward the door when Will's voice sounded behind them. "Quinn, got a minute?"

Quinn froze, then spun around cautiously to find him standing outside the circle of chairs, his hand resting casually on a chair back. "I have a few minutes before my bus."

She turned to Viv. "Thanks. If I miss the 9:08, I'll see you next week."

"You got it." With a jaunty wave and a swirl of skirt, Viv sailed through the door.

Quinn waited as Will said good night to everyone else before turning to her with a smile. "Hi."

"Hi." She could hear the trepidation in her own voice. "Did I..." *It's not always about you.* "Did you need something?"

"I wanted to check in to see how you're doing. We've had about a half dozen sessions together at this point, I think."

"About that, or I wouldn't remember as much as I do."

"And you feel comfortable here? In this room? With everyone? With me?"

"Yes."

"Even tonight?"

Quinn fixed him with a puzzled stare. *Where is he going with this?* "Yes."

"That's good to hear. I wasn't sure. You seem off tonight."

Damn. She'd been trying to make things look like everything was entirely normal. Or at least new normal. She should have known someone trained to notice minute differences in personality and behavior as a way to analyze trauma damage would spot her reticence. "In what way?"

"You've really been coming out of your shell in the last few weeks. Talking more. Sharing more. Just seeming more relaxed. This was more like your first session. You seemed uncomfortable. And you didn't make any notes. In every session, you've made notes when someone gave some advice or said something that particularly rang true for you. But tonight, your notebook stayed in your pocket."

Heat flooded Quinn's cheeks, and she glanced over at

the coffee table, wanting to look anywhere but at Will. "Sorry."

"No need to apologize."

He purposely stepped into her line of sight, and she forced herself not to look away.

"If you want to talk about what's bothering you," Will continued, "I'm a good listener. No pressure, but I can sense something is different with you this week." He glanced at the coffee carafes, then back at Quinn with a wink. "Can I buy you a coffee?"

Quinn couldn't help the smile that twitched at the corner of her lips. "How can I say no to a big spender like you?"

"Exactly. How do you take it?

"Double cream, double sugar."

"Coming right up." Will prepared two cups of coffee and then carried them over to one of the twin couches. He handed her one of the cups and then sat down with his, waiting while she sat at the far end of the couch. If he noted the purposeful distance, he was kind enough not to mention it. "What's going on? Whatever you feel comfortable talking about, that is. You know how this goes—anything you say to me will remain confidential."

Indecision weighed heavily on Quinn. Since the attack, she was so often isolated. Even if she couldn't remember specific events, she knew the overall feeling of separation from the lives going on around her. Much of it was her own choice, wanting to hide her challenges from the world. But here was an offer of assistance from someone who understood the weight she carried, someone who could possibly help her find her way out of the fog.

Quinn pulled her notebook from her pocket, laid it on one thigh, worrying one of the satin ribbons between thumb and forefinger. She looked up to meet his eyes, and immediately felt safe. "The details are a bit fuzzy, but I've reviewed it enough times, including on the bus ride here, to feel sure it happened." She paused for a moment and then forced the words out with enough speed to ensure she wouldn't stop partway through. "I witnessed a murder Friday night."

"You . . . *what?*" His hand jerked, the coffee nearly sloshing over the rim. "Do the police know?"

"Yes. That was a mixed bag. The responding officers didn't believe me."

"How could they not believe you? Wouldn't the body be a dead giveaway?"

"That's where it gets complicated." She opened the book to the page becoming more and more familiar to her—the one with Reyes's name at the top. The book fell open easily to that page, but she ran her hand over it twice, as if to flatten it, but really more for comfort, recognizing that page was her connection to someone who believed her. "I read this just over an hour ago on the bus ride here, but I'm already losing the details." She offered him the book. "Why don't you read it for yourself? Then one of us will remember."

Will stared at the book, unmoving. "Are you sure? Your most personal thoughts are in there. You're okay sharing it?"

"Maybe not all of it, but this part, yes. I don't think I could explain it all to you. My retention is getting better, but it's not all there yet. And while I don't remember everything about you, I feel like I can trust you. And maybe you'll be able to help me figure out how to negotiate this."

"I'm willing to try. Thank you for trusting me with something I know is practically a touchstone for you." He set his coffee down on the adjacent table and took the book. "I don't want to intrude. You tell me where to start and stop reading."

"Start under the contact information for Detective Reyes. I'll tell you when to stop."

For the next few minutes, the only sounds in the room were the flow of traffic around the hospital and the turning of pages. She nearly stopped him when he got to the section on her feelings of guilt and sorrow for letting the dead man fade into the recesses of her consciousness, her hand rising, before balling into a fist and dropping into her lap.

The quick flash of his gaze told her he'd seen it, but when she didn't actually stop him, he continued on.

When he reached the end of her notes on the dream, she said, "That's all of it." Her fingers were practically itching to slip the book from his grasp, just to be able to feel the comfort of the smooth leather cover under her fingers, but she forced herself to intertwine her fingers, leaving them in her lap. *Trust him.*

He laid the book on his knee, then reached for his coffee, swallowing three or four deep gulps so quickly Quinn wasn't sure how he didn't burn his throat. She took a sip of her own, trying to give him time as he considered what he'd read.

"First of all," he said, "let me say I'm sorry you've gone through this. From the terror of witnessing the murder, to the handling of the responding officers, to your struggles with it since. It must have been horrible."

"Pretty much."

"From the perspective of what's happening in your head, how is your recollection of the events?"

"Repetition is making it better. I now remember that I witnessed a murder, and where I recorded those details, but I lose the details themselves."

"To an extent, that's a normal part of memory. The brain remembers the most important things best."

"As a method of survival?"

"Partly. At its core, it's based on our emotional response.

For someone with normal memory capabilities, when something major happens, we experience a bigger emotional response. That's all based in the limbic system in the brain, but the memory centers and emotional centers in the brain are geographically close together. And memory is associated with any big emotional response. As a result, we're more likely to recall frightening or emotional events." He looked down at the book and flipped back several pages. "You've actually done yourself a favor here without knowing it. The way you describe the attack, the details you included, it made me feel like I was standing in that alley with you."

"If I don't write it all down, it's gone forever."

"Maybe. I'm not convinced of that. If your issue is recall versus retention, you may get those memories back some day. But you're working with what you have right now. No matter the cause, you're not able to bring those memories back after a certain window of time, so you're compensating." He tapped the page with his index finger. "Compensating really well. You make notes that cover all five senses. You wrote down that Detective Reyes actually prefers your notes to the average witness testimony because they're frozen in time. They won't change. And because you're so attuned to the fact you won't be able to remember, you notice everything you can so you can record it. Even if it's for a short time, attention really focuses memory, and you gave it that attention." He closed the notebook and handed it to her. "In many ways, you're the perfect witness."

The surge of relief as the notebook came back into her hands was a warm wash of calm from head to toe. She never felt truly secure if the book wasn't in her possession, even if it was only a few feet away. She slid it into her back pocket, the familiar pressure comforting. "As long as a judge is okay with my testimony being that book and nothing more. Because what am I remembering now? I assume just the repetition of what's in the book, not memories of the actual event."

"There's a lot of that. But I'm not sure it's all."

"What do you mean?"

"Let's look at how you're beginning to retain some memories you can access. You knew who I was when you came in today. We call that 'rehearsal'—where repetition strengthens the synapses, which in turn results in better recall. The dream you had was one of two things—either your subconscious is pushing back on all those memories and trying to resurface them, or your brain is embroidering details around what you saw. But you say you made drawings of what you experienced in the dream?"

"Yes, because if I didn't get it down, I knew it would disappear."

"And were they lifelike? I can't draw stick figures, so if that happened to me, I'd be useless at capturing it."

"I can show you if you're interested."

"You can?"

"I took pictures that night to show to Detective Reyes. They're still on my phone." She pulled her phone out of her back pocket, brought up the first of the photos, and handed the phone to Will. "Swipe right to go to the next image."

Will stared at the photo of eyes for a moment before zooming in and then moving around the image. "This is remarkable." Head still bent, he looked up at her. "You're very talented."

"Thank you. It's a useful tool."

He flipped to the next image, to the page of mouths. "Remarkable," he repeated on a murmur. "This could lead the police to an identification."

"If they think it's real . . . maybe."

He moved to the image of the ears. "I'm sure when you

were hospitalized, some of your doctors explained to you what was happening to your memories."

"If they did, I don't remember it."

"That was always going to be a hazard. Here's what I think may be going on. Keep in mind the brain is a complex organ and we only know a fraction of what it can do and how it does it. It's an evolving field and likely will be for this century, if not beyond."

He returned her phone. "Let's start with memory basics. When the brain wants to store a memory for later access, three things have to happen. First, the memory is encoded, which is how incoming sensory information—be it sight, sound, taste, information you learn in a class, or even a thought that occurs to you—is converted into a format that can be stored in the brain. This happens in the hippocampus, which is one of only three locations in the adult brain where new neurons can still be created in a process called neurogenesis. Next, once the memory is encoded, it has to be retained or stored. Memory consolidation is a combination of encoding and retention, and is where the memory is stabilized. I won't get deep into the science, but it involves increasing the signals between synapses. Then, the final memory process is recall—the ability to access that memory." He sat back and considered her thoughtfully. "I've always thought you had a memory consolidation problem following your assault. The memories get made, because they don't disappear immediately, right?"

"Right. My short-term memory is fine, but that's so finite, just a few seconds. It's the long-term memory that's the issue. I remember, but then, given time, the memory just . . . dissipates."

"According to your notes, on the night of the murder, it dissipated faster."

"The one time I needed it to hang on a little longer, and

it poofs off at the speed of light." Quinn's tone carried the sting of bitterness.

"But you guarded against that. You took notes to make sure the scene, as you saw it, was accurately captured."

"Not that the cops believed me. They thought I made it up."

"But this Detective Reyes . . . she seems like she's on top of things."

"I guess? I don't remember *her*. I now know to call her, but I don't remember her."

"As long as she knows your current limitations, she can help you compensate. But back to your specific case. You can retain memories for more than a few seconds, so it's not your short-term memory that's affected. You can retain memories for an extended period of time, around an hour, so it's not strictly a retention issue. It could be a consolidation issue, or it could be a recall issue. Or a combination of the two. How are you sleeping? Have you made notes on it?"

"Some. And with dreams like that? Not great."

"How about before the murder?"

"Not well, overall."

"That could play into memory consolidation. Sleep is crucial for memory consolidation. It's when the hippocampus replays the events over and over during slow-wave sleep and the neocortex helps store away and secure strong memories. Not getting great sleep will inhibit that. Part of the problem here is recall is the main metric to judge memory storage of any kind. When you can't recall a memory, is it because it was never encoded? Because you can't recall it? Or because it was never stored properly?" He chuckled. "Sorry, listen to me lecturing. All I need is a blackboard and some chalk and we have all the makings of a college course."

"No, it's good, really. You're making my own situation

make sense to me. I'm going to make notes on this, because I'll never remember it otherwise, but it will help me understand what's happening inside my own skull."

"We could delve into this more with some one-on-one testing, but I'm sure your doctors have it in hand and wouldn't necessarily want me putting my oar in. However, in my opinion, based on what I've seen during these sessions, you're not consolidating memories as well as you could before the assault. You can recall, though potentially with limited accessibility, which may have to do with insufficient consolidation. That's what's happening in your dreams."

"You don't think I'm making this up out of whole cloth?"

"Not at all. You're only three months out from the assault?"

"Almost."

"You're still healing. You may feel like physically you're fine, but your mental and emotional recovery are ongoing. Your brain is still healing even if the outward bruises are gone. And from what I can see here"—he looked down at the image on the phone—"your brain is doing what it's supposed to do."

"What do you mean?"

"Ever done an activity—say driving to work taking the same route as always—and when you get there, you don't remember the drive?"

"Yes. I remember that from before the attack. I went to college for floral design, and some mornings after I'd arrived on campus, I didn't remember the drive in. It didn't happen often, and I always assumed it was too much stress and not enough coffee that early in the morning."

"That might have contributed, but more likely, it was simply your brain prioritizing things that are important. Remember I said your brain remembers the important things best because of the emotional component? Boredom from the same drive you've been doing for years sometimes isn't sufficient emotional stimulation. You're safely driving and in complete control, but if nothing out of the ordinary happens, you may not actually remember that drive or be able to distinguish it from any of the other uneventful drives. However, if a tractor trailer jackknifes in front of you, crashes, and bursts into flames, you'll absolutely remember *that* drive."

"I bet."

"The murder would be something to remember. Maybe not in its entirety, because stress can inhibit memory formation. You wrote about that in your notebook because Detective Reyes knows all about it. But that was an important event with a kick-ass emotional response. You think you didn't retain anything from it." He handed her back her phone. "I disagree."

"You trust these images?"

"I do. Of course, as good as they are, you're trying to get down facial characteristics of someone you saw in low light from a distance, so your drawings may not be entirely accurate. But they're the best representation you could do, considering. Hopefully Detective Reyes knows that, too."

"I hope so." Quinn drained her coffee cup. "I need to run or I'm going to miss my bus." She checked the time and frowned. "Already did. I'll catch the next one."

"I held you up. Let me give you a lift home."

"That has to be well out of your way. I'm all the way out in Mountain View."

"Actually, that's not bad at all. I'm in Emerald Hills, so it's only a little out of my way." He met her eyes. "Let me take you home. I kept you late. It's getting dark, and . . . considering . . . I'd feel better if I dropped you off at your curb." When she hesitated, he added, "Please."

He looked distressed enough at the thought of her getting into trouble on her way home alone; she reconsidered her knee-jerk response. Two months ago, she'd have never trusted him to take her home safely; she'd still been too on edge and too damaged. Now she was surer in her estimation of the situation. She didn't know Will well, but once again, her inclination was to trust him. He'd been gentle both in his handling of her and in helping work out her surfacing memory. She didn't think he was going to turn on her in the car. And it wasn't a matter of hiding her street address from him; he already knew it from her registration in the support group. More than that, he was right—it was dark out now and waiting nearly a half hour on her own in the gloom could be risky. It would be smarter to let him take her home. "Okay, thanks, I appreciate it. It takes long enough to bus back; I may end up at home at the same time as if we hadn't taken the time to chat."

"Great. Just one more thing—I want you to feel you can always reach out to me if you need to. This is a lot, so if you're struggling with any of it, know you're always welcome to give me a call. Let me give you my cell number. You can write it next to Detective Reyes's, so when you're reviewing that information, you'll see it, as well. The repetition will help you remember it's there so you know where to look for it if you need it."

"That's a generous offer. Thanks." Quinn opened the book—it now naturally fell open to that page from the repeated reviews—and waited, pen poised over paper.

Will rattled off his cell phone number, then stood. "Just let me tidy up the coffee. The deal with the church is they provide the coffee, but I take it all to the kitchen for easy cleanup for them in the morning."

"Sounds fair. I'll give you a hand and maybe we can do it in one trip." She stood and helped him pack up the coffee station before carrying it down the hall to the bright, gleaming kitchen.

The guilt had waned slightly. Maybe she wasn't as useless as she thought and would be able to help the case progress after all. If there was more than she thought inside her head, maybe it was just a matter of accessing it. As horrific as the act of murder had been, maybe it had shaken something loose in her head.

If so, she'd make the best of it. She knew Will wouldn't mind, would even understand, so she'd make some notes in her book on the way home to make sure she didn't forget what he'd explained to her tonight, how he thought the truth was there, being filtered by her dreams. His faith in her, backed by his scientific and medical knowledge, bolstered her.

Maybe she remembered more than she'd ever imagined.

Maybe she still had a chance to identify the killer, after all.

CHAPTER 9

The sun was already beating down from between wispy clouds whisked by ocean breezes when Quinn stepped off the Route 3 bus on Seventh Avenue just south of F Street. She stood for a moment as the bus rumbled away, turning her face up to the sun, enjoying the contrasting play of warmth and wind on her face.

The stillness and heat of the last few nights was gone, swept clean by ocean breezes. It was a fresh morning, and Quinn's mood matched it.

She'd spent the twenty-minute bus ride reviewing the notes in her notebook while a heavy bass beat throbbed behind her from someone's earbuds. Some mornings she would have found the noise irritating and intrusive; this morning, she had the focus to tune it out.

That was progress.

A new note in her own handwriting under Reyes's phone number told her to keep reading, that it was going to be okay. She read on, moving from horror to logic and relief as new people stepped into the situation, lending their aid and expertise. Additionally, though she couldn't prove it with an actual recollection, she somehow knew the horror of the murder didn't affect her the way it had originally. Maybe Will was right that the memories were under there, and her constant repetition and rehearsal of the information was blunting the blow.

Not that it was a good thing to be inured to violence, but in her case, it meant each time she read it over, it wasn't striking her brain as shocking new information. Also progress.

She glanced at her phone—8:12 AM. The shop didn't open until 9:00 AM, but on mornings when she opened, she liked to be there well in front of Jacinta, who was always there about fifteen minutes early. It gave Quinn a chance to review any orders on the books and make any notes she thought she might need. That way when Jacinta arrived, she'd be ready to jump into work.

Someday, hopefully, she wouldn't have to take all these extra steps. But, for now, it helped her get by.

She quick-stepped up Seventh with the light, then waited at the corner to cross F Street. Morning traffic whizzed by, everyone in a rush to get somewhere, from the tourists who flooded the city at this time of year to residents trying to get to work. She caught a break in the traffic and jogged lightly through the crosswalk, dropping to a walk on the far sidewalk.

"Morning, Marco, Luca." She waved at the two young men, both sporting matching hotel uniforms of black pants and red polo shirts, leaning against the outdoor valet desk under a wide red umbrella. For as long as she'd worked at the florist shop, at least one of these young men was at the desk every morning.

"Hey, Quinn." Luca waved back. "How you doin'?"

"Great." She looked up into the brilliant blue sky. "Going to be a good day. I can feel it."

"That's what I like to hear." Marco gave her a grin and a nod as she passed the desk. "Have a good one."

"You too."

Down to Sixth Avenue and across with the light, past

one of the area's rocking nighttime hot spots, infamous for its mechanical bull and Wild West menu, then a few international restaurants. The don't-walk hand had just started to flash at Fifth Avenue, so she stopped to wait for the next round to cross. As she waited, her gaze wandered up the street, over Mediterranean, Japanese, and Persian restaurants, sitting side by side with American taverns and pizza and burger joints. Her gaze came to rest on the front of Casa Morales with its wide burgundy awnings shading an empty patio that would contain packed tables and chairs by lunchtime.

She loved this city. She hadn't been born here; that had been far north in Sacramento. However, after her mother died while she was in college, there was nothing to hold her there. It had been impulse, deciding to look for work here when she graduated, but she'd been to San Diego a few times as a teenager and the lush gardens and all the green had pulled at her even then. She still had friends in Sacramento, but some others were already spread to the four corners of the country. In today's internet age, they knew they could stay in touch.

And they had. Visits and video calls and texts . . . until her attack. If you want to know who your real friends are, have a serious incident in your life. Then you'll see who'd still be there for you, or who was just there because you could put them up for the weekend on your pull-out couch so they could party in San Diego.

Even the friends she'd partied with the night of the attack, it had been a test for them, too. A disappointing test, as only two of the group still stayed in touch with her now she no longer enjoyed the social whirlwind each weekend. It was just too hard. She knew everyone's name and history, but couldn't remember any new stories, so it was like their relationships were frozen in time. She'd only made note of a single outing she'd attempted, outlining a short

evening where she felt disconnected from the first moment. There might have been more; perhaps she hadn't
noted the details because they'd simply been too depress-
ing. On top of that, the exhaustion and fatigue associated
with traumatic brain injury still plagued her. She didn't
have it in her to don her dancing shoes on a Saturday night
to hit the bars after a full day at work.

She was old before her time.

Two of the girls understood. They were the friends who
took the trouble to come to her, or meet her for lunch on
her break at a local restaurant, or for dinner after her shift.
She knew this from her notes and the call logs on her
phone. The rest of the friends had disappeared from her
life since the attack. Not recorded, not there. Just . . .
gone.

*Stop it. Remember what you told Luca. It's going to be
a good day. Don't suck it into a pit.*

Quinn straightened her spine and squared her shoulders
as the last of the traffic flowed through the intersection to
the north as the light went yellow. The light changed and
the orange hand flipped to the white walk symbol. She
stepped into the intersection and started across. As cars
streamed past, making their way down F Street, her gaze
wandered to the green light and the street sign above reading FIFTH AVENUE. And then to the black-on-bright-yellow
seal of the City of San Diego—the seal on every street sign,
with the twin dolphins representing the Atlantic and Pacific Oceans, the flanking pillars of Hercules for Spain's
historical jurisdiction of the area, the Spanish sailing ship
denoting their regional exploration, and the belfry over
all, in memory of the early missions that settled Southern
California.

The memory hit with a flash of pain that knifed through
her skull, and she pulled up short, her gaze fixed on the
circular seal.

But, in her mind, that wasn't what she saw.

In shaded black-on-white was a belfry with an arched, bell-shaped pediment capping the open space containing the bell, with sides sloping down in an expanding curve to the base. Inside, a bell hung from a crossbeam while additional architectural bands supported the beam and a bell weighing likely well over five hundred pounds.

But the image was indistinct, and parts of it were lost in gloom, shadowing even that brief glimpse.

The blast of a car horn jolted her to awareness, bringing her back to the present, where she stood partway into Fifth Street, in the middle of the crosswalk, with the hood of a black SUV less than a foot away as it tried to make a legal right turn on the red, but found its way blocked by some woman who'd unhelpfully planted herself in the middle of the intersection.

Quinn raised a trembling hand, mouthed "sorry" to the irritated man behind the windshield, and ran to the far side, just as the light changed and traffic filled the street behind the turning SUV. Not stopping there, she clutched her bag tighter and sprinted down the sidewalk, weaving around pedestrians and the glassed-in extension of a comedy club, past a hotel entrance, and a quaint Irish pub. She flew by the cursed alley with its metal gate, its security decorously camouflaged as outwardly radiating metal bars, now firmly closed and locked, past classic wooden double doors leading to the law firm, then around the corner and up Fourth Street.

She ignored the looks and the single "Hey! Watch where you're going!" as she wove through foot traffic, not stopping until she reached the shop. She dug in her bag for her keys, unlocked and opened the door, and slammed it behind her. Then leaned back against it, breathing hard, her heart hammering. Her bag slipped off her shoulder, but her hand snapped out to catch it before it tumbled to the ground.

Screw this.

She refused to live in fear. If her hippocampus was sending her a message, she wasn't going to cower; she was going to goddamn listen to it. Taking a firmer hold on her bag, she flipped on the lights by the front entrance, throwing the gloomy shop suddenly into a flood of brilliant, blooming color. She strode down the corridor, through the open doorway to the back room holding the main worktable, and hit the lights. Opening her purse, she dug out an HB pencil and the small sketchbook she'd been carrying for more than a month in hopes her memory might return and she could capture some of it.

Either she just had a flashback to a real memory, or her brain chose that moment to hallucinate. She refused to believe it was the latter.

She bent over the sketchbook and put pencil to paper, stopping occasionally to close her eyes and bring what she'd seen into focus. Her pencil was sure and steady, her eye sharp, making corrections when what her hand transcribed didn't quite match the picture in her mind.

When she was done, she straightened and stared at the sketch. It was the belfry she remembered from the vision, not in a patchwork of shadowed pieces, but as an extrapolated full image. As she stared at it, she realized this was really what she saw in the memory: not an actual architectural detail—and San Diego was lousy with historical religious buildings with belfries, be they churches or monasteries—but some kind of logo. Black-on-white, simple. Meant to be memorable at a single glance.

She pulled over one of the high stools and sank down into it, even as she continued to study the sketch.

Where did it come from?

She closed her eyes and tried to bring the image back.

Focus. The image is there, you just need to draw it out.

She took a deep breath and then blew it out through pursed lips as she let the quiet of the shop and the scents of the blooms she loved so much soothe her.

Slowly, piece by piece, the image built in her mind, until, with a flash of clarity, she knew what it was.

It *was* a logo; one she'd seen inside the van at the end of the alley the night of the murder before it drove away. That's why it was partly in shadow. Maybe not even entirely in shadow; while she couldn't see any people in the memory, according to her notes, the killer tossed in the body and then climbed in himself before sliding the door shut, so perhaps some of the gap was because the killer stood between her and the image?

If she could remember the image, why couldn't she remember the man himself? And why was that image inside the van? Staring at the sketch, tapping the unsharpened end of the pencil in a rapid tattoo on the table, she considered. What if it was a lawn sign, meant for display but not delivered yet? Lots of companies advertised work they did at a residence by displaying a sign while they were on the premises. Usually signs like those also had the company name and contact info, a phone number or website, but those details might have been lost in the gloom and distance.

And terror.

Or what about one of those flat, magnetic signs you could use on a commercial vehicle? Jacinta had matching signs with the name of the shop, its street address, and website in jaunty colors she slapped on her driver and passenger doors when she was setting up for a party, wedding, or funeral. Or sometimes just when she was driving around. She always said it was great advertising. But removable, so when she wanted her personal vehicle to be just that, it could be. What if it was something like that?

The more Quinn thought about it, the more she liked the idea. If you were going to take the company van to do something nefarious—like assist in a murder—you wouldn't want a trail leading directly to you in the form of a street address or phone number where you could be found. You'd take anything identifying off your white panel van so as to be entirely anonymous.

They didn't call them pedo vans for nothing. Identical to ninety percent of the vans out there, with no windows in the back, they were a company workhorse, but could also contain untold mysteries inside. Like carpentry tools, shingles, stacks of lumber, electrical components . . . or a dead body.

Maybe that was why all she could remember was the belfry. If it was a full logo, there would be more information—the name and full details on a company, for example—or a larger image. But those signs were flexible and didn't stand on their own. So perhaps it had been propped up or slipped in behind equipment to stand upright, and she only spotted a corner of it. The corner with the belfry.

Her quick glance at the floral clock on the wall gave her a jolt. She needed to shelve this for now. Her brain had possibly given her a clue she could sink her teeth into, but that had to be later. For now, she needed to put all this away and settle herself into the day's work before Jacinta came in.

She made notes in her book about her new insights, cross-referencing her sketchbook. Then she pulled out her phone and set an alarm for about an hour after she got home. She had every confidence this experience would be gone by tonight, so she'd give herself an hour to go home to make and eat dinner before she gave herself a task. The alarm directed her to look in both her notebook and sketchbook.

She took one more look at the sketch. Should she tell Jacinta? Her boss had been so kind and compassionate, but she was also human, and a businesswoman. There was only so far Quinn could push that. For now, she'd keep this to herself and throw herself into her workday.

She closed the sketchbook and tucked it and the pencil into her bag, then slid the notebook into her back pocket, as if the experience had never happened. But, for now, she knew it had.

The memories were there, but recall was the challenge.

If she could bring more of those memories back, somehow, anyhow, she could do it. She could turn Reyes's investigation around.

CHAPTER 10

Quinn curled up on one end of her couch, her TV on as she scrolled Netflix.

There were advantages to her amnesia. Any movie, series, or season that had debuted since her attack was new every time she watched it. But, for practical purposes, at least for now, she could only watch movies. She couldn't follow a miniseries or any sort of season of a show as it was too long from episode to episode for her to remember the ongoing story. But a movie she could manage. Sometimes she lost some of the beginning by the end, depending on the length, but it usually didn't ruin her enjoyment of it.

She cued up a romantic comedy, in the mood for something light and carefree. She selected the number one movie of the week, assuming she'd likely seen it already, but as it was basically a blank canvas for her, settled in to watch.

She was picking up her mug of tea when her phone alarmed.

She set the mug down, untasted, as she stared at her phone and a message from the past. **See morning's notes and small sketchbook.**

What does that mean? She knew alarm subjects had a restricted length, but that message didn't tell her anything. Just ordered her to do a thing.

"Okay, past me. What's up?"

She rose to retrieve her sketchbook from the bag sitting on the table by the front door and pulled out her notebook. She started with her notes, reviewing what happened that morning, piquing her interest to see the image. She opened the sketchbook, staring at the belfry for long moments. "Where did you come from?" She glanced sideways at her laptop, perched on the side table. "Time to enlist Professor Google."

She booted up, and as she waited to log on, she snapped a picture of the belfry before running it through Google Lens, Google's image recognition software—feed it an image, and Google's AI overlords would try to identify it for you. She checked to make sure she had a clear image, and then hit the eye icon to activate Google Lens, waiting as it went through the discovery phase.

A stream of results came back.

"Good job, Professor." Propping her feet on her coffee table, being careful as always not to dislodge any sticky notes, she set her laptop in her lap and logged in. A sticky note on the palm rest listed her password, but as she hadn't changed it since the attack, she ignored it and typed in the well-remembered string of letters and numbers. She brought up her browser and then picked up her phone, scrolling slowly through the list, knowing it might be like looking for a needle in a haystack, but if the needle was there, she wanted to pluck it out.

Lists on symbols of the Church. Commercial vector and clip art sites. Architectural links leading to a variety of sites around the world. A link to an artist's Etsy page. Travel links to the San Diego area. A site selling rare prints. A number of hits were in Cyrillic type, and Quinn assumed Russian belfry architecture had to be somewhat similar to San Diego's Spanish Mission style.

Farther down the list, she hit pay dirt. Even better, it was local pay dirt because she had a hard time believing someone came from out of town to kill the victim. Especially considering the way the murder happened, it seemed more like a foot chase, possibly a heat of the moment occurrence, not a planned out-of-town slaughter.

She was sunk if it was.

But if it was local, the image of a Carmelite belfry made sense. That Mission style belfry was used all over town as a recognizable symbol of San Diego and its history. It could be seen around town on existing historical buildings like the Old Town Immaculate Conception Catholic Church and the Mission Basilica San Diego de Alcalá.

Cross-referencing the possibilities on her phone, she started looking up potential matches on her laptop.

A local cleaning company downtown that specialized in churches and whose logo featured more of what she'd call a church bell tower topped with a cross. She glanced at the sketch again and then squinted at the logo. Maybe? It seemed a stretch, but her notes proposed a distant, low-light situation, so she couldn't depend on the sketch being completely accurate.

An electrical company in the Midway District that used a similar styled belfry in its logo. Similar, not exact, but close.

A catering company in Barrio Logan, whose logo featured the full front of a mission she wasn't familiar with. Not actually real? And could the image of the belfry she'd remembered only been a part of a larger image? She couldn't discount it.

She kept scrolling, cross-referencing, forming a list.

Then diving into the list to make levels of what she saw as likely possibilities.

A little under an hour later, she finally took her hands off the keyboard and looked at her list. She had six solid possibilities, but she considered three to be the most likely, because of the business type requiring that kind of vehicle. A firm like Santiago Architectural Design might need a large panel van, but it was less likely. Ditto for Emerson Barbers. But everyone stayed on the list, just in case.

However, at the top of the list were the three strongest possibilities, both for style and for function.

Mission Electrical in the Midway District.

Mundo Verde Garden Centers, which had multiple locations, but their main store was on Euclid Avenue in the City Heights neighborhood.

On the Go Delivery out of Five Points, conveniently right by the airport.

That was the short list. Now, what to do about it?

It would be lunacy for her to go to those locations, stroll in, and ask to see their vehicle fleet.

But . . . it wouldn't be lunacy to drop by, casually look around, and see if any of the vehicles matched the description of the van in her notes. She could go after hours, but if any of the places had security cameras, she didn't want to be spotted as the only person on-site. No, it would be better to go late in the day for each company, so any of the trucks out during business hours would be returning, but while there would still be traffic in the area so she could blend in. This would be her best chance to see most of the vehicles on-site and not be noticed specifically by any of the employees.

Because what if one of the employees was the killer?

He didn't see you.

You think he didn't see you. You don't know that for

certain. Your notes say you were in the shadows, but what if there was more light than you think?

She'd be careful. She'd be casual and unassuming. And she'd have to rent a car, because the locations were all over town and she wanted to make sure she could make a quick getaway if she felt any kind of threat. Waiting at a bus stop could be a fatal mistake if she was seen and identified.

Driving was a whole other can of worms. She'd been cleared by her doctors for regular activities, including driving, but it had been a long time since she'd had a car. She used to drive the family car when she needed a vehicle before, but had sold it to pay off debts after her mother's death. She'd kept her license current, though, so this could work.

She looked up one of the many car rental places near the airport and found that for under one hundred dollars, she could do a short-term rental. Pick it up mid- to late-afternoon and start with the electrical company. Head for the garden center, which would be in its last hour or so by that time, and scope it out. Hit the delivery company by the airport last. If employees were still working, by that point, they'd have completed their pickups and deliveries and would only be working on incoming flights. She'd be super careful, but she thought she could do it safely.

And choosing a rental place near the airport meant taking the MTS to and from it would be easy, even if it took longer than she thought and it ended up being late.

She picked up her mug of tea, only to discover she'd already finished it while she'd been researching. This time it wasn't a matter of forgetting; it was a matter of distraction. She'd been so deep into her search, she hadn't noticed she'd drained her cup. Putting down the laptop, she went to the kitchen, put the kettle on, and leaned against the counter as she waited. Her gaze drifted to the laptop and the lines of text she couldn't read, but could still remember.

For now.

She'd have to make copious notes so she'd remember why she thought this was something that needed doing, because she'd forget her purpose along with her plan.

Her plan.

Fear and logic simultaneously grabbed at her with icy fingers. What was she doing? This was madness. She wasn't one of the countless TV cops who not only tracked down a killer, but physically put him in his place. Truly investigating this crime wasn't her job—she didn't have the skills or the network to do so. And why would she get more mixed up in this than she already was?

The answer struck home with sharp surety.

Because life was full of injustice. Quinn was a prime example: struck down in what many would say was her prime, now barely surviving—forget about actually living—while the one responsible for the wreck of her existence still walked free. But perhaps she could find some vicarious justice for herself by helping find it for someone else. If she continued to play the victim, to hide away from the world, staying only on the periphery at best, a slain man's family would suffer. She couldn't help him anymore—truthfully, had never been able to help him—but she could help those he'd loved. And who loved and now missed him. And maybe, just maybe, something she learned could set Reyes on a path to finding justice for that unknown man. Then she'd find some for herself. And, maybe then, she'd be able to start to really live again.

Even though Reyes believed her story, there remained no physical proof it had happened. If she could find any kind of proof, or associate any person or vehicle with the crime, it would give the detective somewhere to start.

Quinn could at least do that.

She turned to the calendar that lived on her counter to consider when to put her plan into action. She checked her phone, found the day's date, and then looked at the calendar. Her work hours were filled in for the rest of the month, which was surprising, as Jacinta from *before* was never a planner and hours were figured out basically week by week at the eleventh hour.

Today was Friday. She was working all day tomorrow, and had Sunday and Monday off and was back to work on Tuesday. Unless something had changed, those were always the two days the shop was closed. She could do this as soon as Sunday, but standard businesses like Mission Electrical wouldn't be open—good for viewing the fleet vehicles, bad for staying out of sight. So . . . Monday it was. She'd make notes and set an alarm in her phone with a reference to a page in her notebook.

At this point, there were so many instructions and references to things to review, she'd taken the time to number the pages in her notebook to make sure she could direct herself efficiently. When time was of the essence, sorting through a few hundred pages—she couldn't remember the exact number now—just wasn't feasible.

She had to hand it to herself. If nothing else, she'd learned a lot recently about how to make her disadvantages work for her.

At her elbow, the kettle boiled, and she automatically reached for the cupboard labeled TEA and pulled out the box in the front. As she dropped a tea bag in her mug and added water, she chased away any lingering doubts.

She could do it safely, with minimal expense, and would feel like she was being proactive.

It was time to do a little off-the-books investigating.

CHAPTER 11

It was a half hour before closing when she pulled into Mundo Verde Garden Center. She parked in a spot a little distant from any other cars and cut the engine. Then forced herself to release her white-knuckled grip on the steering wheel and loosed the breath she'd been holding.

Made it.

It had only been twenty minutes getting from Mission Electrical to here, but Google Maps had taken her west on I-8 and then south on I-805 S. Not a big deal for most drivers. But for someone who hadn't driven in more years than she cared to mention, driving the packed interstate at close to highway speed was nerve-racking. The volume of cars was the trade-off for the slower speed as San Diego continued on its way home after a Monday workday, but too many of them were in an incredible rush, following too close or cutting in front of her to exit, so even what she thought of as the safe right-hand lane had kept her blood pressure sky-high for the entire trip.

She'd never driven in such a big city. The aggression and impatience of some drivers was a revelation.

She wouldn't ever be snarky about the MTS again. Waiting for a late bus was a pain, but once she was on-board, she had time to relax and review all her notes from the night she'd witnessed the attack onward, the minimum twice-daily task she'd set for herself that was making her growing bank of memories possible. Driving the streets of the city she loved made her despise it, at least while she was behind the wheel.

She flexed her fingers a few times, letting the blood flow back into them while she centered herself.

Notwithstanding the stress of the drive to Mundo Verde, the day had actually gone pretty smoothly. Well, from what she could remember. Already, the car pickup was fading, though to the best of her spotty recollection it had gone fine. Her marching orders to herself sat beside her on a yellow legal pad on the passenger seat. The heading *Research Trip* topped the page, followed by step-by-step instructions all the way from renting the car, to the order of her stops. Each stop had a full address, and she'd outlined for herself which bus and trolley she needed to take to get to and from home. Each completed step was checked off with the pen clipped to the top of the pad of paper.

The trip to Mission Electrical had been quick and useless. Located on a quieter industrial street inside the Midway District, it was an unassuming white cinder block, single-story building with a frosted glass front door and an adjacent fenced lot. Several of the company vehicles were in the lot, and while there were several panel vans, each bearing the company logo that included the image of a Carmelite belfry, the vehicles were painted Pacific blue and the logos were permanently embossed.

It was unlikely one of this company's vehicles had been involved in the murder. Not impossible, but in this fleet of ocean-blue vehicles, a white van with no distinguishing marks would certainly stand out as an anomaly. She hadn't taken Mission Electrical off her list, but it was way down at the bottom now.

On to location number two—the garden center. A huge sprawling greenhouse and shop, the parking lot was just off Euclid Avenue, with the greenhouse and associated shop behind it. There were no company vehicles in sight in the parking lot, but during her first pass by the greenhouse, she'd seen the second driveway marked SHIPPING/ RECEIVING just north of the main driveway, curving around the greenhouses and out of sight. She didn't want to be so obvious as to drive into that area of the greenhouse, but figured she could walk it on foot, or, if she was lucky, be able to see the area through the glass walls of the greenhouse.

She reviewed her list, refreshing her mind as to why she was there and what she was looking for. Then she grabbed her bag and climbed out of the car. She slipped her car keys into the pocket of her bag that always held her house keys, knowing if she forgot where they were, the key pocket would be the first place she'd look, and then slung the bag on cross-body. Leaving the parking lot, she stepped into color.

Overlapping wooden pergolas cut some of the glare of late afternoon, partially shading row upon row of plants beneath them from the full strength of the summer sun. Tables of summer vegetables promised fall bounty for the home gardener. A large sign over wooden and metal mesh tables of potted mixed arrangements of bright flowers with a tall center explosion of decorative grasses decreed HELLO . . . GORGEOUS! Shade plants clustered under pergolas covered with a fine netting, and, beyond, a large sign with FUN IN THE SUN! was surrounded by swaths of brightly colored blooms, entirely exposed to the sun they craved.

As a renter, Quinn didn't have space for an outdoor garden, but as a florist, she spotted many familiar varieties— carpets of bright purple salvia, tall spikes of pale pink and magenta lupin, bloodred and creamy white roses bursting from dark green foliage, the sunny smiles of gerbera daisies, and the graceful elegance of calla lilies.

She stopped for a moment to close her eyes and breathe in the complex mix of perfumes, her blood pressure dropping at the familiar scents. Feeling more centered and comfortable, she scanned the space, spotted the entrance to the greenhouse, and changed direction. Double sliding doors parted for her as she stepped out of the sun, yet the heat and humidity barely changed.

Inside, she was greeted by stands of multicolored orchids in various conformations, stacks of decorative clay pots, piled bags of birdseed, terrariums of succulents, and baskets of air plants. Color was everywhere, from bright pillows for garden furniture, to floppy sun hats, to tables of blooms of every shade imaginable. Quinn's eyes only barely touched on them as she studied the layout of the store. The front part of the greenhouse was shaded from the sun by draping arcs of fabric, hung from above, but past the accessories section of the store, the greenhouse opened to tables of plants under beams of sunlight.

Quinn strolled toward the rear of the greenhouse, hiding her true purpose by stopping here and there to consider an orange-and-magenta lantana flower cluster or a trumpet-shaped violet torenia with a bright yellow throat. She was determined not to attract any attention in a store beginning to empty of customers as it approached the end of its business day. Customers who browsed and bought blended in. Those who made a beeline for the back of the store to peer at the receiving dock were incredibly obvious.

Keeping one eye on the time—twenty minutes until closing—she finally made it to the rear section of the greenhouse, where the tropical tables were covered with ten-inch pots of snake plants, dieffenbachia, and hibiscus in full scarlet bloom. She stepped around a grouping of ten-

inch pots of three-foot-tall rubber trees and monstera plants
to pick up a peace lily, admiring the glossy dark green leaves
and pure white, lance-shaped flowers. She put it down and
picked up a second one, mimicking a serious buyer considering which individual plant to purchase.

Anyone in the store would have thought she was looking at the plant, but she was actually looking past it, through
the slightly grimy windows of a working greenhouse to the
receiving dock on the other side. The driveway she'd seen
from the street curved around the back of the building to
where the open receiving dock sat to the left of where she
stood, the driveway angling down so the delivery truck
beds would be level with the dock. A large cube van was
backed up to the dock, its side splashed with a variety of
giant blooms with BELLA LAGO PERENNIALS across the top.

Disappointment filled Quinn. There was no company
vehicle in sight, just a commercial truck from one of the garden center's producers. She'd been so sure this was the best
timing to find a delivery van back at the end of the day.
Maybe she needed to try first thing in the morning—catch
an Uber to arrive as they opened and see if that changed
anything. She set down the peace lily and wandered toward a grouping of birds-of-paradise fifteen feet to her
right, struggling to look casual and as if she hadn't just
had the rug pulled out from under her feet, chiding herself
for her disappointment as she went.

*There was never any guarantee you'd find what you
were looking for at every location. Make notes, leave
yourself instructions, come back.*

She knew she could do it, if only it wasn't so hard to
arrange. Notes to leave for herself with instructions and
reasoning, transportation to arrange, timing to catch a vehicle where she needed it to be.

She turned to look at the plants, and a flash of sunlight
temporarily blinded her. Squinting against the glare, she

stepped sideways, away from the worst of the bright light, and gasped, immediately trying to cover the sound behind a cough. She glanced sideways, checking the area around her for any employees, but the aisles were empty. Trying to maintain the casual look, she strolled to one end of the greenhouse, turned, and walked back the way she'd come, angling so she could see out the rear of the greenhouse.

A white van sat behind the perennials truck.

It was hidden from view from where she'd stood with the peace lilies, but now the front windshield was visible, and at just the right angle to reflect sunlight. But that was all she could see, just the front grille, fenders, hood, and windshield with no sign of any logo.

She needed to get back there to see the rest of the van. But how? That was definitely an employee-only area.

"Attention shoppers, the garden center will be closing in fifteen minutes." The voice on the loudspeakers echoed through the open space of the greenhouse.

She needed to kill at least another ten minutes. Then she could wander back here and see if the truck was gone. Time to pick something to buy so when she left the store, no one would think twice. She was just a normal customer, browsing to make a purchase.

She dawdled to the front of the store, and zeroed in on a selection of houseplants in decorative pots. She picked up a kalanchoe with hot pink blooms, but then spotted the African violets. There were several different colors, but amethyst flowers dotted with pink spots rising over variegated green-and-white leaves caught her eye. "Aren't you pretty?" She selected one in a subtly patterned, white ceramic pot, smiling down at her choice.

"Aren't those lovely?"

Quinn nearly jumped at the sound of a female voice beside her, recognizing she was more on edge here than she would normally be. She turned, laughing, one hand pressed to her chest, the other holding the pot she had managed to not drop to face a young woman with her long red hair tied back in a high ponytail, wearing the store's standard purple uniform shirt. "Sorry, you startled me. Yes, they're lovely. What variety is this?"

"That one's called *Devotion*. It's quite popular."

"I can see why."

"Do you need help finding anything else? The store will be closing soon."

"I want to take another look at the peace lilies at the back. Then I'll cash out."

The employee gave her a smile and a nod and went to make sure the next customer knew they were nearly done for the day.

Knowing her time was running short, Quinn quickly moved to the back of the store. Returning to the peace lilies, she was relieved to find the perennials truck gone and now she had a full view of the van.

She worked hard to mask the surge of triumph that rose as she studied the van—no windows on the side, single side cargo door, black-and-white logo on the side with a Carmelite belfry, the bottom of which was surrounded by an arc of flowers and the words MUNDO VERDE GARDEN CENTER, the address and phone number in block letters beside it. And the nearly invisible rectangular line around the logo and company information told her it was a magnetic sign that could be removed.

Mundo Verde was now at the top of her list. She needed to review all the possibilities, and it still wasn't definitive proof—what if she'd seen the logo as the van drove around town and that image had gotten mixed up into her faulty memory?—but she needed photographic evidence.

She set down the potted violet on an open section of table between the peace lilies and a group of Boston ferns and pulled out her phone. Making it look as if she'd just received a text, she opened her app, called up Jacinta, typed in a reply, and then didn't hit send. A quick sideways glance told her she was all alone at the rear of the store, so she launched her camera app, zoomed in on the plants in front of her, then quickly raised the phone, let it focus, and shot three quick photos of the van. Lowering the phone, she checked the photos—the logo was crystal clear—locked her phone, and put it back in her pocket.

She looked up for one last study of the van through the glass panel and met the eyes of a man standing beside the cargo door. He was short, with a lean build, tanned skin, and dark hair, wearing the same purple shirt as the other employees. But it was his eyes that caught her and held her transfixed. Clear blue and ice cold, they held hers in a flat, dead stare.

Fear shot like an electric shock through her nerves, leaving them jangling in alarm as her heart tripped.

Run.

She clamped down on the urge to flee. Innocent customers looking for their next purchase didn't run in panic when they saw a stranger. She took the time to select a lily and read the care instructions, all the while keeping it high enough to partially block her face from the man, then, as if deciding it would be too hard to keep alive, put it down again, picked up her violet, and turned to walk calmly toward the cash registers. Her hands were shaking—from fear or an adrenaline rush, she wasn't sure—so she clutched the pot against her abdomen, ensuring she wouldn't drop it, as she struggled to keep her face utterly relaxed and her body at ease.

If the pot jittered a few times against the counter when she put it down, the teenage cashier didn't seem to notice. Or hear the thudding of Quinn's heart right through her breastbone. *Get it together, Quinn. You're making yourself obvious.*

"That'll be ten dollars and seventy-one cents," the cashier said.

Quinn paid with a twenty-dollar bill—she tried not to buy anything on credit because she could destroy her own credit rating by forgetting to pay off a card month after month—and pocketed the change before taking her plant and striding out of the store, through the pergolas, and into the parking lot. It was a temptation to look back, to see if the man followed her and those cold blue eyes tracked her progress, but she wouldn't allow herself.

Normal shoppers aren't so paranoid that they check to see if they're being followed.

She got into the car, slammed the door, set the plant on the passenger seat, jamming it in place with her bag, and dug for the car key. Straightening, she scanned the lot around her for any sign of movement; all she saw was staff moving among the plants, getting ready to end their workday, and one or two remaining customers, still grabbing a few items before the close of business.

Seconds later, she was driving out of the lot and down the street, being careful to nail the speed limit, to seem calm, like a typical driver, not one whose world had just been rocked. She didn't know where she was going—she didn't need to know at that second—she just needed to drive. She mindlessly drove for about ten minutes before she pulled into a grocery store parking lot, found a space at the far side, and parked. She lowered her head to the steering wheel, letting her breath come hard and fast, finally allowing herself to react.

Why had he scared her so badly?

To the best of her knowledge, she'd never seen him before. If she took her notes as being truly accurate, he couldn't have been the killer, being too short and not bulky enough for the man she'd seen in the shadows.

But what if her notes weren't accurate? Not because she

hadn't written down what she thought she'd seen at the time, but what if between light levels, distance, and her terror, she hadn't understood what she was looking at?

If that was true, then could she trust any of it?

Panic radiated with ice-cold barbs, sending her heart pounding again. What was she doing here? If she couldn't trust herself to record the events of her life as they happened, how could she think there was anything she could do for a slain man? She was entirely unreliable.

Through the insecurity, logic and backbone battled to the surface.

No. Stop it. You believe what you saw. You just need to prove it. You'll prove nothing if you act like a coward and hide away as if it never happened.

Quinn forced herself to take a breath, to close her eyes and tip her head back against the headrest, to stop for a moment. Stop doing, stop thinking.

Reset.

She opened her eyes, turning her head sideways to look at the pad of paper holding her instructions. She hadn't doubted herself when she'd set herself this task. She might not have been so confident in the flashback that she wanted to tell Reyes, who was already stretched thin with her caseload, but she'd trusted herself enough to put time, effort, and money into this search.

And look what she'd found. A possibility. A white panel van with a magnetic sign with a Carmelite belfry that could be removed, if, for example, you needed to murder someone and didn't want to advertise your business at the same time. Was it *the* panel van? She had no idea, but it was a better possibility than the vehicles at Mission Electrical. She had no idea what the possibilities would be like at On the Go Deliveries; still, it was a possible step forward.

Speaking of a step forward . . . she studied the plant she'd just bought. Her reliable memories from *before* told her she'd had plants in the past, and had enjoyed their bright pops of color around the apartment and tending to her own modest garden. There were no plants now and whether that was because they'd died over her time in the hospital, or if she'd killed them with neglect afterward when she never remembered to water them, she didn't know. But this was something she could work on, something small. Making the effort to keep something alive. She was hopeful her capacity for memory was coming back, even if slowly. If not, she was learning how to manage, how to live life as close to normal as possible. Maybe it took multiple calendars, sticky notes, and alarms on her phone, but she was managing. Now she and her little plant would manage together.

She raised the flowers to her nose to inhale the soft, sweet, slightly powdery fragrance and smiled. "You need a name." She checked out the little plastic information spike in the planter. "It says here your real name is Saintpaulia, but that's a mouthful. Let's go with Paula."

She set Paula down on the seat, picked up the pad of paper, unclipped the pen, and, with more force than necessary, almost tearing the paper, made a check mark next to *Mundo Verde Garden Center*.

Two down, one to go.

"Come on, Paula, let's ride."

CHAPTER 12

Her eyes fixed on her computer monitor, Reyes absent-mindedly reached for her coffee mug, raised it to her lips, and took a sip. The bitter brew hit her tongue like scalding asphalt; she grimaced, swallowed it, half-burning her throat on the way down, and set the mug on her desk, pushing it away as far as she could reach. Maybe that would be disincentive enough.

Who was it who said the definition of insanity was doing the same thing over and over again, expecting different results? She'd always thought it was Einstein until she'd heard that was unlikely. Whoever it was, they'd nailed it. She had to be nuts to keep trying the cop coffee in the bullpen. It was never good, but desperation drove her to keep the hope. Disappointment kept the flame of hope quenched.

It was a travesty in her mind that here she was at police headquarters, and there wasn't a local coffee shop of any kind for blocks. It was practically criminal. She'd give her eyeteeth right now for a cappuccino. Or a caramel latte. Or, her favorite, a caffè mocha. Chocolate *and* espresso . . . how could you go wrong?

With a sigh that she clearly wasn't going to get the caffeine fix she craved—or, hell, even a decent cup of regular coffee—Reyes turned back to the report she was completing. Sometimes murder cases were complicated, like the murder of a family matriarch the year before where there were about a dozen logical suspects with their eye on the family fortune. Sometimes you never got your hands around a murder case, like the one in the F Street alley the week before with no body, no crime scene, and a witness who could only remember shadowed snatches of the event at best. And rarely—sadly, it was only rarely—you got a case where the guilty party might as well have been holding a sign with a neon arrow pointing directly at themself. Like in today's case, where her suspect killed his wife because he thought it would be cheaper than divorcing her, then, after stabbing her to death, he walked through some of the blood in his boots. He realized he'd done it, cleaned it off the floor and the bottoms of his boots . . . and totally missed the blood worked into the grooves in the treads. And there he was, two hours later, still wearing those boots as he worked a dolly in the garage where he toiled as a mechanic.

Maybe if he'd only gone to yoga class and had enough flexibility to see the blood. Maybe if he'd simply changed his footwear and discarded the boots in a dumpster somewhere or given them away to a homeless person. Or maybe if he hadn't been lying on his back with his bloody boots staring right at her when she walked into the garage to inform him of his wife's tragic death, it might not have been a dead giveaway. When she'd called him on it, he tried to make a run for it. When she tackled him to the ground, he started wailing his wife was a tyrant and it was the only way to get her out of his life.

Nothing like a witnessed confession to wrap a case quickly.

She glanced down at the tear in the knee of her slacks. She was still irritated at the damage done to her pants when she tackled him, sliding them both along cracked and gritty concrete. She liked this suit, damn it. It was one of her favorites. It moved with her when she needed to be active and didn't bind her in any way. And now it was going to be just a jacket. Maybe . . . ? Another look and a sigh told her it was doubtful the tear could be mended well enough for business wear. Detectives had to look sharp. The appearance was part of the authority, part of the intimidation, and the most hands-off way to make sure a perp knew who was in charge. Having patched knees somehow didn't carry the same punch.

She'd won this one, but taken one for the team in the process.

At least the perp was downstairs in holding, and it was doubtful he'd have a fancy lawyer making sure he made bail.

She returned to the report, grateful, not for the first time, for the keyboarding course her mother had insisted she take in high school. She glanced sideways at Detective Thom Walker, writing one of his own reports, pecking at the keyboard with two fingers. It got the job done, but the less time spent on paperwork, the better, as far as Reyes was concerned.

She made a mental note to call her mother that night.

She'd just starting typing again when Detective Felip Cervelló paused as he passed by, a pile of stacked file folders topped with a coffee mug in his arms.

"Hey, Reyes, did you hear about the washed-up DB?" Cervelló rebalanced the folders, leveling out his coffee.

Reyes looked up at Cervelló. One of their senior detectives, with gray liberally peppered through his once jet-black hair and deep lines carved into his bronzed face, he was one of Reyes's favorites in the bullpen. Slow to piss off, logical, methodical, he'd always been fair both to her and to any suspect that came into his purview. She knew from conversations in the break room his wife was pushing for him to retire, and he was starting to feel the pull of it himself, though, so far, he was fighting her on it. It was going to happen sooner rather than later, she suspected, and she'd miss him like hell when he was gone. He'd leave a vacuum she wasn't sure any of the other detectives could fill, including herself. No one else had his decades of experience, his contacts in the law enforcement and local communities, or his wily reasoning. Some of the brass had been here just as long, but they were the brass, not one of the guys in the trenches. And though she knew some of the brass well, you just didn't shoot the shit with them the same way, have the same connections to them. She had that with many of the guys in this bullpen, but most of all Cervelló, who had taken the new female detective under his wing when some of the other fossils still didn't like the idea of a woman in their ranks. He'd made her welcome, and she'd always owe him a debt of gratitude for that.

"What DB?" Reyes side-eyed the teetering mug and pushed a bunch of papers and the Columbo bobblehead the guys had given her for her thirtieth birthday out of the way. "Put that down before you lose your coffee. Granted, if it spilled on the floor, it would likely take the top layer of wax off."

"Could be an improvement," Cervelló quipped as he set down his load.

"No doubt. What DB?" she repeated.

"Washed up in Woods Cove."

Reyes's gaze shot to the large, detailed map mounted on the bullpen wall about fifteen feet away. "That must be about sixty miles north of here?"

"I'd say closer to seventy, but yeah."

"That's not our jurisdiction."

"Definitely not. That's Laguna Beach PD's bit, but I thought you might want to know. Seeing as you're missing a body."

Quinn's report.

"That's true, I *am* missing a body. What's the info on this one?"

"I don't know much. The only word that's filtered through the grapevine is it's a male DB in street clothes, and LBPD isn't missing anyone. At least that they know of."

"We have four missing males. One is from weeks before the reported murder, so it's unlikely. One is from just before, two after. I was going to follow up on those three in my spare time." She threw a sour glance at the report on her screen. "Which never materialized because of the eight other cases I'm juggling."

"All fresh?"

"No, two are older, but I'm not giving up on them yet. But without a body, it's a crapshoot as to who the guy might be. My wit didn't get any kind of good look, no judge of age or even hair color, just a general body type. All the missing men could fit it."

"And, God forbid, it's a flat-chested gal with short hair and you're barking entirely up the wrong tree."

"Yeah, that too. So the case is in stasis. However, if a body turned up . . ."

"A violent hit like that would shoot to the top of your list. It occurred to me you might not have heard about the DB because it only happened today, and I thought it might be worth following up on. By this point, LBPD must be working on an ID."

"I'll definitely do that. Thanks, Cervelló. Appreciate the intel." She looked down at the stack. "Maybe do this in two trips so you don't lose your coffee? That would be such a shame if you spilled it all. Tragic."

"At least if you spill some pouring a cup over the sink,

it'll clear out the drains." He grinned when she chortled. "Nah, I got it." He picked up his stack of folders. "Let me know if this DB pops for you."

"Definitely." She watched Cervelló make his way—un-eventfully—to his desk and then turned again to the map, considering.

A body had shown up, and here she was, short one body. Of course, that didn't mean the body was associated with her case. Lots of people fell out of boats or off piers, off surfboards, got caught in currents and drowned, had an accident cliff jumping into the Pacific, and more. But the body was dressed in street clothes, which made it *much* less likely to be a planned swimming excursion that went sideways. That still left boats and piers.

But if the dunking was accidental, the alarm would have been raised and she certainly hadn't seen anything come over the wire or on the news about anyone missing in or near the Pacific. Of course, if it was a suicide, the person might not be recognized as missing yet.

And seventy miles was a long way for a body to float. Then again, it was ten days since Quinn had reported the murder. It could have moved that far in that time period with the prevailing ocean current. Especially since she had no idea where the body had gone into the water. Or when. Or even if.

But in this part of California, the current moved north, so a body dumped into the ocean here would move in the direction of Woods Cove.

She liked Woods Cove. It only had a short beach, but it was surrounded by magnificent houses high on the cliffs. The sand was warm and soft, and the water was so, so blue as it lapped around the exposed, seaweed-covered rocks. It was a great shallow spot to suit up for a dive, and, facing due west, it provided a knockout sunset.

What a shame to ruin that natural beauty with a dead

body. And one that, if it was her missing victim, had to be starting to decompose as well as was likely fish food. The Pacific was the warmest it would be this month; even then, it only topped out at about seventy degrees Fahrenheit. That slowed decomp as did the saltwater environment, which would likely help with victim ID, but it didn't stop it. And the fish and crab would consider a soft body a feast.

She needed to call LBPD. If it actually was Quinn's victim, she might have a proper case to work.

She looked up the number for LBPD Homicide and placed a call to the Major Crime and Intelligence Team.

"Laguna Beach Police Department, Detective Aubert."

"Detective Nura Reyes, SDPD, calling. I'm looking for some information on a deceased male who washed up at Woods Cove. I'm trying to determine if the individual is related to one of my current cases. Is that your case?"

"No, Nick Duncan has that one. Hang on, I'll transfer you." There was a click, followed by ringing.

It was picked up after three rings. "Laguna Beach Police Department, Detective Duncan."

"Detective Duncan, I'm Detective Nura Reyes from the SDPD. I'm looking for some information on the body that washed up in Woods Cove. Have you made an ID?"

"Not yet. Body's at the Orange County morgue and the coroner is working on it. I can email you the photos we have so far if you can do a visual ID."

"Is the body in good enough condition to allow for that?"

"It's not bad actually. Decomp has definitely started, but I think he'd still be recognizable."

"Fish didn't go to town?"

"A little, but not bad."

Reyes opened the case file on her computer and jammed

the phone between her shoulder and ear. "What did you recover with the body?"

"Not a whole lot. No identification of any kind. The pockets were empty. Black jeans, burgundy, long-sleeved button-down shirt. Black socks and boxers. Wearing black ankle boots. You know, the kind with the elastic side panel?"

"Chelsea boots."

"Chelsea boots?"

"Yes." Reyes rolled her eyes. *Men.* "Skin color?

"White. Short buzz cut, blond hair. Blue eyes."

"Stature?"

"Exact measurements will come from the coroner, but tall and lean."

"It sounds like your DB potentially matches a witnessed murder here in the Gaslamp. My case has stalled because there's no crime scene and no body."

"That's a pisser."

"Isn't it, though. Any idea about COD? Any obvious injury?"

"Some scrapes from coming in against the rocks, but that's it. No obvious GSW or knife wounds. The coroner's tech didn't undress him at the scene, just moved the shirt enough to do the incision for liver temp, and with a dark shirt like that, it would be hard if not impossible to see bloodstains, but nothing I saw showed any kind of entry point. How did your guy die?"

"It was a one-on-one scuffle. Wit thinks his neck was broken."

"That would certainly explain the extreme angle of his head. Coroner will confirm if that's what happened. I should get details in a few days."

"Works for me. If I have a positive ID, I'll need the body moved down here and I'll take the case off your hands."

"That works for me. Give me your email address and I'll send you the images I have, and you can start on visual ID. It'll be password protected, so write this down."

Reyes jotted down the password as Duncan recited it. "Appreciate that, thanks. I'll let you know how I do." She gave him her SDPD email address, thanked him again, then hung up.

As she waited for Duncan's email, she opened the local missing persons cases. A quick scan of the women, just to be sure, told her that was unlikely. She moved on to the men, bringing up the four images to study, all provided by the family or friends who made the report.

The first, the one from weeks before the reported murder was the least likely. Short and stocky at 5'8" and 220 pounds, he didn't match Quinn's description of "tall and wiry." Of the remaining three, two men would fit that description, and one was less likely, as well as being considerably older. Quinn said the man had put up a struggle and hadn't succumbed immediately. She also had described his movements as "furtive." Reyes studied the face, clearly worn by years, and doubted this was the man. Still, she would keep her options open.

She studied the two younger men. Neither had hair that matched that described on the body, but hairstyle and length could be easily changed. Both men had blue eyes. The blond man smiled back at her from a dark background like he was taking a social media profile picture, whereas the slightly darker-haired man was caught in a candid pose, surrounded by family and friends.

She glanced at her email, knowing she was being unreasonably impatient and forced herself to simmer down. The photos were coming, and she'd get her chance to compare them to her records.

Of course, if the killing was of an out-of-town visitor or

someone traveling for business, a report might not even have been filed, or might have been filed in another jurisdiction. But that would be Duncan's problem if this didn't turn out to be her vic.

Behind the photos, her email shifted as a new message came in and she glanced at the sender. *Bingo.*

She brought up her email, opened Duncan's message after entering the provided password, and scanned down a repeat of the information he'd already given her, with about a dozen attached image files. She saved the files and then started with the image with the earliest time stamp.

It was a wide-angle shot of Woods Cove taken from near the edge of the water. In the background, two- and three-story houses, all with wide windows and multiple levels of balconies pointed seaward, lined the top of the cliff. Some even dangled right over the edge, supported by stilts at the beach level, the kind of architectural nonsense Reyes couldn't figure out. Why on earth would you build a house on a cliff on stilts when the San Andreas Fault tended to rupture every 150 years and it had been over 200 years since the last Big One? Did you want your house to collapse into the ocean? Was the view that much worse ten or twenty feet back, on nice, solid rock?

Sometimes people boggled her mind.

In the middle of the image, a flight of stairs rose from the beach, angling a few times as it stepped over the rocky cliff face making its way toward the terraced entrance off Ocean Way. Up at the top of the stairs, yellow police tape stopped beachgoers, neighbors, or simply curious onlookers access to the beach.

Protecting the cove, the sea cliffs, composed of continental granite and sedimentary rock, rose thirty feet in the air, though some cliff faces had piles of tumbled rocks at their base. Flat, white beach sand stretched across the nearly deserted cove, except for several large cobbles of igneous rock at the edge of the water that resisted the erosive forces of the ocean.

Reyes shook her head in wonder at the useless bits of info her brain held on to when she sometimes forgot the details of the meeting for the next week she'd booked the day before. *Thanks, Mrs. Gardner. Guess that eighthgrade lesson on local geology stuck better than I thought.*

The only signs of life—and death—were at the water's edge, where the waves still lapped at the dead man's feet. The picture was taken early that morning from the way the light just touched the body as it rose over the houses and cliffs to the east. A uniformed cop stood at the head of the body, alongside a man in a dark suit and tie Reyes imagined had to be Duncan, standing off to the side as the crime techs snapped pictures before the forensic team stepped in. Only after that could the body be removed by the coroner's office.

The man lay face down in the sand, one knee drawn up toward his waist, the other bent slightly. One arm was trapped under his body, the other flung out. The overall effect was that of a rag doll, tossed carelessly away by a child grown weary of playing with it. He lay with his left shoulder jammed against a ragged thrust of multicolored rock—chunks of black and rust locked into place by pale gray igneous sediment.

He'd come in on the tide and snagged on the rough rocks at the shoreline. Lucky, or they'd have lost him for a while longer, or, possibly, forever, which was no doubt the original intent.

She flipped to the next image. It was a close-up of the body, and she got a better look at the state of the corpse from the back, where it was clear that, with the exception of strands of kelp tangled under his collar, the shirt was undisturbed, certainly undisturbed by any kind of weapon.

She leaned in, studying the body position in relation to the head. She'd seen bodies thrown back on land by the sea before—impossible to work homicide in a seaside town and escape it—but this one definitely looked . . . limper. And she chalked that up to the head position, which struck her as an impossible angle for an intact spinal column.

Don't get ahead of yourself. Don't make assumptions.

The next few images were longer shots of the body from different angles before closer shots of the body in situ, including the visible hand and more detailed shots of his head. It was clear the body was in pretty good shape and only his ears and the fleshy part of his hand by the base of his thumb had been sampled by the local sea life.

Then, as more feet entered the images, the body was rolled and the face revealed. The first three images were also long shots before the photographer moved in and the face became clear.

As the first close-up of the face opened on her screen, the head now balanced on his shoulders and staring straight up, Reyes sat back, taking the time to closely examine each feature.

The man's blond hair was close-cropped on the sides and only slightly longer on top, giving him a nearly military attitude. The open, staring eyes were hazed with white, but tones of blue still glowed from beneath in the early-morning sun. The skin was a sickly gray with a waxy appearance, marbled with tiny bluish-green blood vessels just below the surface. His lax mouth sagged open, his lips starting to darken, their edges pocked from fish feeding. But the facial architecture was there, the cheekbones, the high forehead, the sharp nose, the shape of the skull.

Reyes opened the image of the missing blond man and lined the two pictures up.

"Found you."

There was no mistaking the similarities. While the dead

man's face had begun to bloat and discolor, the bone structure was the same. They'd confirm by family ID and by PCR, which would take time, but her intuition said this was the right man.

She pulled up the file to look at the details she hadn't wanted to influence her before. Jack DeWitt, thirty-seven years old, lived alone but was reported missing two days after Quinn reported the murder when his brother, Cam, became concerned because DeWitt couldn't be reached. Cam had used his spare key to get into DeWitt's duplex to find his starving and dehydrated German shepherd. After caring for the dog, he'd raised the alarm with police and the missing person report had been filed.

She scanned through DeWitt's information, stopping when she saw his occupation—a journalist with the *San Diego Union-Tribune*. She looked up his bio page on the *Union-Tribune* website, only to find the same picture as in the missing person report. So, not for social media, but a professional profile image. That explained why it hadn't been updated with his new haircut. It might be a summer cut and they likely only did professional photos for staff occasionally, so the change hadn't been captured.

She sat back in her chair, staring at the byline photo as she propped her elbows on the arms of her chair and wove her fingers together over her abdomen. Beside his smiling face was his position at the paper: *Investigative reporter—breaking news, policing, politics.*

Important topics. Topics that could be high stakes and high emotion.

"Well, Mr. DeWitt . . . what were you investigating that might have gotten you killed?"

CHAPTER 13

Reyes glanced at the old-fashioned analog clock on the wall near where her desk sat at the outer edge of the bullpen—it was just coming up on 4:15 PM—and weighed her next move. Even though she knew it would likely not lead anywhere, she grabbed her cell phone, called up a number, and dialed.

She'd watched Quinn put the contact into her phone with Reyes's name, which was why she was using her cell phone. She wanted her name to come up. Hopefully, Quinn would remember her at this point. If not, they'd manage.

"Hello?" The voice at the other end of the line was a little tremulous.

Doesn't remember, or not well enough to be sure. "Quinn, it's Detective Nura Reyes. Do you remember me?" The silence of Quinn's pause answered the question for her, so she didn't make Quinn admit it. In a few sentences, she ran through the events with Quinn, and told her to look in her notebook for Reyes's name.

"I remember parts of it," Quinn said, "but not all. Not you."

"That's okay, you will. Quinn, are you at work?"

"Yes."

"When are you done?"

"Six . . . but I often stay a bit late." Her voice dropped to a murmur for the last part.

"To make sure you get it all done. I remember you saying that. Do you think you could cut it a little short today and come down to SDPD headquarters? We're on Broadway, only about a dozen blocks away. It's a fifteen-minute walk, but I'd be happy to pay for an Uber for you. After the assault . . . I can understand you wouldn't want to walk here alone."

"It's okay, it's still light out. I can be there by about six thirty, after we lock up."

"Sounds great. I won't tell you how to get up here once you arrive, so you don't have to remember it. Just ask at the front desk. I'll text you a Google Map to get here. Can you put an alarm in your phone so you know to come?"

"Yes."

"See you then. And Quinn?"

"Yes?"

"Thanks for doing this. I'll either drive you home after or set up that Uber for you so you don't have to bus home. That way you won't lose so much time or have to bus home later than usual. Deal?"

"Deal. See you around six thirty."

Reyes set down her phone. She had two hours to pull together everything she could find on DeWitt, which meant starting with a judge and getting a search warrant for DeWitt's house. Cam DeWitt had a spare key, but that didn't denote ownership and she didn't want to wait for the will to be read—if there was one—to start looking for DeWitt's killer. Easier to get a signed search warrant. She needed to do a full property search and get access to his electronics. If he was working on a story, that might lead her right to the killer. Which reminded her to add access to his computer and files at the *Union-Tribune* to the warrant.

Reyes also needed to collect samples for DNA comparison. Perhaps Cam DeWitt would confirm the identification, but he might not be willing to carry that last memory of a beloved brother into the rest of his life. She felt secure in the identification of the body as DeWitt, but wanted a secondary confirmation of some sort, even if it took time.

The next question, however, was, how Jack DeWitt's body washed up in Laguna Beach.

She pulled up a map of ocean currents in the area, and had her confirmation. The warm waters off San Diego were part of the Southern Californian Eddy, the circular current just under one hundred miles across that ran north up the coast, past San Clemente, Santa Catalina, Santa Barbara, and San Nicolas Islands before hitting the cold water of the southerly California Current just west of Los Angeles, arcing west, and then flowing southward past those same islands with the California Current before breaking off to head east to run the circle again. Perhaps the plan had been to take the body out by boat and toss it into the Southern Californian Eddy knowing it would get caught in the California Current and head south.

If it made landfall in Mexico, that was their problem.

Reyes studied the map, quickly spotting a potential problem, had that been the plan. The Southern Californian Eddy lay about fifteen to twenty miles off the southern coastline. But between land and the Southern Californian Eddy lay the California Countercurrent, which brought warm water from Baja California up to join the Southern Californian Eddy. In fact, it was the influx of warm water from the south and cold water from the north that caused the eddy in the first place. However, the countercurrent flowed closer to shore near San Diego before joining the eddy proper closer to Los Angeles. Worse, at Laguna Beach, Catalina Island was precisely placed to split the two flows of ocean current, with the Southern Californian

Eddy to the west and the California Countercurrent to the east.

Which meant, if someone dropped the body into the ocean from a boat to make sure it cleared the San Diego area, but didn't go out far enough to make it well into the Southern Californian Eddy, they'd miss it, and drop the body in the California Countercurrent, which ran close to the shore.

Close enough that if the tides ran right, the body would wash onto the shore. And had.

The pieces are starting to fall into place.

She sent off her request for a search warrant and then spent the remaining time before Quinn arrived studying DeWitt's missing person report, and any information she could lay hands on right away.

"Hey, Reyes! Visitor for you."

Reyes looked up at the call, blinking at the clock to find it was 6:25 PM. She found Renfrew standing inside the bullpen door with Quinn.

She'd initially thought Quinn's appearance—willowy, with long blond hair and delicate features—was a good representation of her mental strength. She didn't think that anymore. Quinn was terrified of the blankness in her mind, and still kept trying to claw her way back to knowledge.

Time to see if there was anything for Quinn here today.

She closed the windows on her desktop, then walked over. "Thanks, Renfrew. And thank you, Quinn, for coming." She turned and led the way to her desk, snagging the unoccupied chair from the next desk for Quinn. "Please have a seat." She sat herself and waited as Quinn settled. "Do I need to explain again why you're here? Reinforce it?"

"I guess that depends on why I'm here." Quinn shifted restlessly in her chair, her hands clasping, then unclasping nervously.

"You're not in trouble, Quinn, in case you need reminding. You've done nothing wrong."

"Good to know. I'm never quite sure."

"Let's go over it again, because it doesn't hurt to drill down on the details. I know you're reviewing the case regularly, and it's getting cemented, but let's make sure it's crystal clear for you." She quickly took Quinn through the details as they'd been reported. "So . . . all that in mind, a body just washed up on shore at Woods Cove in Laguna Beach. I'd like you to look at some photos to see if he looks familiar."

Quinn's hands gripped tight, and she held very still. "Of the body?"

"I have pictures of the body, but I was thinking more along the lines of who I think he might be. I know there are some challenges here, between the distance, and the lighting—"

"And my memory," Quinn interjected.

Reyes refused to be anything but honest with her. "And your memory," she repeated. "But there's starting to be some leaking there. Think about your dream. Something is emerging. Maybe the shock of witnessing the murder shook loose some block in your brain. I'm not a neurologist or psychologist, but with a decade under my belt as a cop, I have a sense of people and how they work. I've seen them at their worst, and I've seen unimaginable strength and resilience." She studied Quinn, who'd turned her face away to stare at the floor. "That's the category where I'd put you."

Quinn's head shot up, surprise shining in green eyes that edged toward turquoise. "You haven't been paying attention."

"That's where you're wrong, because I *have* been paying attention. I have a feel for you now. Some people wouldn't have reported the murder. You did. Some would have ignored the visions that came to you in dreams. You didn't. Some wouldn't come here to do what you're about to do. You did that, too. So don't tell me you don't have strength. Life dealt you a lousy hand. Strength is not succumbing to the pressures of life. Strength is fighting back to whip life's ass. That's what *you* do."

The color rose high in Quinn's cheeks, so Reyes shifted the conversation back to business, not wanting her to be embarrassed. "Take a look at this with me. This is simply from comparing photos of men missing in San Diego with the photos of the deceased victim on the beach. I expanded the search to include anyone missing in the two weeks before the murder, all the way to today. That gave me four possibilities. Of that, two were not a fit for age or body type. Of the two it might be, one for me was the clear winner." She opened the folder on her computer with the images and found the one of DeWitt. "Ready?"

"Yes."

"Tell me if there's anything that strikes you as familiar. I don't know when this picture was taken, so certain aspects may have changed over time."

"Like weight, or whether he'd just gotten a haircut?"

"Exactly like that." Reyes opened DeWitt's byline image and rolled her chair out of the way so Quinn could draw closer. "Take a minute to look at him. Don't make any snap judgments. Consider all his features."

Instead of leaning in, Quinn sat back in her chair, her eyes locked on the image, still as a rabbit trying to avoid notice. A full forty-five seconds passed before she shook her head. "He's not familiar."

"Not in any way?"

"No. From my notes from that night, I was pretty far away. If I'd been close enough to see details, I think I'd have written them down. I made more note of his overall stature. I'm sorry."

"No need to apologize. I knew it was a long shot you'd recognize him for multiple reasons, none of which have anything to do with your memory. But I had to try."

Quinn parted her lips as if to speak, then closed them, pressing them into a flat line, their color leaching away.

But Reyes caught the motion. "What?"

Quinn glanced at the monitor again before turning to the detective. "Can I see the pictures of the body?"

"You want to?"

"God, no." The horror in her voice was unmistakable. "But maybe I'll see something there. I want to help, and I feel like I've done nothing but complicate things from that night."

"Not at all. Let's just look at you being here now. A body washed up in Woods Cove. That's the jurisdiction of the Laguna Beach PD. We wouldn't have paid any particular attention to it right away. Sure, whoever has the files on the missing persons would have gotten notification of an unidentified body at some point and DNA would have to be compared, but everyone in this room knows I have an open murder case with no body, so when it washed up, word spread back to me. We're looking at it now because you"—she made air quotes with her fingers—"complicated things. Quinn, the colder a case gets, the further people move away from it, and the weaker the recollections. You've moved this investigation way up the timeline, and that's good. Now . . . are you sure you want to see the dead man? It's not pretty. He'd been in the water for a week and a half, and while the water temp is colder than the air temp, decomp has started. And the fish have been at him."

Quinn winced.

"I just want you to be sure. You seeing it could be useful, because there are differences between the man in the photo"—Reyes indicated the image on-screen—"and the one on the beach. But this could be upsetting. I need you to know that before I show you."

Quinn nodded, her lips still a folded pale line, and pointed at the monitor.

Gutsy.

"Okay, then. This is the man on the beach." Reyes opened one of the shots from farther away, wanting to give Quinn a few moments to take in the environment, not just the ruined body.

"The clothing is right," Quinn said. "I said I had trouble seeing him in the shadows because he was in dark clothes." She contemplated the image a little longer. "He seems like the right stature, but I can't tell how tall he is."

"We'll be getting info from the coroner in the next few days, and that will include his height. I'm going to show you his face now."

"Go ahead."

Reyes opened the close-up shot on the man's face.

Beside her, Quinn inhaled sharply, but didn't blink, keeping her eyes fixed on the photograph. After about ten seconds, she let out a breath and then leaned in, bracing her forearms on the edge of Reyes's desk.

Definitely gutsy.

"Can you put the other picture beside it, please?"

"Sure." Reyes lined the photos up so they were side by side. "Does this jog something?"

"No."

Not that she expected anything, but that single word still carried the weight of disappointment for Reyes.

"But I think you have the correct identification," Quinn continued. "Whether this is the man I saw die, or not, I think this is the correct match."

"How so?"

"In art class, when it comes to sketching real people in figure drawing, you're taught not just about what you see on the surface, but what's beneath. The structure of a face, the shape of the skull, the layers of muscle and fat . . . it all contributes to the overall appearance. I look for that when I'm studying faces if I want to draw them. And while there are differences between these two images—like the hair is much shorter and the skin tone and texture is all wrong because, well, he's dead—I'm seeing the similarities that don't change."

"Like?" Reyes knew this already, but wanted to hear the thoughts of someone looking at it from a slightly different perspective and expertise.

"See the underlying bone structure? It's hard to see some of it because of bloating, but the basics are still there. The face is long and narrow, more of an oval, not square or heart-shaped. The jawline isn't soft but isn't as pronounced as in many men. He has a tall forehead, and his eyes are relatively close-set. Sharp cheekbones, though they're a little hidden here." She pointed to the image on the right of the dead man. "And his ears are uneven."

"Uneven?"

"The left is higher than the right. I mean, none of us are symmetrical, but some of us are worse than others. That stands out to me."

"I hadn't noticed that aspect. Good eye."

Quinn's smile was shy, as if she wasn't used to praise. "Thanks." She sat back in the chair. "I agree with your analysis. The photo on the left is your deceased victim."

Quinn turned her face away from the photos as if she couldn't take any more, so Reyes grasped the mouse and cleared her desktop. "I thought so before, now I'm only more certain."

"Who is it?"

"I can't tell you that yet. We need to inform next of kin first. I'll tell you as soon as I can, but that can't be right now. But the media will grab hold of it soon." *Sooner, once the warrant comes through to search his work elec-tronics. The* Union-Tribune *will be all over this as it's one of their own.* She stood. "Thanks so much for your time, Quinn. This was very useful. I'm going to order you an Uber now."

"Are you sure?" Quinn's face clearly telegraphed she'd appreciate the safe ride home, but didn't want to impose.

"Totally. Do me a favor? Make notes on this on the ride home. I'd like you to be able to refer to this if you need to."

"I'll do that."

"Give me your home address?" Reyes pulled out her cell phone, called up the Uber app, and ordered a car to take Quinn to the address she recited. "I'll text you the car and driver info when I have them, so you know you're get-ting into the right car. It will pick you up at the corner of Fifteenth and E where they can pull over. You'll text me when you're home safely?"

"I will, thank you."

Reyes stayed in place as Quinn crossed the bullpen and disappeared through the door. Then she sat down and brought up both images again.

She should have the search warrant by tomorrow morn-ing, so that was first on her list. She needed a DNA sample from DeWitt's home to not only compare to a sample from the body, but also the urine taken in the alley. It could take weeks or even months, and chances were smaller that they'd get a hit there, but maybe for the first time, she'd catch a break in this case, connecting that man to that alley. Naming the dead man was one thing, but placing him in the alley was key.

She felt secure in her identification of the body as that of Jack Dewitt, but she would contact Cam DeWitt to see if he'd be willing to do a visual ID of his brother as confir-mation. As much as she hated to do it to him, if he was willing, it would be a faster ID than DNA, which could also take months. But maybe she could pull strings there. She'd see what she could manage.

She studied the two faces, then pulled out her phone and looked at the images Quinn had texted her after her dream in the middle of the night. They hadn't discussed it, but as she reviewed the rage-filled images, Reyes didn't see a similarity. Maybe the images only captured the killer. She'd seen him in the van, so perhaps that was the face that stayed with her that night, even if she didn't know it.

She set her phone facedown on the desk.

Either way, they'd made tangible progress today. Now she had something to run with.

The open door of possibilities of the case beckoned.

CHAPTER 14

Quinn put the last clean dish in the dish drainer, let out the water from the sink, and towel dried her hands. She started to hang the towel over the bar across the top of the oven door, but it slipped from her fingers to tumble to the floor. With a groan, she hung her head, her eyes closed as she gathered herself.

She felt jittery and unsettled. And surprisingly, she knew why.

The face of the dead man had stayed with her. For once, she'd actually like a memory to go away, but the image seemed to take up residence in her mind, and her constant focus on it only reinforced it.

What was it she'd noted after that talk with Will? The larger the emotional reaction to something, the more the brain prioritized it?

She'd had an emotional reaction all right. Horror and sadness and fear, all rolled into a gut punch that had taken her breath. She remembered the reaction as well as the face . . . again underlined by the force of the emotional blow. She had no concerns it would still be with her by tomorrow morning—a good night's sleep would wipe her recollections clear. But for now, it hung over her like a dark mist.

Her gaze flicked to the open sketchbook on the drafting table in the corner. A face looked back at her, sketched in pencil with pastel shading. It almost looked otherworldly, carrying vague hints of muddy aubergine with bluish-green blood vessels streaking under waxy gray skin, and cloudy, staring eyes.

She'd drawn it when she came home. Not able to clear the vision from her mind as she made notes in the Uber on the ride to her own neighborhood, and, though her stomach gurgled with hunger, she sat at her drafting table and tried to exorcise the vision from her brain by pouring it out with graphite on paper. Then, when that hadn't seemed to capture the horror because he just looked too . . . normal in black and white, she'd reached for the pastels. Even just that subtle shading had brought out the horror in spades.

What it hadn't done was excise the horror from her mind. Even after making and eating dinner and cleaning up afterward, she still dwelt on it.

She thought she'd been brave to offer to view the face, to see if she could add anything to the investigation. No matter what Reyes said, Quinn felt she put up more roadblocks to the investigation than she took down. And she hated making trouble for people, hated not being able to offer any assistance in clearing up her own mess.

It's not your mess.

She picked up the towel, successfully hanging it to dry this time. Returning to the living room, she flopped down on the couch to stare at the African violet sitting on the coffee table, its bright flowers a cheerful burst of color over the small sticky note stuck to the pot reminding her she'd named the plant. "I sure hope your day was better than mine, Paula." She straightened the pot, turning it slightly so she'd see more blooms in an attempt to bolster her mood, then frowned at the remote sitting beside it. She didn't feel like TV tonight. But after having sketched that horror across the room, she didn't feel like working on her art, either. Books were out for now, because she couldn't remember the story from day to day. Maybe if she reread an old favorite? If it was one she'd read often enough, she'd always know where she was in the story.

She looked down the darkened hallway toward her bedroom to where her bookshelf sat stacked to overflowing with hardcovers and paperbacks. But it seemed like such a long walk right now.

Some days the post-concussion fatigue Will talked about at every meeting seemed worse than others.

Will.

She knew from the name, phone number, and instructions beside those for Reyes, he wanted her to call if she needed to talk. Her memories of Will weren't focused enough for her to know if it was a sincere offer, but why would she have written it down otherwise? The note was in her handwriting, so unless she'd done it under duress, she'd left it there as a helpful note to herself.

Before Quinn could think about it more, and possibly second-, third-, fourth-, or fifth-guess herself, she pulled out her notebook, picked up her phone, and dialed the number beside Will's name.

"Quinn, is everything okay?"

His use of her name startled Quinn momentarily before reason kicked in. *He has your number. If he expected you to call, he could have put you in his contacts so when you called, you were identified.* "Hi, Will. Is this a bad time?"

"Not at all, I was just sitting down with my book. What's up?"

"I'd love to talk something out with you." She was sud-

denly filled with awkwardness. What was she doing interrupting his personal time after work like this? People came
home and wanted to put their feet up and relax, not deal
with someone else's issues. "You know what, I'm interrupting your evening. We can discuss it tomorrow after
the session. I'll talk to you then."

"Wait!" Will paused for a few seconds, as if listening for
her breathing to make sure she was still on the line. "Still
there?"

"Yes."

"You're not interrupting my evening. Did you find my
name and number in your book?"

"Yes."

"I asked you to put it there. For just this reason—for
when something was bothering you and instead of bot-
tling it up, you could talk it out. It would also give you
someone else with memory of an event, even if it didn't
happen to me personally. Would you like me to pop
over?"

Alarm made her sit bolt upright. Here? In her apartment
covered with memory prompts? Checklists and sticky
notes and calendar listings? He knew about some of her
strategies, she was sure, because they must have discussed
it in session, but the sheer volume might catch him off
guard. Might leave her seeming less in his eyes.

She was already so much less now than *before*; she
couldn't bear to add to it. "Want to grab a coffee somewhere? I could meet you."

"Or I could pick you up. I know where you live and can
call when I'm outside so you're not waiting in the dark on
your own. Where do you want to go?"

Luckily, Quinn had lived in the area long enough to
have an opinion. "There's a nice little indie coffee shop

down on Thirty-Sixth and National. They'll be open for a few more hours."

"That's nice and clo—" He cut himself off. "Wait, is that the little joint that makes its own small-batch donuts?"

"That's the one."

"Suddenly I have a hankering for an apple fritter. Or a double chocolate glazed. So many choices. Thanks. Now I get dessert out. Win-win."

She chuckled, feeling lighter now.

"I'll leave in about two minutes," Will continued. "Remember, I'm coming from Emerald Hills, so I'll be there in about ten. Call you from the car."

True to his word, Quinn's phone rang nine minutes later, and she told him she'd be right out. After tucking her sketchbook in her bag and switching off all but the living room light near the front door, she closed and locked the door behind her, and then jogged down the half flight of steps to the front walk. Will's silver sedan was parked at the curb at the bottom of the walk. She noted that coming from his own neighborhood to the northwest, he'd pulled a U-turn so he was facing east again, all so she didn't have to run across the road to meet him.

Sometimes, it was those little kindnesses that really said something about a person.

"Thanks for picking me up," Quinn said, as she buckled into his passenger seat.

"For a chance at a gourmet donut?" Will rubbed his abdomen. "We men are simple creatures. Dangle food in front of us, and we'll show up. Especially if we don't have to make it ourselves."

She returned his smile. *Keeping things light to keep the pressure off. I can do that . . . for a while anyway.* An image of a pale face with opaque staring eyes swam into her mind. She gave her head a shake as if to clear it.

Will's eyes narrowed slightly, as if in question, but he didn't push. He pulled away from the curb, took the jog down to 41st Street, and then hopped onto National all the way to 36th Street. They parked in the busy lot and headed toward the shop.

Quinn eyed the nearly overflowing patio. "I don't remember ever being here in the evening before. This place is hopping."

"It's all about the donuts. Let's see what today's selection is."

The scents of yeast, sugar, and espresso hung fragrantly in the air as they entered the shop.

"Forget about actual food," Will said. "If they could bottle this scent for my house, they could just take my money."

"Yours and many others, including me."

They approached a glass case with three levels of shelving piled high with brightly iced donuts in neat lines.

Quinn scanned the offerings, recognizing some of the flavors. As a small-batch shop, they had some standards they made all the time: apple fritters, old-fashioned cake, double chocolate dipped, and more. But most of the flavors were custom and changed with the season: peaches and cream, butterscotch toffee stuffed, raspberry habanero, chocolate berry, strawberry-lemonade filled . . . and the list went on.

"What can I get you?"

Quinn looked up to find a college-aged woman with her long dark hair tied back in a low knot smiling from behind the cash register. She did a quick scan of the coffee offerings. "Could I get an iced white chocolate mocha, please, and a butterscotch toffee stuffed donut?"

"Is that everything?"

"No." She turned to Will. "Made up your mind?"

He reached for his wallet. "I can get this."

"You could, but you're not. You came out to help me. Let me get this." When he hesitated, she insisted, "Please."

His hand dropped to his side. "Thanks." He turned to the barista. "I'll get a cheesecake brownie donut and . . ." He studied the coffee menu overhead. "A cappuccino." He glanced over his shoulder. "There's a booth free by the window. Why don't I grab it?"

"That would be great, thanks."

Quinn joined him a few minutes later bearing a tray with both coffees and thick white ceramic plates, each loaded with a massive donut. She slid it onto the table and then rotated it so Will's coffee and donut faced him. "If I'd known I was coming here, I might have passed on dinner. This is a meal unto itself."

"Sure is." Will set his cappuccino in front of him and then picked up the plate bearing a huge donut, iced with a smooth white icing and covered with a chocolate zigzag, a full-size brownie perched on top. "This is like dinner with a dessert chaser."

Quinn set her coffee and donut on the table, then whisked the tray away to a nearby stand before sitting down. "I may only be able to manage half of this."

"That's okay. I understand they have takeout boxes, because you wouldn't be the first. Here goes." He took a huge bite of his donut, catching the corner of the brownie and part of the donut. He chewed, closed his eyes, and hummed in pleasure.

Quinn couldn't hold back the chuckle. "Would you and your donut like some private time?"

He finished chewing, swallowed, and waggled his eyebrows at her. "It's practically an out-of-body experience. You try."

She picked up her fat donut, filled with butterscotch toffee, iced in white, and crowned with a pile of butterscotch shavings. She took a much more modest bite, and had to wipe toffee off her lips when it burst out of the center. Her mouth exploded with the flavors of sugar, butter, molasses, and vanilla. She fought the urge to close her eyes in pleasure as he had.

His eyes twinkled from across the table. "I told you it was an out-of-body experience." He took a sip of his cappuccino and nodded in approval. "So . . . what's going on?"

Some of her pleasure trickled away. She knew this was coming, but the distraction was delightful, though apparently not enough to clear her memory of that face. "Not sure where to begin."

"Something happened today that unsettled you, or else you wouldn't have called. Let's start with that and work our way backward. Or forward."

She glanced sideways, out of the booth, to make sure no one was listening, but all around them was talk and laughter. No one paid them any heed. Still, to be safe, she leaned toward him, and dropped her voice. "I saw a dead body today."

He had raised his cup to drink again, and froze with it just short of his lips, balanced in both hands. His gaze flicked from the artistic leaf the barista had sculpted in the foam on the top of his cappuccino to Quinn. "Pardon me? Did you say . . ." His gaze shot sideways, to the table across from their booth.

"Yes."

He set his cup down into its wide saucer with excessive care. "Where?"

"San Diego Police Department headquarters. With Detective Reyes. And not in person. In photos." A shudder snaked down her spine as the picture once again filled her mind. "It was awful." She gave him a smile she knew had to be crooked. "But memorable. That was hours ago. I remember what you told me about the mind prioritizing things with a big emotional impact. Apparently this one had a big impact."

Clinical calculation slid into Will's expression. "You still remember what he . . . she . . . looked like?"

"He. And yes, which is unusual for me. Normally it would be gone by now. Why is that?"

"I think we can work that out. But first, who was it? Was it related to the case?"

"Yes. Detective Reyes thinks it's the victim."

"Does she know who it is?"

"She thinks so. She showed me a picture she used to compare to the photos of the dead man. Someone who was reported missing two days after I witnessed the murder. I agree with her. That's who the deceased man is."

"She showed you both images?"

"Yes."

"Who is it?"

"She hasn't told me yet. She said she needed to notify next of kin, which is totally reasonable."

"Yes. Just frustrating from your point of view, I'm sure."

"Extremely."

"Where was he recovered?"

"The body washed up on shore in Woods Cove?"

Will's eyebrows winged up. "All the way up there? Do they think he was dumped overboard?"

"I think that's the idea."

"Probably hoping it would go out to sea and never be seen again. Backfired on them."

"In a big way. Although right now, it kind of feels like it backfired on me, too."

"Because you can't get those images out of your head?"

"The one time I was looking forward to my brain letting go of something, it's doing the opposite. I prepared myself for not remembering. I made notes on the ride home, then when I was home, I drew the face. Then when that wasn't enough, I colored it."

"Trying to expel the memory," Will stated.

Quinn shrugged, a careless gesture, but one too full of tension to be smooth. "Didn't work."

"That will come in handy tomorrow. You won't have it by then." Will pushed her plate toward her. "You've gone pale just thinking about it. Take a bite. The sugar will do you good."

Quinn took more of a nibble and washed it down with her iced mocha. "Do you want to see it?"

Will was mid-bite himself, so he chewed and swallowed before responding. "The photos?"

"No, the sketch. I don't have access to crime scene photos."

"You brought it with you?"

The surprise in his voice brought heat to Quinn's cheeks. Of course he was right, this wasn't the place, and why would he want to see that anyway . . .

His hand came down over hers, squeezed lightly before letting go. "It's okay if you did. If you wanted to share it with me, I'm honored."

"To see a dead man?"

"To see something that has so greatly affected you that you reached out for my help. For my friendship. I'd like to see it."

"You'd like to." Her flat statement brimmed with disbelief.

"Not to see him. But to see what you saw. Does that make sense?"

"Yes." She opened her bag and pulled out the ring-bound sketchbook. She scanned the area around them, but no one was paying any attention. She opened the book, flipped to the page, and then angled the book toward the window on their other side, so no one could see unless they had their faces pressed to the glass. She passed it to him.

He took it, maintaining the slant of the angle. "*Christ*," he mumbled under his breath. When she reached for it, he intercepted her seeking fingers, clasping her hand, and holding it as he studied the image for long seconds. Then, releasing her, he closed the book and handed it back to her.

She slipped it into her bag and turned back to him, studying his face as he appeared to be taking a moment to put his thoughts together.

Finally, he spoke. "I can see how that stayed with you. By the way, I need to say that if that's a lifelike representation of what you saw, you may have missed your calling."

"I didn't. I'm a very good florist."

"If you're as good at that as you are at this, you must be damned good. But again, that stayed with you because of the horror of it, and then you unwittingly reinforced it. There was repetition in making notes, in drawing the sketch, in coloring it when it didn't seem complete to you. You've kept the memory alive instead of clearing it out."

"I should have known that."

"Why?"

Surprised, she looked up into his eyes. "Because it's my injury. No one is going to know it better than me."

"True. But as someone who is learning the boundaries of your injuries and the journey to healing, I'm seeing those boundaries moving."

Something akin to hope lit in her chest like the smallest of flames, buffeted by the wind. "Really?"

"Really. You won't remember the details of our first

meeting, but you couldn't remember my name for the length of the session. You couldn't hold it for even the hour. Several meetings later, you still didn't remember me from the week before, but you had my name at the end of the meeting. Now you remember me from one week to the next. More than that, you knew to call me when your day was overwhelming and you needed to talk it out. Maybe you don't, but I see the progress. Recovery rarely comes in giant leaps, but in small steps that don't always move forward. You have to look for the trends. Your trend is definitely moving toward recovery."

"But I don't know if I can trust the memories that come as part of my recovery."

"You mean the dream?" he asked.

"Yes." And the flashback. And the search it had spawned, leaving her with one strong possibility, and two others moved way down the list as the delivery company vehicles didn't match the profile of the one she'd seen. But she didn't mention any of it to Will, still not feeling secure in how real that image was.

"You'll learn what you can trust and what you can't. I don't think what's coming back to you are confabulations—false memories—brought on by stress, but I can't prove it."

None of it may be real. That thought had a chill racing through her veins. Maybe it was all false? She covered her reaction by taking the time for a slow sip of her mocha. "Confabulations. That's a real thing?"

"It is. And while healthy people can produce them, the frequency from those suffering from brain injury is increased. The memory is real to them, but entirely untrue." As if he could see the growing horror in her eyes, he quickly tried to clarify. "But I don't think that's happening here."

"As you said, you can't prove it."

"No, but everything I see, everything I know, says that's not what it is."

"Maybe I'm just incredibly believable."

"Detective Reyes certainly finds you believable. She's been your advocate all along."

"I know. Thank God for her. According to my notes, she believed me when no one else did. Then she stayed on it. And we're finally making progress."

"You definitely are. And don't let the repetition stop you when it comes to your art. The reinforcement isn't bad; just make a note that what you focus on will stay with you. There are so many benefits from art to individuals suffering from TBI. I think we talked about it in your very first session." He considered her thoughtfully, and she could tell his mind had traveled. "Though, that first time you didn't make notes, not like you did later, so this may be new to you, as you don't have notes to review."

"The art is good for me? It helps speed healing?"

"It does. On multiple levels, depending on the extent of injury. For those who have muscle spasticity and coordination issues, it can help tune fine motor control and hand-eye coordination. For those with attention issues, it strengthens focus. As well, artistic expression has been known for decades to decrease depression and anxiety, improve communication, and give an outlet for emotional expression. It also lowers cortisol, the stress hormone, which would be specifically good for you, especially now. It helps you center yourself after these repeated psychological jolts." He glanced at her nearly untouched plate. "We're ruining these superb donuts with this discussion. Let's enjoy our coffee and donuts, and help clear your mind of all this." He leaned his chin on his hand, a smile spreading wide. "Tell me about what you do at the florist shop. You must be amazing at it if it's better than your sketching."

She let him lead her into conversation and away from death.

But now she knew the name of her biggest challenge of all.

Confabulations.

Because if no one could trust her memory, if *she* couldn't trust her memory, what hope was there of ever solving this crime?

CHAPTER 15

Reyes was making progress, even if it was slow. She stood at the door to DeWitt's duplex, the spare key in hand care of Cam DeWitt, and the search warrant in her pocket. It was already 1:00 PM and she needed to get through the initial search in time to meet Cam at 4:00 PM at the office of the Orange County coroner. Cam had been nothing but helpful, offering to ID his brother first by photograph so he wouldn't hold up the investigation while she made arrangements, but he wanted to see Jack in the flesh, to have that final knowledge that his brother was gone.

It was going to be incredibly hard, but Reyes respected his decision. If it had been her sibling, she'd have needed to know for sure. Not photographs, not a detective reporting a match, but a visual confirmation her world would never be the same.

Reyes was sure the world would never be the same for Cam DeWitt. But he'd done the photo identification of his brother, and she was grateful that allowed her to jump straight into the investigation.

The search warrant had come through first thing. Reyes hadn't bothered to get her car and drive to the *Union-Tribune*, which was only a handful of blocks and a ten-minute walk away. She'd gone through his desk, talked to his coworkers, been given access to all his digital notes for current stories. There was nothing on paper at his desk, and it was going to take hours to search through his digital information to discern if something in his professional life had led to his death.

Interviews with his coworkers gave her an excellent picture of DeWitt the man, as well as DeWitt the journalist. Everyone liked him and was genuinely shocked and saddened when Reyes broke the news of his death. By all accounts, they painted a picture of a man who was smart and driven, and who had worked his way up the ladder fairly based on his own skills. It was a newsroom, so of course there was the odd personality clash, but no one bore any long-lasting grudges. He'd been known to go toe to toe with his editor from time to time, but they all did. It was a competitive business, where everyone wanted the big scoop, but overall, the newsroom ran pretty smoothly. He lived alone, except for his dog, and the general consensus was he loved his career more than he was interested in finding a partner, so he was perpetually, and happily, single. Reyes took notes on everyone's name, position, history with the paper and with DeWitt, but she was sure DeWitt's coworkers weren't the key.

One interesting fact was that DeWitt's coworkers reported he practically lived his life as a journalist on his phone. He didn't do notes with pen and paper, was one hundred percent digital, and often said the only useful tech was the one you had with you at all times. For recording notes, for reviewing, even for some writing—though he did his major writing on a full keyboard—his phone was his life. And if it wasn't in his hand, it was in his back pocket. He went nowhere without it.

Standing outside the newsroom, she'd called Duncan at the Laguna Beach Police Department to confirm that no phone had been recovered. He hadn't mentioned one, but she had to make sure, even if after more than a week in salt water, it would likely be beyond redemption.

No phone was recovered with the body.

Then the question remained: If he had his phone with him the night he was killed, was it lost in the struggle, fell out of his pocket on the road while he was being loaded into the van, was left in the van when his body was removed, taken intentionally because of what might be on it, or had it dislodged from his pocket as the current swept his body northward and was now somewhere on the Pacific seabed?

Her money was on the phone being intentionally removed. Considering the story Quinn told of DeWitt's murder, he'd been trying to evade someone, but was caught and killed. He'd done something or knew something that had made him someone's enemy. If that person also knew he lived his life on his phone, they'd have been sure to have removed it from the body in case it contained any link to the killer.

Even knowing the likelihood of DeWitt having left his phone behind in his home before going out for his last night was infinitesimally small, it was still her number one priority. That, and any computer equipment.

She wanted to talk to his brother, Cam, about the possibility that DeWitt used a cloud backup service. Anyone who spent his professional life on his phone wouldn't trust his data just to a portable device that could be dropped on the sidewalk, or in the toilet, or could simply have a hard drive failure. People like that had backups, either physical or in the cloud. DeWitt's coworkers only knew about the newspaper's backup system, but she had to hope that Cam knew more than that. If there were cloud backups, she was going to a judge ASAP to get a warrant.

She had gloves and evidence bags with her, ready to collect a DNA sample to compare to the urine in the alley, and would ensure chain of custody from the sample in situ all the way to the lab. A toothbrush would be perfect for this; if not, a brush with hair with the root bulb still attached. She'd cover her bases and grab both if they were inside the duplex.

DeWitt had lived in a two-story duplex in the South Bay Terraces area. Far enough out from downtown to allow for a small patch of grass for his dog, and close enough that it was less than a twenty-minute drive to the *Union-Tribune* offices. The duplex was faced with beige stucco, a matching brick chimney rising from the rear of the house to tower over the slanted roof. The residence shared a single wall with the other half of the structure, with part of the common wall on the ground floor occupied by a single car garage.

She knew that garage would be empty, as once she had a name for her victim, she'd looked for him in police records, and had found his car had been towed from a lot downtown the day he was reported missing. She didn't blame the investigator in the SDPD Adult Missing Persons Unit for not putting it together. They were a small unit, terminally understaffed, with their hands full. They'd have made the connection in the next few days, Reyes was sure. She'd seen the relief in Detective Adlawan's eyes when she told him Jack DeWitt had been identified and had the case transferred to her. Sometimes, there was simply too much work, and no one wanted a victim to fall through the cracks simply because they were human.

The front entrance was on the side of the house, two-thirds of the way toward the rear of the house, hidden from the road, the adjacent neighbor, and any other prying eyes by a tall, neatly trimmed boxwood hedge. Reyes slid the key into the lock, and opened the door.

And stopped dead.

Two days after DeWitt had been murdered, his brother

had come to this house to retrieve DeWitt's dog. Had something been amiss, he would have said something because it would have kicked the missing person's case up to the top of the list.

Someone had been here since Cam DeWitt and had trashed the place. She stood in the front entrance, not wanting to go farther until she'd returned to her car for shoe covers, but took the time for a long look.

The entrance opened to a living-dining space with a soaring ceiling that angled clear up to the second floor. Above, a railed balcony peered down on the main floor from under a skylight. Down on the ground floor, a sofa and twin chairs flanked a fireplace. A large, flat-screen TV hung over the mantel. Beyond, across gleaming oak floors, a table surrounded by four chairs, with two more against the far wall flanking a buffet, sat in front of sliding glass doors leading out to the backyard. Directly across from her was a kitchen all in shiny stainless steel and soft gray cabinets.

Or that's what Reyes's brain translated as she stared at the chaos. In reality, it looked like a whirling dervish had spun through the space. A whirling dervish with a razor-sharp blade leaving no stone unturned.

The couch cushions were hacked open, scattering foam and tatters of upholstery. A basket of dog toys was overturned, scattering toys into the detritus. The chairs were upended, their fabric lining sliced, the coffee table and end table kicked sideways. The TV lay face down, shattered, on the hardwood, the remnants of its mount over the mantel hanging drunkenly, the drywall behind it cracked and crumbling. The dining room chairs, all rich upholstered cream, were sliced open and tossed around the space. The table was still standing, but shifted to clear enough room to open the oak buffet and drag out its contents. Ceramics and glassware lay shattered all around it, the twin doors ajar. The kitchen was a similar scene of open cupboards, scattered and shattered possessions.

Were they looking for something, or sending a message? And if they were looking for something in particular, did they find it?

Reyes pulled out her phone and called for the crime techs. She wouldn't wait for them to go in, but she'd need to be especially careful. She returned to her car to grab nitrile gloves and shoe covers, put them on in the doorway, and then stepped in.

Nothing stood where it had originally, as far as she could tell. Every item, be it furniture, crockery, or ornament, had been displaced. Knickknacks were thrown, pictures pulled from walls and carelessly dropped, books lay crushed underfoot.

She stepped into the living room, glass from framed photos originally mounted by the front door crunching underfoot. She methodically moved through the space, examining items visually, not wanting to move anything until the crime scene photographer had done their thing. Rock-solid certainty was settled in her gut that there was nothing for her to find. Had there been, it was long gone.

Down the hallway that ran alongside the garage, she reached the master bedroom. It faced the street and had a bank of windows only feet from the front walk and perhaps fifteen feet from the sidewalk, so she was unsurprised to see the wood slat blinds were closed, sinking the room in gloom even in the bright light of midday. She pulled a pen from her pocket and tapped one corner of the rocker-panel light switch to avoid any latent prints as much as possible. The overhead fixture flashed on, flooding the room with light, and though Reyes expected the same level of chaos, it still took her breath away.

Every drawer in two dressers was pulled out and tossed on the floor, the clothing inside pawed through and thrown to every corner of the room. Bedding was pulled off, and pillows and the mattress—foam exploding out of multiple slashes—were tipped off the bed frame. The mirrored twin sliding doors of the closet were shattered, with only a few wicked shards still clinging to the top border. The two flanking lamps as well as their bedside tables were over-turned, twisted, and crushed. A shredded dog bed was tossed carelessly into the corner. Down from the pillows covered every surface.

She didn't dare enter, because she didn't want to disturb the down or track it all over the house, especially not be-fore the crime scene techs arrived. She could only see a sliver of the en suite bathroom, but it also looked wind-swept. No quarter spared, apparently.

Trying to find DeWitt's phone would be like finding a needle in a haystack.

She still needed to find his other electronics, though she had a bad feeling about what she'd find, if anything re-mained. A flight of stairs led from near the bedroom door up to the second floor. At the top of the stairs, the hallway split both left and right. Reyes followed the short hallway to the left to find a combination guest bedroom and li-brary. The shelves lining the long, windowless wall were empty, every book piled on the floor, and the bed looked similar to the disarray in the master bedroom downstairs.

Shaking her head, Reyes retraced her steps to the head of the staircase and beyond to the balcony. And there she found the electronics.

DeWitt had turned this space into his office, brightly lit under the skylight slanting over his desk, with the open space beyond the railing giving the area a light, airy feel. His dark wood pedestal desk was still in place, likely too heavy to move, but all the drawers were removed, the con-tents flung wide. A classic, green-shaded banker table lamp lay on the floor and the rolling, ergonomic desk chair was tipped on its side.

But it was the computer she focused in on where it lay partly under a broken desk drawer. A sleek black laptop, it lay in two pieces beside one of the desk's pedestals, the monitor snapped clean off the keyboard. The screen had an unnatural twist in it, and cracks radiated out from a crushed indent near one corner. The keyboard itself was pockmarked with missing key caps, one palm rest was cracked, and the other had a gaping hole. Stepping closer and bending down for a better look, Reyes realized the gaping hole wasn't just due to damage.

A slot the size of a laptop hard drive lay empty under the palm rest.

Whoever had done this must have been afraid of what information DeWitt had in his possession. Killing him wasn't enough; they'd needed to ensure there was nothing anyone else could find. So they'd searched for physical proof and destroyed any digital proof. Then taken the hard drive, just in case the breathtaking violence wasn't enough.

Reyes stood, staring at the wrecked laptop. Why not simply take the whole thing? Whoever did this could have simply tucked the laptop under their arm and gone out the door. There was no need for this destruction. Unless . . . yes, that might be it. What if they tried to get onto it and it was password protected and they didn't know if they could crack it? Or maybe simply didn't care to? Maybe not knowing what was on the drive wasn't an issue as long as no one else could learn it either? And they didn't want to be seen leaving the duplex with the laptop; that might have made them memorable.

Perhaps timing was part of the issue. When had all this been done? Clearly sometime during the previous week in the days following the report of a missing person, but when? It would be impossible to do this much damage without making any noise, which made her think someone must have risked a daytime search. Doing this in the middle of the night, especially with a joined wall between the houses, and worse, between the kitchens, where most of the breakables were located, would have reverberated through the entire structure to the owners of the other side of the duplex. But during the day, when many were out of the house at work, as long as they could get in unseen, and then block any outward-looking, exposed ground-floor windows—as they had in the master bedroom—the searcher had the chance to take his time. To be efficient.

He'd certainly been that.

The timing also made her wonder. Whoever had done this had waited until the dog—not a miniature breed, but a full-size German shepherd—was removed and no longer a threat. Had they tried to get in earlier and the dog had warned them back? You could shoot an attacking dog, but if a scared and hungry dog had gone for a stranger as soon as the door opened, the shot wouldn't even be muffled within the confines of four walls. And, contrary to what you saw in movies, a suppressor didn't actually muffle a gunshot much. It maybe dropped the sound twenty or thirty decibels at most. Between the barking dog and a gunshot, chances of discovery would have gone way up. However, if they waited until the dog was either rescued and removed, or simply died from neglect because they knew DeWitt wouldn't be coming home himself, they could have been watching the house and waiting for the opportunity.

She would add canvassing the neighborhood to see if residents had seen anyone suspicious hanging around.

She took one more look down over the balcony at the destruction below before she went outside to await the crime scene techs. This was overkill in the extreme. Whoever did this could have done a quiet search, or one that had left things disturbed, but not destroyed. The destruction had been a conscious choice.

Was it a message sent to someone associated with De-Witt? To his brother? To a coworker? To someone else with a different connection?

This wasn't a typical reaction to a man who was generally well liked. This was the reaction of someone who was trying to erase an individual. Or make the point that a life could be erased.

She could only hope whoever it was didn't know there'd been a witness to the killing, and who that witness was. This was a person who showed patience and strategy as well as brutal violence. Running on the assumption it was the killer himself who'd done this, it was clear he didn't have any trouble at all murdering with his own bare hands.

If he found out Quinn had seen him, even if SDPD tried to protect her, sooner or later, her life could be forfeit.

CHAPTER 16

Quinn slipped silently into the alley. In the silence, everything was magnified: the scurry of rodent feet and the drip of water from a downspout, a remnant of last night's rain; the nearly suffocating thickness of the warm night as air filled her lungs; the putrid stench of rotten food and garbage mingling sickeningly in her nose with the scent of lilies and roses; the flash of headlights as they streaked by on F Street, transiently lighting the alley before it sunk into gloom again; the sour taste of unease on her tongue.

She shouldn't be here, but she wasn't sure why.

The slick plastic of the garbage bag clenched in her fist was too slippery to hold securely, and she struggled to keep her fingers around it as she crossed the alley to the click click click of her heeled sandals on grimy pavement strewn with garbage. She needed to get rid of the bag and get back inside.

Evil things lurked in the dark.

Reaching the garbage bin, she moved to hurl the bag into it, but it abruptly felt weighed down when she tried to drag it off the ground to heft it into the air and over the lip of the bin. With a groan, she released the bag, wondering how it could suddenly be so heavy. Grasping both hands *around the knot at the top, she put all her strength behind lifting it, and it came off the ground two inches, then four, before the plastic tore just under her fists, leaving her holding the knot as the bag tumbled to the ground.*

With a growl of frustration, she bent over the bag, reaching for the ragged edges to gather them together and try again, when a horrible odor rose from the contents, assaulting her nose and making her eyes water. Blinking, she leaned in, unsure how the refuse from the shop—scraps of ribbon, plastic sleeves, disinfecting wipes, and miscellaneous trash—could smell that bad. All their scrap greenery and spent flowers went into the organic waste bin, not the garbage, but what was inside the bag smelled like rotten eggs or meat spoiling in the sun. Also, it shouldn't be that heavy. She folded back one edge of the bag to see what was amiss.

Her scream echoed endlessly off the brick walls.

The murdered man lay inside the bag, his body contorted in ways no live person's ever could. His head lay tipped back, his eyes, frosted white with death, staring up at her, as if pleading for help. His skin was almost ghostly white in the pale light, yet still she could see the undertones of green and purple—the muted tones of death almost glowed in the gloom. As she watched in horror, pale, wriggling maggots began to pour from his open mouth and out through his nostrils, filling the bag as if to drown him.

She screamed again as bitter vomit rose in the back of her throat.

A noise from the end of the alley had her jerking her head up. A lone figure stood backlit by the lights on F Street. The figure was huge, muscular, male, and had his eyes locked on her.

Quinn whirled, and ran. Miraculously, the dead end of the alley melted away, and light glowed softly at the end of a tunnel. She just needed to get there. She sprinted with everything she had, but her heels impeded her stride. The end of the tunnel was getting closer . . . closer . . .

He was on her.

She crashed into the ground hard enough to knock the wind from her lungs as she cracked the side of her head against concrete. But she got a view of the man on top of her as he pulled back to strike her, his joined fists raised over his head, ready to smash her skull into the unforgiving concrete again as she lay stunned and breathless beneath his slender, wiry frame. She had a brief glimpse of a high forehead, narrow nose, light eyes, and a dark mark trailing over the left side of his jaw and down his throat to disappear under the torn and frayed collar of a grimy shirt.

She wasn't going down without a fight. Lurching up, she reached out with both hands, aiming to claw down his cheeks and throat. In her dizziness, she completely missed him with her left hand, but hit home with her right, scoring a triplet of scratches down his cheek, blood welling dark and red in her wake.

He roared in fury and pain. Then his fists slammed down and agony exploded—

Quinn woke with a strangled cry, thrashing in tangled sheets, trying to free herself from the attacker. She had to get away, she had to get help . . .

Quinn's frantic struggles slowed as she came to, realizing she was in her own bed, as dawn peeked between her curtains, blown by a soft breeze. She was half on her stomach, half on her side, both hands braced on the bed as her hair fell in sweaty tangles around her face. She dropped down on a pillow damp with either sweat or tears—she couldn't be sure which—her breathing hard and ragged. She rolled onto her back and closed her eyes in exhaustion.

And saw the face of her dream attacker again. The whole face.

She lunged for the lamp, blinking against the blinding light and fumbling for the sketchbook, pencil, and eraser, right where the sticky note beside her lamp said they should be left.

Levering her body upward, and pressing the pillow against the headboard, she dropped the book and pencil in her lap and pushed her palms against the damp sheets several times to dry them as best she could.

She took a deep breath to steady herself. Then she picked up her pencil, and drew as if lit from within, needing to get the vision in her head onto paper before it dissolved into mist. When black-and-white wasn't enough, she threw back the covers and strode to her drafting table, yanking out the chair to throw herself into it, and digging into her case of colored pencils. She pulled back the curtain by the table, and the first fingers of dawn light spilled into the room to light her way.

It was another twenty minutes before she was satisfied. She sagged into her drafting chair, the black cherry pencil falling from her lax fingers to roll over the angled surface and drop to the floor.

She was exhausted. But as she stared at what she'd produced, it was perfect. She'd nearly gone into a fugue state to get there, but had she just identified the killer?

The facts of the murder were now solid in her memory. She knew the details of what had happened, even if she couldn't remember the actual event. But the dream . . . it had been like she'd been back in that alley, feeling the heat and the dampness in the air, smelling the garbage, and hearing the rats and the bass thump of some far-off music.

The shock and terror had certainly seemed real. The way her sleep tee and shorts still clung damply to her skin spoke eloquently of that.

She had to hand it to her brain—it had taken this situation and juggled some neuroplasticity into the mix. Yes, it was taking a lot of work to build the memories she needed in this crisis situation, but it was working. Maybe she was finally healing, maybe it was as Will described, and the emotional content of what drove her learning was key. Either way, she'd take it.

She needed to call Reyes, whose number she now knew could be found in her book.

Her book. She needed to make detailed notes before she called.

Write it all down. Check it. Then check it again. It was a strategy that hadn't failed her so far.

Taking her sketchbook, but leaving the colored pencils in disarray on the table and floor, she padded into the dim bedroom. She pulled back the curtains, and took a deep breath of clean morning air before sitting on the side of the bed and picking up her notebook. She took several minutes to make detailed notes, review them, then added a few additional descriptors before she was satisfied she'd captured the dream. Flipping back a number of pages, she found Reyes's number.

She placed the call with a quick look at the clock— 6:23 AM—and sent out a silent apology.

"Quinn." Reyes sounded awake already, sharp, and ready to meet the day. "Are you okay?"

"Yes. Well . . . mostly."

"Explain." The single word was all business and straight to the point.

"I had a dream. A bad one. Well, a bad one to experience, but I think some good came of it. I have a face."

"Whose face?"

"I think it might be the killer. Can I send you a picture?"

"Absolutely."

Quinn took a picture and texted it to Reyes.

When Reyes spoke again, she sounded distant. *Put the call on speaker.* "That's quite a face. Quinn, I'll say it again, you have considerable skills. Tell me what happened in the dream."

Quinn took her through it from start to finish. "Clearly, I'm embroidering on the truth."

"It could be your brain's way of working out what happened, especially a brain like yours which is still healing."

"Will might be able to explain a bit better what's happening here."

"Will?"

"Will Dawsey. I go to a TBI group therapy session every Wednesday night. He leads the session. I know from reviewing my notes I've told him what happened. He's helping me make sense of how I'm remembering, and what and why it's happening."

"He might be good to run this by. But some of what you dreamed here didn't happen. The body was never in a garbage bag, but the bag was why you were out in the alley in the first place. You feared you were heard in the alley, which amplified that fear and the potential consequences." There was silence for a moment. "I'd like you to come in. Now, if possible, while the memory is still as fresh as it will be in your mind. I'll call you an Uber because time is of the essence, but I'd like you at headquarters."

"Why?"

"To look at mug shots. The kind of person who does what you described, an organized kill like that, leaving no trace? That's not that killer's first kick at the can. And people like that have arrest warrants and charges. And we have their pictures. I'd like you to look at some faces. Can you do that? Right now? You'd still be able to get to work on time if you came now."

"I can be dressed and ready to leave in fifteen."

"We'll do the same thing as last time. I'll text you the car and driver when I have it so you know you're getting in the car I ordered." Quinn heard rustling in the background, and a low murmur. "One more thing," Reyes said into the phone. "Give me a rundown of the basic physical characteristics of the man you saw."

"Like hair and eye color?"

"Start with that."

"His hair was dark, so were his eyes. And he had a mark, a dark red mark that started on his cheek and ran over his jaw and down his throat."

"Like a gang tat?"

"Honestly, I'm not sure."

"Okay. Build?"

"Slim."

"Age?"

Quinn paused, bringing the face back into her mind. Grooves were carved deep around his mouth and eyes, but she read it as a combination of rage and rough living, rather than age. "That one's harder. In his thirties?"

"I can throw the net wider there and do twenty-five to forty-five. We can run it again after that with an even wider age range if needed; it will just return more hits and will take longer to search. Weight and height?"

"Can't even take a guess at that. I didn't see him full figure in the dream. And it's not like this was me seeing him in real life. It was a dream."

"I get that. But this may be the most accurate portrayal of what you saw that we'll get. Anyway, clock is ticking. See you downtown in thirty. Bring the sketchbook."

"I will."

Quinn ended the call and gave herself twenty seconds to sit and take it all in before she hit the ground running.

Had she done it? Had she identified the killer?

CHAPTER 17

Quinn stepped into the nearly deserted detectives' bull-pen at San Diego Police Department headquarters and quickly found Reyes—whom Quinn didn't recognize but who stood out as the only woman—sitting at a desk near the edge of the room.

Reyes was working on her computer, but must have had one eye trained on the door because she looked up the moment Quinn stepped in. She stood and waved her over. "I'm Detective Reyes. Do you remember me?"

"I know who you are from my notes. Your voice is beginning to sound familiar. The rest of you . . . not yet."

"Baby steps. Your ride went fine?"

"It did, thanks. Let me reimburse you for it."

"Nope. Don't worry, the SDPD is picking up the tab. I'm not risking a witness in a case, so I'm expensing the rides. Just like I did the last time you came."

Quinn scanned the room, as if looking for any familiar landmark. "I don't remember being here before."

"Not enough times for you to build the memory. I'm getting a good feel now for what it takes for you to remember things. Still reviewing all your notes on every bus ride to and from work?"

"Yes."

"And that's why you can remember them. One recent visit here won't do it, not enough time yet for repetition, just like you haven't seen me in person enough times yet. And hopefully there won't be enough times for you to actually ever remember this room." Reyes motioned to the second chair at her desk and sat down in her own.

Quinn sat down. "Do you want to see the sketch first?"

"No, I don't want you to see it again quite yet." She glanced at the clock on the wall. "It's been forty-five minutes since you called me. I want to see what you can make from what you do remember. If not, we'll review the sketch and start again." She turned to her computer. "I wrote down what you told me, and had the computer narrow the search based on those parameters, which took a little time, but it's done. I didn't want to waste any of your memory retention time running the search. This is the first batch of shots. Seven hundred and thirty-five in total."

"Seven hundred and thirty-five! That's the narrowed down pool?"

"You should see the original. This also goes back a ways, but yeah, it's a lot of people. Pull closer to the desk, here's the mouse. Look at the first set of shots carefully, then move to the next. I didn't include the mark you noted on the right side of his face, because it could be a tattoo or a recent injury, and depending when the shot was taken, it might not be in the photo. I didn't want to limit the pool based on that."

"I guess that makes sense." Quinn rolled up to the desk. "Okay, I'm ready."

Reyes opened the first mug shots—side by side front and profile, head and shoulders photos of a man who looked to be in his mid-thirties. The man looked tough and angry, and while he had the prerequisite dark hair and eyes, the shape of the face was all wrong and the eyes were too wide-set. "Not this one."

"Then click through to the next." Reyes indicated how to progress to the next pair of photos. "You don't need to tell me if you don't see him, only if you do. Take your time. Want an absolutely terrible, gut-melting cup of cop coffee?"

Quinn's gaze slid sideways, trying to judge if Reyes was making a joke or not. From her face, she was not. "It's pretty early and I haven't had any coffee yet today, so I'll say yes as long as I don't have to finish it if it's as bad as you say it is."

"Deal. How do you take it?"

"Double cream and sugar."

"I'll make it triple for you."

"Might be a good idea."

Quinn spent long moments studying each face, scanning each facial landmark and characteristic for anything familiar. She started slow, then got into a rhythm allowing her to move faster, still confident she wasn't rushing the process. Reyes returned with two coffees. Quinn took a cautious sip of hers and shuddered. It was exactly as bad as Reyes had warned her it would be, and similar to how Quinn imagined liquid tar might taste, with cream and sugar only making a negligible dent in the overwhelming notes of burnt charcoal.

She'd been at it for over a half hour, and was cognizant of Reyes looking up at the clock often—clearly worried time was ticking away along with any hold she had on the memory—when she stopped dead.

The man's face was squared off, with a well-defined jaw, a wide forehead below a straight buzz of dark hair, and muddy greenish-brown, close-set eyes. More notably, running over his jaw in the side profile shot was a dark-red port-wine birthmark.

This was him. She was sure of it.

"This one."

Reyes had been gazing out the window on the far side of the nearly deserted bullpen, but whipped back to face Quinn as she studied the photo. "You're sure?"

"As sure as I can be. None of the other ones were remotely familiar. This one rang the bell first time." She dug in her bag for her sketchbook, pulled it out, flipped past the face of the victim to the man who had attacked her in her dreams. She held the sketch beside the monitor. "Yes. This one."

The likeness was striking. Not the same expression—the one in the sketch radiated rage whereas the one in the photo simply showed a glum boredom—but the features were the same. Same eyes, same narrow nose.

Same mark with the same unique borders running down over his jaw and throat.

"Well done." Reyes nudged closer. "Let me get in there."

Quinn rolled back a few feet, allowing Reyes to get closer to her computer. "You have more information on him than just his picture?"

"Some data is more complete than others depending on what kind of record he has, but we'll at the very least have the basics on him." She clicked through to another window, scanned down a list of information. "This is Dylan Hobson. Mr. Hobson has quite a sheet over his three-plus decades on this earth. Armed robbery, assault and battery—"

"Sounds like the kind of guy to attack someone in a dark alley."

"His latest charge is . . . wait." Reyes was silent for a moment, scanning down the information on-screen. Then, "Damn."

"What?"

"This isn't Jack DeWitt's killer."

"That's the name of the man killed in the alley?"

Reyes slapped the heel of her hand against her forehead.

"Sorry, I meant to bring you in on the identity once the family had been told, but things have been crazy. Yes, his name was Jack DeWitt, and he was a journalist with the *San Diego Union-Tribune*."

"But I didn't dream about his killer?"

"No."

Quinn's shoulders sagged in disappointment as her hopes crashed. "Why not?"

"Unless he can manage to be in two places at once—in which case I'd like to know how he does it, because that would be hella handy some days around here—it's not possible. He was in Centinela State Prison, being considered a flight risk due to his history, so he's being held without bail awaiting trial on the charge of raping a minor female. He's been in custody for the last six weeks." She met Quinn's eyes. "I can check with the prison, but if there'd been a break, we'd have heard about it. He only went in about six weeks ago, so it's not like he was paroled out."

Quinn collapsed back in her chair. Disappointment filled her to the brim and then overflowed. She'd thought she'd nailed it. She thought she'd been able to identify the man who'd done this horrible deed. And now . . . nothing. "I was so sure."

"Yeah, you were. Hang on." Reyes dug into the file, flipping through screens, then starting another search.

Quinn took a sip of her coffee, instantly regretted it, and put it down on the desk.

Confabulations. What if none of it was true?

Maybe she'd seen that face at some point in a newspaper article about his arrest for the rape. Maybe she'd seen him on the street.

Maybe he'd walked into the florist shop to buy flowers for his girl and his birthmark had caught her eye, had startled her, and that had created the memory of his image.

Innocent until proven guilty.

She looked up when Reyes patted her arm.

"You're thinking this has been a waste of everyone's time," Reyes stated. "It's not." She pointed to the sketchbook, which Quinn had laid on her desk. "You came up with this for a reason, and I think I know why. Take me through the dream again, as much as you remember, because a couple of things are now standing out for me. Use your notebook if you need to."

Quinn did the best she could in recounting the dream—it was already beginning to blur badly in her mind—then went back and added more information using her notebook.

"Yeah, it's definitely making sense to me now."

Reyes looked pleased, but Quinn simply felt confused. "It doesn't to me."

"There were a couple of clues in your dream. Not a lot, but enough to steer me." She scanned down Quinn's body and then up again. "Is that what you wear to work? Jeans and a casual top?"

Quinn jerked slightly at the abrupt change in topic. "Well . . . yeah. I'm going to go in as soon as we're done here. We don't dress up because we regularly get wet and dirty. Everything is wash and wear."

"And that's what you normally wear for shoes?"

Quinn stuck out one sneakered foot. "I can be on my feet for eight hours at a stretch. I like something comfortable."

"And flat."

"Definitely."

"And we know that alley is a dead end."

"Yes."

"You can't have identified the murderer because this man"—she pointed at Hobson—"was behind bars at the time. But three months ago, when you were assaulted and left for dead, he wasn't. That's the perp you identified.

I'd be willing to place a good-size bet you just solved your own open case."

Quinn opened her mouth to speak, but her brain simply short-circuited and words evaporated, leaving her gaping like a fish.

Reyes crossed the room to the water cooler, drew her a paper cup of water, and returned with it. "Drink this. Don't torture yourself with that swill we call coffee." She pressed the cup into Quinn's hands, closed her fingers around it. "Drink."

Quinn did as instructed, mechanically taking first one sip, then another. Then her brain reengaged. "You think this is my attacker? But I never had those memories."

"You don't think you did. But the assault began before you had your head injury. Possibly only seconds before, but before. Unless you were knocked out first thing, you experienced the assault." She lightly tapped an index finger twice to Quinn's temple. "I say that memory is in there. Fighting to get out, apparently. So much so it altered the dream. Both your assault and the murder you witnessed were traumatic for you in different ways. Your brain is still healing from significant trauma, and it's mixing them up.

"Most of what you re-created was grounded in what you witnessed that night in the alley. Taking out the trash, only in this case the trash was the body of the victim. Seeing the killer far away at the end of the alley. You describe the alley in great detail, like your senses were heightened. Everything was more vibrant, the sights, the smells, the sound of your heels on the pavement." She glanced down at Quinn's feet. "Sneakers don't click. But I've gone over the file Detective Barrow put together on your assault. The heeled sandals you wore that night would have made exactly that sound. Then there's the alley. That first day I came to the shop, I checked it out myself. Walked it from end to end. Stood where you said you'd taken cover and looked to the far end to see what kind of view you had. It was a long way. And the alley wasn't open at both ends. In the dream, you described it as a tunnel, open in two directions. Just like the construction tunnel you were assaulted in in front of the hotel."

Quinn sat deadly still, not daring to breathe as Reyes connected the dots which, to her, seemed crystal clear.

"The last part that brought it home for me is the detail." Reyes picked up the sketchbook, studied the face. "Your skill makes this a possibility most others wouldn't be able to manage. They might be able to work with the department's forensic artist to create a face, but this one came directly from you, while the image was still fresh." She put down the sketch and met Quinn's eyes. "As I said, I stood where you did and looked out toward F Street. I have twenty-twenty vision. Even if I could draw—which I can't—I'd never have been able to see the kind of details you've included here. It was dark, they were struggling, and it was about seventy-five feet away."

"But that night in the construction tunnel, he had to be right on top of me," Quinn breathed. "Unless he knocked me out before I could see him, I got a look at his face. Possibly a good look."

"Which puts something else in mind . . ." Reyes pulled out her cell phone and flipped through image thumbnails before selecting one. "Look at this." She held up her phone with the page of eyes Quinn had sketched a week and a half before. "Some of these eyes match the sketch you did this morning. You assumed these images were from the murder, but it seems to be the catalyst for your brain pulling out images from multiple events."

"I never thought of that."

"If you remembered you'd done the sketches a week or so ago, you likely couldn't remember them in detail. But it's all good, because I can." Reyes looked back at the mug shot. "It sure didn't hurt that his face has a very distinctive mark. Guess it never occurred to a man to use a tone-matched cover-up to help hide his identity." Reyes rolled her eyes. "Then again, the night of the rape arrest, he was high as a kite on PCP. PCP, incidentally, is known to cause violent and aggressive behavior."

"In other words, he got high and took it out on whoever walked by. He didn't rape me though." For a moment panic streaked through her. *Or did he, and you don't remember?*

But Reyes's next words calmed her fears. "No, he didn't. Maybe that was his intent, but he beat you so badly you passed out, and maybe that ended the fun for him. He took anything you had worth any value and rabbited."

"He didn't have a sapphire ring on him, did he?"

"Let me check." Reyes scanned the record. "Not according to this. You were wearing one that night, right?"

"Yes. My mother's ring. One of the only things I had left of her."

"She's gone now?"

"Yes, died when I was in college."

"I'm sorry. Do you have any pictures of the ring?"

"I'm sure I do, on my laptop back in my apartment. I'd have to look."

"A detail like that likely got lost in your assault and injury investigation, and you weren't missing it at the time because of the trauma. But let me see what I can do. The Robbery Unit here in the SDPD has connections to local pawn shops and others who might buy that kind of jewelry. We may be able to track it down."

Hope rose to fill Quinn's chest in a warm, comforting wave. "Really?"

"Really. Set an alarm in your phone to remind you to send me the most detailed photos you have of it, and I'll see what we can find." Reyes looked back at her monitor as Quinn pulled out her phone and set an alarm. "Back to this guy. When he was arrested more than a month later, he was caught just after an assault. The victim called for help and a couple of units happened to be nearby. And because he was high, he wasn't overly smart about staying out of sight, and they nabbed him."

A sudden thought occurred, and dismay punctured Quinn's growing swell of joy. "This is all well and good, but just because this makes sense and we think it's real, doesn't mean it is. That's not how the legal system works. No court of law is going to take the word of a woman who can't remember things from one day to the next without a huge amount of effort."

"Sadly, you're right. It's not how the legal system works. Otherwise, a bunch of people I have hunches about would be in jail instead of free in the world to commit their next crime. But for this? We have rock-solid evidence. We have DNA."

"We do?"

Reyes's grin was full of satisfaction. "We do, because you fought back. There were skin cells recovered from under your nails. You scratched him during the struggle. They've been run, but there were no matches. And while the rape victim visually ID'd him, rape kit samples were taken at the hospital to nail his ass through DNA. Which is still ongoing because of backlogs, but I expect it to be completed anytime now. But if Mr. Hobson here turns out to be a match to you, too . . ."

Quinn's breath caught on a little jolt of hope. "Then he's the one who did it. And will go to jail for it, as well."

"You got it."

For a moment, all Quinn could do was sit and stare at the mug shot as disbelief, relief, vindication, and elation combined to crash over her, nearly sweeping her under. It hadn't been her intent, but she might have found the man who had, possibly irrevocably, changed her life. The man responsible for her feelings of inadequacy, and all the work she had to do just to appear normal, even when she was shrinking inside. All the things she'd lost—independence, friends, her vision of her future, her memories of any individual event in the last three months. All gone.

She wouldn't get any of it back, but he'd pay. And he'd never touch her again.

Safe.

As long as she hadn't been seen at the end of the alley by a man who could end human life simply with a twist of his hands.

CHAPTER 18

"Quinn?" Jacinta stuck her head through the back door of the flower shop, her long dark braid dangling over her shoulder as she held the door open with one hand. Her gaze landed on Quinn, who had set one of the lunchroom chairs just outside the range of the door to sit in the sun, her sketchbook open on her lap, one pencil in her hand, a second and third pushed through her messy bun as if they were decorative hair sticks. "What are you doing?"

"Enjoying the sun on my lunch break." After an initial glance upward at her name, Quinn had casually flipped the page in her sketchbook and begun a new sketch, focusing on Alberto, leaning against the far brick wall. One of Casa Morales's longest employees, he always indulged in a cigarette in the alley on his lunch break. But for her purposes, he was a perfect model. "Do you need me? I can come in now."

"No, it's okay. The McBride order is almost finished, and no one is in the store. I just wondered where you'd gone. I thought you were in the lunchroom, and then you weren't there. You're sure you're okay?"

Quinn set her pencil down and smiled up at Jacinta.

"I'm good. It's such a lovely day and I wanted to get some light and air."

"But . . . here?" Jacinta's dark eyes slid over the various doors to shops, some propped open, some closed, the garbage bins, the litter lining the corners, and the older man smoking across the alley. Pushing the door open farther, she stepped around the squat plastic bin they left by the door to prop it open. She made sure it remained lodged in the doorway so she wouldn't lock herself out, and stepped out into the sun, picking up the long skirt of her colorful maxi dress so there was no risk of the hem dragging through something unmentionable. She grimaced as she inadvertently kicked a loose chunk of concrete from the crumbling pavement. "Wouldn't you be more comfortable sitting out front?"

"With all the sidewalk traffic? You know what Fourth Street is like at lunchtime. It's a zoo. This is . . ." Quinn wracked her brain for a word that was truthful but would still satisfy Jacinta. *Peaceful? Not anymore. Scenic? Not even close.* "Quiet. I can hear myself think back here." She picked up her pencil, sketching the long lines of Alberto's relaxed body as he leaned against the sun-warmed bricks, his legs crossed at his ankles. "Will says my art could help speed my recovery. It helps manage anxiety and increases coordination and focus." She looked up again. "I made a note so I couldn't forget and put it in my lunch bag." She indicated the open bag sitting beside her on an upside-down florist's crate, beside which sat her phone with a timer counting down to the end of her half hour lunch break. "I want to get better. I don't like living like this."

"I know, honey." Jacinta laid her hand over Quinn's shoulder and squeezed. "Is there anything I can do to help?"

Quinn paused her sketching to squint up into Jacinta's face, backlit by the brilliant blue sky overhead. Quinn couldn't make out her expression, but she knew by heart the kindness she'd find there. She covered Jacinta's hand with her own and held on for a moment. "You're already doing everything. I know because I write things down. I know because you're standing here with me. You came looking for me. I don't know that anyone else would do that." That thought put a lump in Quinn's throat, but she barreled on, not wanting to contemplate her losses. "You let me continue the work I love, and that work keeps me centered. And puts food on my table. I owe you everything."

Jacinta blinked, as if pushing away tears. "I think of you as family, *mija*." She gave Quinn's shoulder another squeeze. "Did you put on sunscreen? You know how you burn."

Quinn laughed and patted Jacinta's hand before picking up her pencil again. "Yes, Mom. SPF 50."

"Good girl. Okay, I'll see you inside."

Quinn watched her go into the shop, waited a few moments, and then flipped back to the previous page. She studied the mouth of the alley as she imagined she'd seen it that night, in the gloom and from the far end, as two shadows grappled.

She hadn't wanted Jacinta to see that image, hadn't wanted her to worry. Because she would. Quinn had been honest—Jacinta had been unfailingly kind to her, a mother figure when Quinn's own was years gone. But right now, she needed the freedom to do what she felt would be best for her. And while Jacinta couldn't control Quinn, she could cramp her style, though Quinn knew it would be with love. Jacinta had called her *mija*, a Spanish term of endearment for a younger female who wasn't actually related by blood. Jacinta wasn't just a boss; she was a friend, and one who'd stood by her. When the attack had occurred, she'd been told Jacinta had been the one to come, to stay, to visit daily. And she loved Jacinta for it.

But it was best for now for both of them if Jacinta didn't know Quinn's real intent—to use her art to push her memories.

If what she'd noted Will said about memories being made more important based on emotional impact was true—and God knew, witnessing a murder had one hell of an emotional impact—then maybe those memories were there, just beyond her reach. For now.

What if the scene she thought she was creating with the help of her imagination was really being helped along by recall? That while she couldn't remember aspects of that night except through storytelling, visual aspects of what she saw were actually consolidated in her mind, just stuck in place? Could those aspects be revealed by art? If art improved focus and attention, and allowed emotions to flow, perhaps they could flow toward truth.

She didn't know if it would work, but she was going to give it a shot.

She studied the sketch in front of her, then pulled the two pencils out of her bun, selected the 5H, and started shading with it. The long lines in the alley slowly sank into gloom as she filled in the gap with shadows. She looked up again, judged where those shadows would lie based on the lighting in the alley and out of the street, and dropped the sketch further into dimness.

But it was the two shadowy figures that called to her most. The one, tall, slender, clearly at a disadvantage; the other, tall, bulky with muscles, overpowering his prey. Both men were faceless, though she noted she'd added in DeWitt's sharp nose in profile. The other man . . . Was it memory or creativity? She had drawn him as the taller of the two, his chest and limbs thick with muscle, a large head on a sturdy neck, with just the hint of the shape of hair. One thing was for sure—this wasn't the man from the garden center as she'd described him in her notes.

She glanced at the time to find she had ten minutes left. She could finish the shading at home with a full pencil set. She didn't want to add color; black-and-white fit the gloom of the scene better, and more strongly represented the starkness of the scene.

She flipped past the sketch of Alberto and then to the next blank page. She sat back in her chair, focusing on the end of the alley. Closing her eyes, she tried to conjure the image of the white panel van filling the gap, the killer standing, feet planted wide, his bulk filling the space as he stared back at her, searching for her in the shadows, a crumpled, lifeless body at his feet.

A shiver ran down her spine.

She opened her eyes, and drew.

CHAPTER 19

Reyes collapsed into her desk chair, exhaustion crawling through her, knowing she must look the part. But at least she had coffee. *Real* coffee. Professionally roasted with expertise and care, mixed with just the right amount of hot milk, topped with foam, and sprinkled with cinnamon, not burned to a crisp and brewed into mud. She picked up the extra-large cup, labeled with the logo of a boutique coffee shop several blocks away, sipped, savored, and sighed in pleasure.

"Where's our coffee?" Chong asked from two desks over.

Reyes only swiveled her head to look in his direction. "What coffee?"

Dressed in a black suit with a radiant, swirling yellow-and-red tie, Chong stared at the tall, covered cup in her hand. "That coffee. You went out and bought real coffee and left us with the swill."

Keeping her eyes locked on his, Reyes took a slow sip, then smiled. "I don't know what you're talking about. You must be imagining things."

With a grin, she turned back to her computer and set her very real espresso creation down beside her keyboard, her spirits lifting as Chong continued to grouse about there being "no 'I' in team." She deserved this latte. She'd caught a case just before end of shift yesterday when a body was found at the base of one of the cliffs off Sunset Cliffs Boulevard. From the call, she'd thought it might be another body washing up on shore, but she put the story together fairly quickly once she was on scene. The car pulled onto the shoulder of the boulevard, its driver blithely ignoring the NO PARKING AT ANY TIME sign, a mere fifteen feet in front of the hood of his car. He'd climbed over the railing, stood at the edge to take a selfie against the setting sun, and had apparently taken one step too far backward and had careened several hundred feet to his death on the tumbled boulders below. Recovering the man—and his cell phone, which luckily landed in an exposed crevice, cementing what had happened—had required marine assistance and some climbing, for which she wasn't wearing the right shoes.

She'd been damned late getting home by the time the body was packaged and moved by the coroner's techs and the initial paperwork was done, and here she was, back at her desk. She *deserved* this coffee, and the other detectives could go stuff it. She wasn't sharing.

She turned to her computer, opened her email, and scanned the long list of incoming messages that never seemed to get any shorter. But two emails caught her eye.

Jackpot!

It was like the heavens knew she deserved a break and were willing to give it to her in spades, as one email was from DeWitt's cell phone company and one was from his internet service provider. She'd contacted both a few days ago, armed with a warrant, requesting access to DeWitt's records. Both had been more than willing to help once she'd supplied them with copies of the warrant, but both needed time to collect the past three months of data she'd requested.

That was a good place to start.

She'd met with Cam DeWitt last week to do a final ID on his brother, a truly heartbreaking task, but Cam had done it with courage and determination. He also gave Reyes full access to anything that might help, including his own home, as he was the sole recipient of his single, childless brother's estate. Reyes had no real concerns Cam was responsible, but conducted the search anyway so there would be no questions later. She then spent several hours with Cam, learning about their childhood as brothers and anything he knew about Jack's current work, which was limited. Like most investigative reporters, Jack kept his cards close to his chest until he published, not even discussing these stories ahead of time with his own family. Good for ensuring nothing leaked to jeopardize your scoop, bad for tracking who might have killed you afterward.

She suspected the most important information she'd learned was that Jack DeWitt had a professional Dropbox account to which he backed up his laptop weekly, but, more importantly, he used to back up his phone at least daily, if not more often. The warrant had already been served to Dropbox; now she waited for them to deliver the data, which she suspected could be weeks away.

She hated waiting, so getting these emails gave her something to sink her teeth into.

Ignoring the rest of her emails, she opened the phone company message and printed the attached document, and then did the same for the ISP. Both were multipage documents that were going to take some digging, and Reyes resigned herself to a day at the computer sorting through potential leads. She considered the list of phone numbers, wondering how many other calls had been made from his phone at the paper, information they had yet to deliver. Though she assumed if there was any competition at the paper—and it sounded like there were some limited tug-of-wars for the juiciest stories—DeWitt would be more likely to do any sensitive calls from his cell phone away from the newsroom.

She scanned down the list—outgoing location, time, incoming location, phone number, call duration. The earlier calls tended to be local, with the odd call to centers with government offices she'd confirm later. But when she got to the more recent calls, Chicago phone numbers filled the roster, and the length of the calls extended. The calls ended on the day of his death, the final call being just before 9:00 PM, with several repeated calls to the same number.

Those calls fell just before Quinn reported his murder.

What had attracted his attention in Chicago, and who was the last person he'd desperately tried to reach out to in his final moments?

Reyes took another fortifying slug of her coffee, mentally rolled up her sleeves, and got to work putting together the last months of DeWitt's communications.

It was hours later when she finally needed a break. She reached for her coffee cup, tipping it back farther and farther . . . empty. "Damn." She cast a flat stare in the direction of the coffeepot to find it half-full, then discarded the idea. *Not worth the gut rot. That latte doesn't deserve that kind of chaser.*

A picture was beginning to form, but God help her if she knew exactly what it was at this point. What she knew for a fact was Chicago was key in some way. First there were the calls to Forest Glen Academy, a ritzy private school in one of the richer neighborhoods in Chicago, then several calls to private lines in the Chicago area as well as a few in the same time period to New York City, Boston, and Seattle.

His browsing history—for which she was grateful he didn't use an anonymizing VPN to hide his traffic—also had an odd concentration in Chicago. Forest Glen Academy showed up again, but so did the *Chicago Tribune* and the *Chicago Sun-Times* as well as several top-notch Chicago country clubs. And, in the same time period, a lot of research into the San Diego mayoral race, an off-season race to fill the seat left vacant after the unexpected death of the mayor following a short illness, with Election Day next month. As there was more than a year before the next scheduled election, city council was required by the by-laws to call a special election and to denote the president of the city council as the interim mayor in the meantime. Signs had immediately sprung up all over town, and the soapboxing had begun.

She went back to look at DeWitt's byline, just to make sure she hadn't forgotten anything: *Investigative reporter—breaking news, policing, politics.*

Politics. Any reporter was going to be neck-deep in politics during the local election, so his traffic didn't necessarily mean anything nefarious. She'd keep those links in mind, but they were likely just a reporter doing his municipal duty.

But Chicago. That intrigued her.

She checked the time to find she'd missed lunch and classes were likely just back in session, so it would be a good time to call Forest Glen Academy. She dialed the phone, pulling out a pad of paper and a pen for notes as the call rang in her ear.

"Forest Glen Academy, working with you to create your child's future. May I help you?" The voice sounded as upper crust as Reyes imagined the school population to be.

"Detective Nura Reyes, calling from the San Diego Police Department."

"Oh." Surprise laced the single syllable. "What can I do for you, Detective?"

"I'm investigating a homicide and your school came up

in my victim's phone records. I'm looking for anyone who would have spoken to Jack DeWitt from the *San Diego Union-Tribune* in the last three weeks."

"I did, for starters."

"You did."

"Yes. I remember him because we don't get many calls from out-of-state reporters." She paused for a moment. "Or any, now that I think about it. He wanted information on our historical yearbooks."

"Did he say why?"

"No. But I forwarded him on to our media center."

"You have a media center?"

"Of course. To manage our public relations, social media accounts, and our technology department."

"They do the yearbooks?"

"They help the kids produce the current year's edition and are currently digitizing past years. Our alumni have been asking for us to do this for years. It's a process."

Alumni. Somehow Reyes had never considered herself an alumna of her public high school. "I'd like to speak to whoever he spoke to in the media center, if I could."

"That would be Caroline. I can forward you to her."

"I'd appreciate that. Thanks."

There was a click and then tinny strings played over the line.

Even the hold music is classy.

It only lasted for about six seconds and then a chirpy female voice said, "Forest Glen Academy, working with you to create your child's future. Media center, Caroline speaking."

This place is a walking slogan. "Hi, Caroline, I'm Detective Nura Reyes from the San Diego Police Department. I'd like to ask you about the phone call you had with Jack DeWitt of the *San Diego Union-Tribune*."

"The police." Ninety percent of the chirp disappeared,

and Caroline sounded baffled with a heavy helping of suspicion. "I'm not sure I should be speaking with you. Do you have a warrant?"

Reyes rolled her eyes. "That's not required for me to ask you a few questions, ma'am. You're not in any trouble. If you need to clear this with your administrators, we can loop them into the conversation. But I know Jack DeWitt called the school a few weeks ago." She ran an index finger down the list, found the entry, and read out the date and time. "I'd like to know what he called about."

"Wouldn't it be easier to ask him?"

"No, ma'am, it wouldn't. Mr. DeWitt was the victim of a homicide."

"A homi—*He's dead?*" The voice went shrill.

"Yes, ma'am. And you would be an immense help to the investigation if you could share what you discussed."

"You don't think—"

Reyes cut that thought off at the knees. "No, ma'am. I don't think you were involved. But he called you for a reason. It may not have anything to do with his death, but it was an unusual call in the phone logs we legally obtained, so I need to follow up on it. Would you be willing to tell me why he called you looking for information on yearbooks?"

"He wanted access to certain years of the yearbook. Wanted to know if we had digital copies."

"Do you remember which years?"

"Hold on, I document all external calls. Let me go back to that one."

Reyes repeated the date and time.

"I have it here. He wanted access to the years 1984 to 1987, which would have covered students from September 1983 to June 1987."

Reyes wrote down the years, staring at them in surprise. "That's a long way back."

"Yes. Decades."

"He didn't say why he wanted to see them?"

"No."

"You make that information accessible to the public?"

"Yes. All the yearbooks are accessible for everyone to see, though I can't imagine who'd want to see them besides our alumni. The 1980s are almost ready to go public, but aren't live yet, so he couldn't find them on our site. I had to give him a private link to them. He sent me an email and I returned it with the links for those years."

"And that was all he wanted?"

"Yes. He was very polite and appreciative that I could supply that information to him."

"Would you be able to supply that information to me?"

Caroline paused for so long, Reyes knew what she would say before she actually did. "I'm not sure I should without a warrant."

"We have Mr. DeWitt's electronics, so we'll eventually dig out your email, but if you'd like me to clear it with the school principal, I'd be happy to do that."

"Why don't you let me do that? I just want to make sure it's okay."

And cover your ass. "That would be great." She provided Caroline with her email address. "I hope to hear from you shortly. I appreciate your assistance." She purposefully applied a little extra pressure. "As does Mr. DeWitt's family, who just want to see justice for their loved one."

"Of course. I'll call Mr. Emerson now to clear it."

Giving her thanks once again, Reyes hung up, feeling even more exhausted after having to deal with Caroline than before.

Five minutes later, the forwarded email from Caroline

was in her inbox. The email contained four links to the requested editions of the yearbook. Reyes opened the first link and paged through the virtual 1984 yearbook.

It looked like something had happened more than thirty years ago that set DeWitt on the trail of something that eventually got him killed.

Who had done what so many years ago a man had to die for to keep it a secret?

CHAPTER 20

Chair legs scraped and people stood, wished each other a good night, and started to break up.

"You busing home?" Viv asked Quinn from where they still sat side by side, gathering their bags and coffee cups.

"I'm going to touch base with Will for a few minutes. See you next week?"

"You bet." Viv gave her a bright smile. "You're going to remember me next week, too. You're really coming along."

Pleasure and satisfaction surged through Quinn. She'd recognized Viv the moment she'd walked in the door—knew her face and had her name, for the first time, according to Viv. "I'm starting to feel hopeful."

"I wonder if I should try using art the way you are. Not to specifically help my memory, because I don't have holes like you do, but for focus and to keep my fine motor skills sharp."

"It wouldn't hurt. What's the worst that's going to happen, you spend twenty dollars on art supplies?"

"The worst thing to happen would be if anyone is forced to view said art." Viv flashed her a grin. "It's not going to be pretty. But, for me, the result isn't the point. The act of creation is the important thing. For *you*, it's the result."

"The process, too. Sometimes, especially lately, I get into a fugue state when I'm trying to draw the memories out. I look up and I should have gone to bed a half hour before. If I do it on my lunch break or before work, I always set an alarm on my phone or else I might miss my shift. My boss has been amazing, but I'm not going to make her lose my time because I'm off sketching. She's already gone above and beyond. I won't penalize her further."

"Did she say you're penalizing her?"

Quinn paused for a long moment before answering. "Well . . . not that I recall. But I remember what a good worker I used to be. I know I'm not up to that standard all the time but—"

"Has she complained?" Viv interjected.

"I don't think so."

"Then you're making assumptions about her opinions, which is unfair to her. You're already working extra unpaid hours—"

"Did I say that here?"

"You did. A few meetings ago when we were talking about positive and negative compensatory strategies."

"What was that one?"

"Pretty sure everyone thought extra unpaid work under the table was a big ol' negative." The curve of Viv's eyebrow told Quinn Viv certainly considered it that. "Anyway, keep doing what you're doing, but give your boss the benefit of the doubt. Also, have you been open with her about all this?"

Quinn stared blankly for a moment, shocked. *How does Viv know about the murder?* Then her brain kicked in and she realized Vivian was simply talking about her struggles at work. "Some of it."

"Maybe think about sharing more of it." Viv glanced at

the clock on the wall. "And that's my cue to scram. See you next week."

Quinn watched Viv stride through the door and wished for just a moment she had more of Viv's confidence and openness. She knew she had moments of grit—notes and instructions to herself made that clear—but she wondered if she hadn't carried through with any of them, because present Quinn wasn't as strong as past Quinn thought she could be.

She'd have to review her notes from beginning to end to see if it had happened.

She was getting better on some of the details now, but still made a point of reviewing it all daily in case any of the information started to slip away. When she was about to start sketching, she would review again, going over the specifics to bring the scene into her mind before putting pencil to paper and letting either her imagination or her memories guide her.

She still had no idea.

"Good session tonight."

Quinn turned at the sound of Will's voice. "Yes, very."

"I'm glad you tagged your book with information you wanted to share. I think your thoughts on art and healing could help numerous people in the group."

"It's not new information. You've talked about it before."

"There's a big difference between me talking about it and someone in the middle of their own recovery describing how it's actively helping them. Yes, I'm a TBI survivor myself, but I'm too far removed, look too 'normal' for anyone in the group to remember it. They don't mean to, but many of them still see me as an outsider. For you to talk about it and how it's working for you in obvious ways, that makes an impression. Personally, I'm impressed by your forward use of your artistic skills specifically to try to tweak your memory capabilities. I'd love to see what you've done. Did you bring your sketchbook?"

Quinn reached for the information, only to find a blank space in her mind. It had been too long since she'd left the house. "Not sure. Let me check. Hopefully I did." She set her bag on a chair, opened it, and pushed through the contents. No sketchbook. "I didn't." Disappointment twined with annoyance at herself. This would have been the perfect time to show the sketches to Will, to get his take on the actual items, not just to discuss it with him. He'd have better guidance if he saw her work. She'd have to set an alarm on her phone to remind her to bring them next week. "That was stupid."

"Hey, none of that. With everything you're dealing with, forgetting to bring a sketchbook is nothing."

"I would've liked for you to see a couple of the sketches. You might have some tips."

Will laughed. "I'll have no tips on anything having to do with fine art, let me assure you."

"But you might have had some tips on how to draw any memories out more if recall is the issue. If it's consolidation . . ."

"The memories probably aren't there, depending on how bad the issue was at the time of creation and then consolidation."

Quinn's gaze skittered sideways to study the circle of chairs. "If that's true, then it's a wasted exercise."

"Hey." Will waited until she looked back at him. "You're doing all the right things. You're retraining your brain on recall using rehearsal, which is great. But what you're most hung up on is a single moment in time."

"A moment I can't go back and change. If the memory was never encoded—"

"It was. You held on to it long enough to write it down and then a little longer after that," Will clarified.

Quinn started again. "If the memory was never consolidated properly, or at all, even if recall is my issue, there's nothing to recall. And the whole attempt is for nothing."

"Sure." Will kept his voice light, as if fighting to keep the discussion from sinking into depression. "But what if it's not? The only way to figure this out is to keep working at it. Let's put it this way: People have strokes and lose the use of parts of their body. With therapy, we can help them regain the use of those muscles to bring them back to their normal life, or one that's close to it. Is that wasted time?"

"Of course not."

"And the brain is no different. You're very focused on this one event. In some ways that's great—you've worked hard to learn the details of it, and, in doing so, learned you can teach yourself other information as well. But the negative is you may never get the details of that night back. You need to be prepared for that, but you can't let the risk of that keep you from making the attempt." He paused for a moment, considering. "You know, if you want me to see your sketches, I could drive you home and you could show me."

Panic rose in a wave and Quinn took an involuntary step backward. To the best of her knowledge, no one had entered her apartment once she'd come home from the hospital. No one had seen all the hoops she had to jump through just to survive the day. He thought she was managing, because that was the image she projected, but even Will, who knew more about her challenges than most, didn't have a full grasp of the sheer enormity of them. How could he not think less of her when he saw the crutches she used just to get through her days and—

"Quinn."

She knew from the way his face softened as she met his gaze that he could see her reaction.

"It's only an offer. It's not a requirement. I understand if you're uncomfortable with someone else being in your space. But I hope you'd know no one would understand more than me. Those of us who've been there before ourselves understand the kind of accommodations we might have to make in our more basic and personal lives. You've talked about what you do at home to manage, so likely most if not all of your accommodations won't be a surprise to me. On top of that, nothing you do at home to get through is wrong. I won't judge, but if you're not comfortable with me seeing your place, I can wait in the car, and you can bring the book out to me. If you want me to see it tonight, that is. If not, bring it next week. The offer wasn't meant to add any more stress to the load you're already carrying. But I'd like to think you consider me a friend. Friends don't judge friends over what they need to do to get by. Whatever it is, it's not wrong. It just is."

Quinn made herself take a step toward him. "Let's start with this. You drive me home and that will give me time to think about it on the way."

"Fair enough."

Together, they tidied the room, cleaned up the remains of the coffee, then headed for Quinn's apartment. Will stayed quiet for the fifteen-minute drive, letting music fill the space, not pushing Quinn in any way. He found a street parking spot just down from her building and cut the engine. He turned to her but didn't say anything.

Quinn had spent the entire fifteen minutes arguing back and forth with herself. But now, as she looked at him, she made the call that no one would be safer than Will. And maybe it was time she stopped hiding. "Why don't you come in and I'll show you?"

He nodded somberly, pocketed the car keys, and climbed out. She met him on the sidewalk and then silently led the way to the walk that lined the east side of the building, up the flight of steps, and to her door. She'd left the outdoor sconce beside her door on, and the brass apartment number softly reflected the light.

Quinn pulled her key out of her bag, unlocked the door, and then opened it, stepping into darkness. She dropped her keys into the basket on the table by the door and tapped the light switch, flooding the apartment with light. "Come on in."

Will stepped into the open-concept living, dining, and kitchen area, and Quinn closed the door behind him. And then waited for him to say something. Anything.

Facing into the living room, his eyes scanned the space, from the narrow table by the door with instructions of what belonged there, to the couch with her grandmother's vibrant quilt, to the TV, and coffee table, with a remote control sitting beside the potted violet. And over all the sticky notes and their reminders.

"Nice space," he said simply. "Very comfortable."

"Thank you."

He turned toward the kitchen and her art nook, then froze, his jaw sagging in shock as his eyes went wide.

Alarmed, Quinn turned to follow his gaze, unsure why he'd react that way, and gasped.

Sometimes, her lack of memory could be a real problem, not only for her, but for others in her life.

She knew about the sketches, but her memory hadn't held on to all the information about them. She knew she'd drawn the images and they'd come from her sketchbook, but her mind hadn't held on to the sheer number of them. Worse, it hadn't held on to the fact that to be able to see them better, to be able to see them all together, she'd taped them onto the walls surrounding her corner-set drafting table.

There were so many sketches.

To hell with the sticky notes and calendar. *This* was

what she should have considered when deciding whether to bring Will inside her home. But this was too new, and she'd forgotten she'd done it.

For once, her skill with pencils played against her in life-like portrayals of unspeakable violence. Of death.

Humiliation burned through Quinn. She couldn't imagine how badly Will must think of her. Only a monster could create this kind of display.

She should never have brought him home. She should never bring anyone home. She was entirely too unpredictable. Life was safer when she lived it solely on her own. She'd prefer gut-wrenching loneliness to this kind of shame.

"You know . . ." She had to clear a throat gone husky with embarrassment to try again. "You know, this probably isn't a good idea." She moved to stand between him and the drafting table, blocking part of his view. Stepping into him, she tried to get him to step back. Then she could reach for the door, get it open, and shuffle him out. Lock the door behind him, and then consider never going back to the group therapy sessions again. But Will wouldn't shift, and Quinn just ended up half pressed against him. "Why don't I bring a few next week for you to—"

"It's okay." His voice was quiet as he reached between them to take her hand.

There was no way he could have missed the way her hand trembled in his, deepening her embarrassment. Heat flooded her cheeks, and she fixed her eyes over his shoulder, staring at the forest scene above her couch, wishing she was there, standing in solitude in sun dappled woods, just her, the birds, and the trees. At peace and at ease with herself, which was diametrically opposed to how she felt at that moment.

Keeping hold of her hand, Will stepped around her and

toward the sketches, coaxing her along with him, pulling with a gentle tug when she dug in her heels and didn't want to get any closer, though finally relenting.

When she tried to pull free of him, he held on, not letting her retreat as they stood in front of a story of brutal violence played out in varying shades of graphite.

For Quinn, it was like seeing them for the first time, and she had to suspect it was like this every time she came home as they simply hadn't been up long enough for her to learn they were there, and, even if not remembering each individual image, had a sense of the whole. Enough time to learn to brace herself for the onslaught before setting eyes on it.

The sketches were hung in random order. She'd started by lining them up, and then as more and more needed to fill the space, they overlapped, angled so each image was still visible. There had to be fifteen images in total, some from a distance, some more like figure studies. The distance sketches showed the figures as dark shadows, but the closer shots were detailed to varying degrees, the early images short on minutiae, but each repeated portrayal brought out additional details.

Will stood silently in front of them, studying one, then the next. Beside him, Quinn stood braced, every limb rigid, waiting for the inevitable blow. *The one where he lets it slip he knows there's something wrong with you. Would have to be, to produce all of this.*

"You hung them where you can see them. Can stay familiar with them. That's smart." Will's voice was calm, and, to her shock, there was no disgust in his tone. He'd slipped into his role as a logical clinician. "As I've said before, your skill is remarkable." He finally looked at her. "You had no idea this was here."

Apparently, she'd given herself away, so it wasn't a question. "No. Obviously I put it here, but . . ."

"It's not been long enough since the pictures went up. Not enough exposure to them, not enough times where you've walked into this room for the repetition to take hold."

"If I'd remembered, I'd never have asked you to come in."

"Why? So I wouldn't be exposed to these images? You asked me to come see them."

"But I didn't remember they looked like this. What kind of person would come up with these images?" Quinn's tone was rising on a harsh edge, but she couldn't calm it. "Would spend time immersing herself in it again and again?"

"The kind of person who's trying to answer a question. No one who knows you, Quinn, would think you revel in this. You're working through a thorny issue."

"But most people wouldn't work through it this way. It's almost like I enjoy it."

"Anyone who took the time to look at you wouldn't think that. I caught your face when you saw them. You were as shocked and horrified as I was. Death and violence aren't your jam, that's very clear. Don't even consider I'd think you're doing this for fun. You're not trying to create images out of nothing more than your imagination; you're trying to re-create an actual event. And yes, you're right, most people wouldn't work through it this way. Most people wouldn't be able to because they wouldn't have the skills. If I was attempting what you are, nothing would come of it because it wouldn't look like anything at all. What you've created is lifelike." He looked back at the sketches. "And then some."

He gave her hand another tug, pulling her forward another few feet, then released her to step up to the sketches, not forcing her to go farther with him. "You told me about the murder, told me what happened, but now I feel like I was standing in the alley with you as it happened. How far away were they from you?"

"Seventy, maybe seventy-five feet."

"That far?" Will turned back to the sketch of the grappling figures down at the far end of the alley. "I'm amazed you saw any details in the dark."

"A lot of it is just those few seconds when they were in the light of the open doorway from Casa Morales. My vision is really good, but I admit it was a long way away."

"Did you draw this one hundred percent from memory?"

"I'm using my notes as much as I can."

"You're reviewing everything you're doing regularly now?"

"Pretty much. I don't know if that's what I always used to do, but it's now part of my routine. I ride the bus to and from work, like I used to, but now instead of listening to music, or browsing on my phone, I read my notes. Everything I've done from the night of the murder, over and over again. I can't remember, but I suspect it used to only be a short part of the ride. Now I wouldn't be surprised if it's the whole thing. What I've done, instructions for what I need to do, that kind of thing.

"Anyway, I sat outside at lunch one day and drew the alley as it was in daylight and then transformed it into what I thought it would look like at night." She gave an unhappy shrug. "I don't know if this is a useful exercise. I could be making up every detail that wasn't in front of my eyes. I could be making up every detail that *was* in front of my eyes because I don't remember it."

"You absolutely could."

Will's answer caught her off guard, and she turned to him in question.

"But I'm not sure that's what this is. I agree with your assessment that while this may all have come out of your head, you're using a different technique to stimulate recall. Of course, this might not be recall in its most technical sense."

"What do you mean?"

"From a memory perspective, there are multiple ways to

bring out a memory. Recall is what you do when someone asks a question, and you can pull the answer out of your memory with no other cues or prompts. What's the capital of California?"

"Sacramento."

"See how fast that came to you? That's information encoded and stored before the assault that you can freely recall on its own. That's what you can't do with these memories right now. Which makes me still think it's a consolidation issue. But without intention, you're doing a few extremely useful things. Starting with the fact you're using the relearning process every time you review your notes— you're relearning information you knew previously, allowing for faster recall." He stepped up to the wall and raised a hand to pull down one of the sketches, but stopped and glanced back over his shoulder. "May I?"

Quinn nodded.

Will pulled down a sketch of the alley and the paired men from about half the initial distance. "It's like you started out from where you stood and you're zooming in on the salient details. What you're doing here is a combination of recognition and recollection. Recognition is when you remember something when you see some aspect of it. Remembering what happened in the alley while you sit in the alley, sketching it, that kind of thing. Or what happens when you take a multiple-choice test versus short answer, which is a recall test. Whereas recollection is when you piece a memory together based on bits of memory and logical cues." He looked down at the sketch. "That's what you're doing here."

He moved forward to return the image to its place on the wall, when his gaze tracked sideways, and then his feet followed until he stood near the oil painting that hung above the table. "The initials in the corner say *QF*. Is that you?"

"Yes."

"It's lovely." He spent a long moment studying the two peonies, their full, multi-petaled blooms a vivid hot pink in the center fading out to a delicate blush above a cluster of dark green leaves, all against a smoky blue-gray background with a subtle metallic shimmer. "I didn't know you painted."

"Not as often as I use pencils or pastels, but occasionally. I enjoy it, it just takes a long time." Her gaze flicked to the canvas. "I don't imagine I've done any since the attack."

"Maybe not. But maybe it's something to loop back to when you're ready. Do you have the supplies still?"

"I'd assume so. I keep my oil paints, spare canvases, and easel in my linen closet, since it's just me and I don't need that much space for sheets and towels."

"Something to think about someday, then." Will walked back to the sketch wall and tacked up the image in his hand before selecting another one. This sketch was pinned on the periphery, but showed the face of a man with a dark mark that began on his cheek, skimmed his jaw, and dripped down his throat. Will glanced from the sketch in his hand to the others on the wall. "What's this one? And it has a name, which the rest of them don't. Dylan Hobson. Who's that?"

Quinn studied the sketch, which seemed only vaguely familiar, but the name she knew from the two or three daily reviews of her notebook. "Detective Reyes thinks it's the man who attacked me."

Will's head snapped up. "She found him?" His gaze dropped to the sketch. "No, wait. You drew him. Is your memory of the attack coming back?"

"Parts of it? I dreamed the face one night, seeing the image from close-up so I could draw it in more detail. I assumed it was one of the men from the alley murder, but when we found a mug shot that matched it, he was in jail at the time. Held without bail on a rape charge. Detective Reyes thinks it might be the man who attacked me."

"Is there any way she can prove it? Did you include that in your notes?"

"She told me skin cells were found under my nails from fighting back during the attack. They're testing if that DNA matches his." Her gaze dropped to the sketch. "She says I may have solved my own assault case."

Will laid a hand on her shoulder and gave it a light squeeze. "That's amazing. *You're* amazing. Just look at all you're doing here. It's like you're opening the floodgates." He released her and tacked the sketch of Hobson up again, and selected another, one of the more detailed images of both the killer and victim. "This reminds me of a recent paper that might be relevant. They've been doing studies with mice that were purposely sleep deprived to put them at a deficit for memory consolidation. After putting them through tasks and proving they couldn't remember aspects of the tasks the next day compared to the control group, they stimulated the mice with light to activate the neurons stimulated during the initial learning of the task and that allowed the mice to remember." He met her eyes. "The interference with memory consolidation didn't mean the memory was never kept, it simply made it challenging to retrieve. But the information was there and could be pulled out under the right stimulation. Your use of art may be the stimulation needed to retrieve the information. It might be short-term, and literally may only be while you're in the process, but these tangible images may be your best recollection of the event." He glanced at the sketch of Hobson. "Events."

"You really think so?" Hope carried clearly on Quinn's tone.

"I do. The brain is a massively complex system, and we

only understand a fraction of it. Even with all we know about what section of the brain does what and how injury can affect those areas, we still don't have a great handle on it because of two hemispheres and overlapping systems. Two people can have nearly identical injuries and the effects can be significantly different. Every TBI is unique, as is the person suffering from it. Have you shown these to Detective Reyes?"

"I don't think so, but I'd have to check my notebook." Quinn studied the sketches again, trying to consider them with fresh eyes. "I don't think I would have. This is still a work in progress. There's not enough to show her yet. I need to drill down a bit more, zoom in closer, try to draw out more details. I need to get closer to a possible ID. Then I'll show her. Maybe in a few days or a week."

"I don't think it will take as long as a week. You're already getting close." He indicated a sketch where two men battled, the larger man grasping the shorter man, who struggled to get away.

Of the two, the shorter man was more fully sketched, with fear radiating from every feature. "This one is the victim," Quinn said. "I'm sure some of my depictions of DeWitt are influenced by photos I saw of him. Or could easily look up online."

"You never saw the killer anywhere but here?"

"Not that I know of." Her laugh was full of derision. "Of course, we'd never know for sure with me."

"You know, I think you need to give yourself a break. It always seems to be your first instinct to put yourself down." He looked back at the wall. "Like this. Your first inclination when I saw this was to assume I'd think you were crazy. I don't. Learn to trust those around you who understand your struggles. We may be able to help you. I can help you now. Pull out your notebook."

Quinn slipped it out of her back pocket. "Why?"

"Let's look closely at these images and compile information you can carry with you to review. Let's look for the clues in these sketches, the ones you may not have noticed you added if you were really in the zone. Yes, there'll be more details coming, but let's start with what we have here." He tacked the sketch on the wall and then stepped away a pace, his hands on his hips, taking it all in. "Knowledge is power, so let's arm you as much as possible."

CHAPTER 21

Quinn checked the time as she waited in a crowd of pedestrians at the G Street traffic light. She had intended to catch the 5:46 PM bus after fitting in a little extra work at the shop after closing. But Jacinta had scuttled those plans when she wanted to finish some invoicing in her office instead of heading home at 4:00 PM as per the schedule, and Quinn lost her opportunity to catch up without Jacinta's knowledge. Instead, Jacinta had come out of her office in time to help Quinn clean and lock up, and had just wished her a relaxing two days off before walking north to catch her Route 2 bus at Broadway and Third to take her home to her South Park neighborhood.

Quinn had walked south on Fourth, crossing to the west side at F Street before continuing south, heading for her Route 3 stop at Fourth and G. The Gaslamp was already hopping, revving up for a fun-filled Saturday night. It was a mix of tourists, many with their phones out, following mapped paths on-screen, or working folks like herself, finished their shift for the day and headed home. Not to mention, the party crowd, already decked out in their skimpy Saturday finest.

A sudden burst of laughter and then a bump to her right

shoulder had Quinn quick-stepping to her left as she looked right. Beside her, three girls in their early-twenties were dressed to the nines, all sleek hair, smoky eyes, short skirts, and heels. From their unsteadiness on those heels, they were either new to them or they'd started the evening early with a little pre-drinking at home to save money once they got to the bar. She was pretty sure it was the latter.

The girl who bumped her giggled again and gave her a wide smile. "Sorry."

"No problem."

The girl turned to her friends, and laughter burst forth again.

Quinn couldn't help a quick glance down at her cropped jeans, sneakers, and the simple blue tee she'd worn to work, still wet from the water she'd accidentally splashed refilling some of the large buckets up front.

You used to be them. Now look at you.

She pushed the thought away. It was useless to dwell on what used to be. The now was all that mattered—not to mention pretty much all she had—and dwelling on the person she used to be didn't help her in any way.

The light changed, and to avoid being shoved at again, Quinn let the trio precede her across the street. Stepping up on the curb on the far side, she arced around them when they turned to cross Fourth Avenue to head deeper into the Gaslamp to find the hottest spots. Passing behind the line of weeping fig ficus trees with their pale gray trunks and thick canopy of pointed oval-shaped leaves, she hustled down the redbrick interlock sidewalk until she got to her bus stop for the 5:26 with a few minutes to spare. Standing beside a tall wrought iron lamppost with three frosted-glass lights that wouldn't be coming on for a few hours yet, she pulled out her phone to check for messages and emails that might have come while she was working—nothing—then slid it away again and pulled out her notebook. In what was becoming a habit, she opened it to the dog-eared page and started her review.

The murder didn't leave her cold-blooded anymore. It was familiar, and she'd desensitized somewhat to the violence as a written description. A small silver lining, she supposed, not that she'd ever thought she'd consider that kind of desensitization a good thing. But in this case, it spared her the severity of the extreme emotional blow each time. It was almost like her brain was practicing self-care.

The blast of a car horn drew her eyes from her book to the intersection where someone who didn't know San Diego traffic was slowing down in the right-hand lane of Fourth with his blinker on to turn right onto G, a one-way street going the other way. The car behind was making his impatience at the incorrect stop more than clear. The driver in front must have figured out he was about to turn directly into traffic, stuck his arm out the window, waved his apology, and then drove through the intersection and past Quinn.

Tourists. The one-way streets through downtown helped with traffic flow, but it confused a lot of visitors.

Quinn was about to turn back to her notebook when she caught sight of the bus still a few blocks away. She put the notebook away and was happy to just people-watch for a few minutes, while passing her weight from side to side on feet aching from her eight-hour shift. She loved her job, but looked forward to being able to sit for the twenty-five-minute bus ride home. The bus stop was getting more crowded now, and she took a slightly tighter hold of her bag as people shifted closer, trying to stay in line while keeping the sidewalk clear. She glanced over the faces, but didn't see anyone she recognized, knowing unless it was a regular rider from the *before* times, she wouldn't.

The bus had to wait at G Street, but then pulled up to

the light standard bearing the MTS sign, brakes shrieking. The doors opened, a half dozen people got off, and then Quinn was the third person on, her fare card in hand.

"Quinn, how you doin'?"

As the second person moved to the rear of the bus, Quinn was delighted to recognize the driver, one of the regulars on Route 3 for years. "Chuck, nice to see you. I'm good." She tapped her fare card. "Donna and the kids are doing well?"

"They're great." Chuck looked her up and down. "You look good. Recovery coming along?"

She didn't remember, but she must have told him something about it. Chuck had driven this route for a long time, and when the bus was quiet, she used to sit up front and chat with him. He would have noticed when she disappeared for weeks before returning. He was always unfailingly kind to her *before*; she could see that was unchanged. It gave her a warm glow. She smiled at him gratefully. "Slow, but making progress. Really good to see you." Then she moved down the aisle, allowing the passengers behind her to climb on.

As on most late afternoon buses in downtown, this one was near capacity, but Quinn managed to find a seat two-thirds of the way back, just in front of the rear doors. Sliding in beside an older gentleman who sat with his eyes fixed out the window, she pulled her bag around to sit in her lap. For the first few minutes, she watched the world go by—busy summer sidewalks, packed street-side patios attached to bustling restaurants, colorful flags whipping in the ocean breeze, and brilliant rainbows of flowers tumbling from pots everywhere.

She really loved her city.

On that happy thought, she pulled her notebook from her pocket and went back to her review, angling the book so the man beside her and the teenage girl standing nearby with one hand on the overhead rail in the standing-room-only crowd couldn't see her words. She settled in for the ride and started at the beginning again.

No such thing as too much review.

She was so deep into her notebook, at first she didn't pay any real attention to the prickling at the back of her neck. But as the bus braked to a stop at Market and 25th Street, she looked up to check her location and the prickling became more insistent.

Someone is watching.

She knew she wasn't being paranoid. Deep in her gut, she felt it. She dropped her eyes back to her book, and then casually looked up as people got off the bus, clearing a little space.

From the dad across the way with his two school-aged kids with their noses pressed to the window, to the senior couple farther down, who seemed to look everywhere but at each other, to the teenage boy chewing gum with his mouth open as he bent over his phone, no one appeared to be looking at her. But she still felt it. Whoever it was, he or she was still on the bus.

The bus started again, and she dropped her eyes, shifting to cross one leg over the other, twisting her body slightly, so she was holding the back of the notebook to face the aisle, no longer caring what the man in the seat beside her saw if he ever took his eyes off the world whipping by. But from this position, she could see the people at the rear of the bus in her peripheral vision. A couple of acne-prone teenage boys rough-housing in the back corner, an older Black woman in nurse's scrubs, likely on her way home after a long shift from her exhausted slump, and a man with a baseball hat that hid his face, his head down over his phone. There was also a young mother with an infant in a stroller that took up three-quarters of the aisle just behind the rear exit—not the best place for her, but likely the only spot she could grab as more people piled onto the bus and she moved toward the back to keep out of the way of the busy doors.

It was a picture of San Diego on its way to wherever it needed to be. Nothing stood out.

Her heart clearly didn't think it was nothing from the way it kicked into overdrive.

You're being ridiculous.

Am I? Do I normally feel this on an average ride home?

Who's going to be after you?

Normally, no one. But what if I was seen?

And that was the real question. What if she was seen that night in the gloom? What if they figured out it was someone who had to have worked in that area, because who else would be in the alley? Okay, sure, *they'd* been in the alley, but who knew how long the gate had been left open? Normally it was only employees. What if someone figured out it was her?

The garden center.

What had happened there? What was her brain telling her? She remembered she'd gone there, but the details weren't ingrained yet. Trying to look relaxed, she flipped pages, scanning as she went, until she got to her notes on the Mundo Verde Garden Center. She searched the notes she'd left for herself, her gaze freezing on the information about the man standing beside the van who'd seen her, possibly even seen her snap pictures of the vehicle.

Knowing she had to make it abrupt or else she'd give someone time to look away, she raised her head to look behind her into the back. Almost everyone was in the same position, but she was in time to see the man in the ball cap drop his head too quickly for her to note any of his features. Now the brim blocked his face.

Was the killer on the bus with her? Or the man from the garden center? If so, what did they have to do with each other? Either way, what if someone was trying to follow her home?

Get off the bus.

But on the heels of that thought, immediately came another.

And go where? Where will you be safe?

She forced herself to calm down and think. *Before*-Quinn would have been able to come up with a plan; *after*-Quinn simply needed to do the same thing. She dug deep for the confidence and clarity of her past self, remembering how that version had it all together. *Before*-Quinn was her, just with a few bumps and bruises. She could do this.

You love this city. You know this city. You can't lead anyone home. So where do you go?

She knew this route like the back of her hand. It had been unchanged for years, and she knew every street, every store, every church along the way, every intersection.

Every intersection.

Imperial and 25th. The Central Division of the San Diego Police Department. It was right there, kitty-corner to the bus stop, and while it might not be open to members of the general public at 5:30 PM on a Saturday, it would be staffed. She could find help there if anyone followed her. But just the sight of it might be enough to hold someone back from trailing her.

Now to get off the bus without being followed.

Another casual scan of the front of the bus to double-check. No, she was sure that wasn't where the threat was. It came from behind. She couldn't prove it was the man in the ball cap, but currently who it was mattered less than how to shake any tail that could follow her off the bus.

If she was wrong, she was delaying her arrival home. If she was right, she'd make it home tonight and not end up in a ditch somewhere.

She didn't think she was paranoid, but if she was, she was willing to bet it all on black.

They sailed past the Island Avenue stop as they continued south down 25th Street, but then someone called for a stop at J Street where two people got off. Moving again, she counted off stops in her head from the memory she'd held for so long. Two more stops. One at K Street, and then the one she needed at Imperial.

She slid her notebook into her pocket and tried to figure out her exit. She could move to the front of the bus, maybe to talk to Chuck, but she might not have enough time now. Not to mention the front of the bus was still packed and she'd have to push through. Or she could exit through the rear doors, but if whoever was behind her saw her pull the cord, her intent would be telegraphed. Still, the police station would be right there, and she'd sprint for it if needed. If anyone tried to stop her on her way there, they'd be in clear sight of the bus and a constant stream of traffic flowing by in two directions, not to mention any pedestrians. Lots of people wouldn't want to intercede in what they might see as a physical altercation—which it would be, because she wasn't going down without a fight—but some would. Quinn had been on the short end of the stick when it came to violence, but she refused to think there weren't good people in the world who would help. Just like the bartender going home at the end of his 2:00 AM shift.

They passed the stop at K Street, which meant Imperial Avenue was next. She had no choice; she was going to have to pull the signal cord above the window to indicate the next stop was required. Just as she was getting ready to reach for the cord, a bell sounded and the light mounted on the roof behind the driver flashed NEXT STOP.

Someone else needed to get off, so Quinn just needed to be ready to move and move fast. She shifted her bag to hang off the edge of the seat at her hip, but relaxed back as if she hadn't a care in the world. Below the casual posture, she was coiled, ready to spring.

The bus slowed, and then came to a stop just short of Imperial Avenue, and both doors opened.

Wait . . . wait . . .

Up at the front, two men said thanks to Chuck as they passed him and climbed down the stairs and onto the sidewalk. As the second man went through the doorway, and Chuck reached for the button to close the doors, Quinn jumped to her feet. Wrapping her left hand around the curved bar that ran along the top of every bench seat, she swung herself around the back of the seat and down onto the stairs leading to the rear door. She took the stairs two at a time, going sideways to squeeze through the gap just as the doors closed behind her with a thump. She power-walked down the sidewalk just as the bus started moving again, and was into the intersection on the walk signal as it went past.

Looking up, she saw the face of the man in the ball cap staring down at her for just an instant before it pulled back. She didn't get a great view of him, but the fury in his eyes was unmistakable.

Chalk one up for the gut. Once again, it was correct.

Her knees felt a little shaky by the time she got to the far side of the intersection and waited to cross 25th. Across from her stood the relatively new building for the San Diego Police Department Central Division, built in the Spanish Colonial style with a red tile roof and a three-story watchtower on the corner facing the intersection. As soon as the light changed, she crossed, still in view of the bus, heading directly for the front steps. Then the bus turned onto Oceanview and disappeared from sight.

She climbed the front steps of the police station and sat down, drained, her heart hammering, her breath ragged.

She wasn't about to sit out here and wait for the next bus twenty minutes from now. She was going to call an Uber to get her home safely where she could regroup.

Part of that regroup needed to be calling Reyes before she got in over her head. She needed to come clean about the belfry logo, the garden center, and the sketches. And now this.

But what are you going to tell her? What evidence can you show her? Can you definitively say you saw the belfry that night, or only that you think you might have? That a panel van at a garden center might be the one in a city of panel vans? That the belfry symbol identifies it, even though it's a symbol used citywide? That a handful of unfinished sketches tell a true story? And can you prove that man was following you? Did he chase you off the bus and down the street? Can you substantiate your feeling?

Or is she just going to think you're unstable? That your flashback and the memories you think are informing your art aren't dependable? That they're confabulations?

Because you don't know they aren't.

Her blood, heated from the scare on the bus, chilled.

This was the crux of the matter. If she had hard and fast evidence, she'd have already told Reyes about it. But what she had was conjecture and possible imaginary embroidery.

No actual facts. And the sketches certainly weren't absolute depictions of reality. She couldn't prove she wasn't coming up with the images out of thin air, and Reyes was too busy to be sent on a wild goose chase based on Quinn's wild imaginings. This wasn't her only case, and others needed her to bring justice for them as well. She couldn't allow her weakness to stand in the way of someone else's justice. That would be unforgivable.

She just needed a few more days. She was off for the next two, and she was going to spend them safely locked in her apartment, sketching anything that came to mind, trying to stimulate her memory and push her recollection. Then she'd have a better story and she'd talk to Reyes.

The only way she could help with this case was to identify the killer. If—and it was a big if—she'd been identified, they didn't know where she lived. She'd be safe at home.

And, hopefully, by the time she reemerged, she'd have a face that would inform the rest of the case.

CHAPTER 22

"Dios mío, Reyes. What's all this?" Cervelló stopped in the open doorway to look into the small meeting room across the hallway from the bullpen.

Reyes looked up from the printed document she was reading and scanned the room, seeing it with the fresh eyes of someone stumbling across the chaos. The rectangular conference table was covered with printed documents, file folders, photos, four binders containing the printed versions of the four yearbooks, an open laptop, a pad of paper, and a handful of pens, along with a box of paper clips, a stapler, and several differently sized pads of sticky notes in blinding neon colors. It looked like a Staples had vomited all over her table. "I'm trying to put my victim's notes together to figure out what happened. Do you know how much research investigative reporters do?"

"The good ones, a mountain. The crappy ones, they report on whatever social media says is God's own truth."

"This was one of the good ones."

"Which means you're fighting an uphill battle." His gaze tracked to the clock on the wall. "You know your shift ended twenty minutes ago?"

"I know. Yours, too."

"So what are you doing here?"

"I could ask you the same thing."

"I was wrapping up for the day and getting ready to ship out. That's *not* what you're doing."

"I'm going to need a few hours to start figuring out what my questions are so I can ask them tomorrow. Just trying to get a leg up."

"Where's Frank tonight?"

"On shift. They're shorthanded, so he grabbed an extra noon to ten PM shift."

"Handy if you want to work late."

"Oh, you know Frank. He gets it. If I have to work late, he knows the drill. Just like I know the drill when he takes an extra shift or has to stay late at the ER. We knew what we were getting into when we hooked up."

"A cop and an ER doc . . . it's a good combination."

Reyes grinned. "We think so. Though, to my great regret, Frank can't cook like Maria."

"Few can. We need to have you guys over for dinner again sometime soon." He winked at her. "Personally, I think Maria has a soft spot for Frank."

"Your wife has excellent taste." Reyes's eyes narrowed as Cervelló pulled out a chair, sat down, and surveyed the whirlwind of paper. "Isn't Maria cooking for you as we speak?"

"It's like you think she's new at this. She's been married to a cop for thirty-two years. She doesn't start cooking until I call her from the car to tell her I'm on the way home. Even calls from my desk don't count. A few ruined meals early on taught her that lesson."

"Smart lady."

"The smartest."

When Cervelló didn't move, Reyes said, "Isn't your smart lady waiting for you to get home?"

"She knows I'll be home at some point. Looks to me like you could use a hand here. What are we looking for?"

We. What are we *looking for.*

She loved this man and his willingness to step in. Maybe it was old school, maybe it was just *him*, but he clearly wasn't going to leave her here to drown in details when another pair of eyes could cut the job in half, even if it meant doing it off the clock.

But she knew this drill, too. Shut up and take the help without making a big deal out of it, just like she wouldn't expect a big deal if it was her jumping in to help him. They'd both done this for the other in the past.

Teamwork, for the win.

"You know the body you put me onto, the one that washed up in Woods Cove?"

"Yup."

"He turned out to be the missing vic from the Gaslamp alley murder, the one with no evidence, including the body. Well, now we have a body."

"Handy. Now you can actually dig in."

"Exactly. The vic was Jack DeWitt, an investigative reporter for the *Union-Tribune*."

Cervelló winced. "That's the kind of guy who might stick his nose where it wasn't wanted."

"I think he did. I've done interviews with everyone around him. His parents are gone and his only brother was the one who reported him missing. It seems like they were close. His colleagues at the *Union-Tribune* seemed to like him. Some friendly competition, maybe even occasionally not so friendly, but I didn't get the vibe it ever got nasty. More of a win-some-lose-some kind of thing. No personal partner of either sex, didn't even really seem to be dating. Last serious partner was last year, according to the brother. He and she lived together for about eighteen months—she finally got tired of him being essentially married to his job, and split. Cam said Jack took it hard and dove even further into the job and hadn't been looking for anyone since. No addictions—chemical, sexual, or gambling—and was living within his means, but didn't have enough to make it look like his finances were the motive. His brother will inherit everything and he's better off than Jack was. Nothing here is an obvious lead to someone who needed to break DeWitt's neck in a dark alley."

"That's official?"

"Yes. Got the prelim coroner's report earlier today. Neck broken at the C4 vertebra, severing the spinal cord. Death was instantaneous."

"Small favors," murmured Cervelló.

"No kidding. While it's not a clean one hundred percent, I'd say at this point we're at a solid ninety-eight percent that the motive for his killing came from his work." Reyes flipped back a page on the pad of paper. "What was he working on at the time of his death? His beat was politics, policing, and breaking news. I spent a bit of time earlier sorting through the different stories, printing out his notes on them, and organizing them. At least on this first round, I've kept it to anything controversial. Personal interest pieces about fundraising that put in a new playground at a park, or how a giraffe and an ostrich at the San Diego Zoo have become inseparable buddies, aren't included. There's more than enough here without that stuff." She selected a folder, checked the label, put it down, and selected a second. "Which leaves us with things like an investigation into the use of excessive force by an SDPD officer during the arrest of a young Black man who wasn't putting up a fight. Charges were laid against the officer, but also against a second officer who failed to intervene to stop the excessive force, and instead just stood back and watched." Reyes put down the folder and picked up another. "Or this story, which was breaking news the day he died, about the Romanian organized crime group operating in the city, but that story broke in the *Times of San Diego* and the *Union-Tribune* was following their lead."

"So that one's less likely even though it involves organized crime."

"That's what I think. We have some other local stories that are in real germinal stages, but the majority of what he was working on was the mayoral election—who the candidates are, what their backgrounds are, what party they'd represent if the municipal election wasn't nonpartisan, that kind of thing. Six candidates are registered for the primary next month before the top two go on to the general election in November. He was working on all of them for background. Keeping that in mind, and that we can't rule out any of these stories as the motive for his murder, there's one thing that's weird. I'm just not sure how to connect it yet."

"What's that?"

"Something was pulling him toward Chicago. He contacted some ritzy high school to get their yearbooks, and placed a bunch of calls to that area. I'm following up, but am getting a blank. According to his files, he was looking for information on some guy named Alf Williams. Some of the people who went to school with this guy—he was a rich kid, spoiled only son of some Chicago upper-crust types—don't know anything about him now. Moved out of the area to go to college, never came back, never stayed in touch. I've hit a bit of a wall in Chicago, but I know there's something there."

Reyes pulled a binder closer, opened it to one of the bright sticky notes, and pushed it toward Cervelló. "This is Williams. He's in every yearbook, but this is the most mature picture." On a page that was mostly filled with girls with big hair wearing brightly colored blouses and sweaters with shoulder pads, she tapped the face of a dark-haired boy with slightly overlong, center-parted hair that winged down over his temples and into his eyes. He sported a thick beard, neatly edged, with a high cheek line. He was wearing a white shirt, a charcoal sport coat, and a striped tie.

"The poor kid." Cervelló pulled the binder closer and leaned in. "Look at the acne. And that's not just any acne, that's cystic acne. I had a buddy who had that. It was the worst. Wasn't a great way to win over the girls."

"He may have had enough money that it wasn't a problem."

"Maybe. He's certainly trying to hide it with the long hair and, especially, the beard. Which at least has the advantage of not having to run a blade over it daily when your skin is a minefield." He studied the photo. "But all the hair makes it a lot harder to identify him if we try to imagine what he'd look like now."

"The nerds are trying."

"To age him?"

"Yes. I gave them all the photos to see if they could work their magic on one of those. The acne is in the early photos, too, but the trade-off to the shaved face is the younger look. Nothing from them yet, but they said they'd have something for me today."

"Day's not over yet."

"Very true. Another thing to know about DeWitt is he was a totally digital guy. He didn't have piles of printed paper on his desk, didn't have a whiteboard full of writing, or a corkboard with images and red string. He did everything on his laptop, and, when he was in the field, on his phone."

"Did you get any of that?"

"The phone disappeared, and I think it's either at the bottom of the Pacific or has been destroyed by whoever killed him after finding out what's on it."

"Guy may have been dead, but still had a face and a thumbprint to get onto a locked phone."

"Exactly. Whoever killed him may have kept the phone to find out what he knew and who else might have known it."

"Then probably have tossed it in the Pacific."

"Possibly. But I learned from his brother that DeWitt religiously backed up his phone data to the Dropbox cloud."

"Getting a warrant for it?"

"Already served it. But I'm still waiting. You know how these big companies need to pass everything through their bank of lawyers to make sure there's sufficient probable cause. And then they have to decrypt his personal files. It's coming, but I have to wait for it."

"Any other electronics?"

"I found the laptop when I got the warrant for DeWitt's residence. Laptop was smashed, and then the hard drive was removed for good measure so the nerds didn't even get a crack at it."

"Too bad for the nerds. They love a challenge."

"Don't they though? So all of this"—Reyes threw an arm wide—"came from the warrant for his notes at the *Union-Tribune*. We got everything—which was a lot, because he's been there seven years—but this is what he's currently working on. I assume if it's already been published, the risk to him ended at that point."

"Agreed, this is the kind of death that happens when you're trying to bury a story, not when you're pissed it got out. Divide and conquer?"

"That works. I was going to Uber Eats in some grub. Want in?"

Cervelló checked the time again, pulled out his cell phone. "Let me tell Maria I won't be back until later. Then, yeah. What are you getting?"

"I'm easy. What do you want?"

"I could go for a burger and rings. As long as you don't tell Maria. She's always on me about my cholesterol."

"My lips are sealed. How about Little Tony's? They have that knockout loaded Mexiburger."

"Sounds good to me."

"Two loaded Mexis and rings, coming up. I'm also getting coffee delivered. No way am I drinking any more of the tar in the bullpen. I think it's slowly eating a hole in my stomach lining. Let me get you one of those, too."

They placed their orders, divided the folders, and dove in. They worked for almost a half hour before Reyes got the text to meet the driver for the food and coffee. She came back and they settled into their meal, and for a long time the only noise was the sound of chewing, paper flipping, and the scratch of pens.

Because it was the bigger stack of files, Reyes tackled the mayoral election and its many candidates, while Cervelló began with the Romanian crime group and then moved on to the policing issues.

Reyes had seen the signs around the town, but with the mayoral election still weeks away, she hadn't taken the time to look at the candidates yet. She dove into them now.

Two birds, one stone. I may be ready to place my vote by later tonight.

There were six candidates, from a variety of walks of life:

Abigail Featherstone—a city council member who was running on her significant municipal experience.

Danilo Gomez—the owner of a local construction company running on a platform of cutting red tape at city hall.

Saul Moore—a startup angel investor wanting to make San Diego a new offshoot of the traditional Silicon Valley tech playground.

David Soto—the current San Diego County District Attorney, the law-and-order candidate.

Jia Chen—a financial analyst campaigning on fiscal re-
sponsibility.

Greg Wheeler—a former state assemblyman wanting to
end partisan hostility in all levels of politics.

Knowing the only way to tackle the sheer volume was
to jump right in, she pulled over the first file and started to
read, making notes about anything a candidate might not
want exposed.

By the time she'd gone through everything in the files
she didn't want to vote for any of them. DeWitt had actually done a great job of collecting information like he was
setting up to write a balanced biography of each candidate, either to all go together in the *Union-Tribune*, or
possibly one sketch a day leading up to the special election. The information was quite in-depth, from their current family life, to their business acumen, to their degrees
and educational backgrounds—Gomez was the only one
without a degree; instead, he apprenticed as a framing car-
penter and branched out from there. But along the way
were bumps in the road for every one of them: Featherstone had a messy, contentious divorce with allegations of
spousal abuse; Gomez had been accused of corner-cutting
to save a buck; Moore of being selective in his investments
with an antisemitic bent; Soto of prosecuting more crimes
against minorities than the white population of the county;
Chen was surrounded by rumors of insider trading; and
Wheeler was reportedly a hound, going after the women
in his office.

Reyes sat back in her chair, pushed her hair out of her
eyes, and looked at the clock—8:39 PM. She felt like she
was getting nowhere fast. "You know, maybe I'll sit this
election out."

"They all suck?"

"I'm leaning that way."

"Look at it as a sliding scale. Who sucks the least?"

"I guess that's one way of thinking of it. They've all got at least one red flag, but nothing is jumping out at me as something DeWitt needed to die for. Some of the information is out—Soto's prosecution stats, for example—and some isn't—Featherstone is going through a divorce as we speak, and there's rumors of spousal abuse."

"If she's the victim, there's nothing to be ashamed of. It sounds like she's getting out."

"That's the problem. *He's* the victim and *she's* the abuser. That isn't something that's public knowledge."

"That could be a problem that could lose her the election. I'd see her wanting to keep it buried."

"She sure as hell wasn't the one who killed DeWitt. But she could have hired someone to do it." Reyes scanned the images that grinned at her with overbright smiles from campaign flyers and brochures. "Keeping that in mind, any of them could have done that. They're all rich enough, and with enough connections if they'd needed a job done, they could have made it happen. Might have considered it a good investment. It could make this much harder if the killer has no direct motive other than a monetary payout. Tracking the suspect was always going to be hard due to the lack of evidence, but if there isn't even a motive . . ." She trailed off, pensively studying the faces again.

"It's an extra challenge. From what I've seen so far, nothing is jumping out at me."

"I have concerns that until we get that Dropbox data, we're missing big pieces of this. Everyone at the paper said DeWitt was never without his phone in his hand. Some of the most important notes may only have been on that device depending on how often he backed up his data. If he was only backing up daily, we may never know some of the details, or the leaps of knowledge he took because of them, because he never had time to do that last backup before he was killed."

"If it was something he figured out, then it's something we can figure out. Clearly, there are connections. We just need to uncover them."

"I guess I'm constantly hearing a clock ticking in the background." When Cervelló looked up, confusion in his dark eyes, Reyes continued, "It's my witness. She's not sure she wasn't seen that night. If she was, she could be in danger. I may not have the luxury of time for those connections." She checked her email on her phone, and sighed. "Still nothing from the nerds."

"Give them time. They'll get it done."

They went back to work.

Twenty minutes later, Reyes raised her cup to her lips and drained the last of her now cold coffee. Then she picked up her phone to find an email from one of the computer forensics guys.

"You're right. They got it done. The nerds got back to me."

"Stellar nerds, every single one of them."

"Don't I know it. Not sure what we'd do without them some days." She set her phone down and angled the laptop a little before opening her email. "They attached an image, which will be easier to see here." She opened the email, then opened the attachment and waited while it loaded. Then blinked. Then blinked again to ensure she was seeing correctly. "Oh, my God."

Cervelló braced his hands on the edge of the table and half rose from the chair. "What?"

Reyes waved him down and turned the laptop so he could see the aged face on-screen. Looking back at them was a man with blue eyes, a short forehead with a widow's peak, wide cheekbones, and a slightly rounded jaw.

She'd seen that face before, or one very like it, here in the pages she'd been reading. Though in those photos, the mouth was smiling, revealing straight white teeth, and the eyes were either looking directly into the camera as if there were no one in the world but the person staring at the image, or into the eyes of a voter or their baby.

"David Soto didn't know Alf Williams," Reyes said. "Soto *was* Alf Williams."

CHAPTER 23

Quinn stepped out into the last rays of twilight and the soft breezes of the coming night. She took a deep breath of warm summer air, just beginning to cool, scenting roses and lavender from the gardens lining the front of the church. "What a lovely evening."

"Gorgeous." Viv slid her a sideways glance. "You didn't want to hang back and wait for Will?"

They started through the parking lot, walking along the line of cars toward Front Street.

"I didn't want to interrupt. He was talking to Marilyn about her mom. She needs a lot of support there and some one-on-one advice would be good for her. I'm not sure she's sharing everything with the group. As an older lady, she might not feel it was proper, but she might be willing to share those details with a medical professional. Though, if the group was led by a woman, I think she'd prefer it."

"I agree on Marilyn, but you've stayed late after the last two meetings to talk to Will." Her smile was sly, the curve of her eyebrow stating her intrigue. "And here I was wondering if you guys have a thing going."

"A thing?" Quinn looked at her blankly for a moment before her brain kicked in. "You mean *a thing*?"

"Sure."

It was so ridiculous, Quinn laughed. "Honestly, if we're having a thing, I wouldn't know, because it's gone from my memory. I'd like to think if I was carrying on with someone, I'd remember." She threw up her hands. "Who am I kidding? Of course I won't remember. And that's a very good reason no one would want to be with me. Especially Will."

"Why *especially*?"

"Because outside of myself, no one knows better than him how broken I am."

"You're not broken. You're just a little . . . dented. Temporarily."

"Dented, that's one way to put it. And temporarily is being hopeful."

"You gotta be hopeful. If not, it can be hard to get out of bed in the morning."

They stepped onto the walkway that connected the parking lot to the sidewalk lining Front Street. "I guess that's the one thing about not being able to recall memories. If you get discouraged, you forget about it by the next day. That's why I have that ribbon in my book."

"The good-and-useful-things-only ribbon?"

"Close. Good and necessary things. Because reviewing details on a regular basis seems to finally drive it into my brain, so I form a memory, even if it's of the written material and not of the actual event. But if it's negative written material, I'll form a memory about that, too."

They hit the sidewalk and turned left to where the long silver and glass bus shelter lined the far edge of the sidewalk about ten feet down.

"That might not be that helpful," Viv said. "And it's probably what you'd remember first. Why is it when someone pays us a compliment we forget about it in ten minutes, but when someone makes a dig, we fret about it all day and then proceed to never forget it?"

"I know that was certainly me before the attack." Quinn considered the four-seater bench inside the bus shelter and then opted to stand on the sidewalk in front of it where she could enjoy the delightful breeze. "Feel free to sit. I want to stand for a while; I've been sitting for the last hour."

"Me too."

Quinn peered up one-way Front Street, which, even at this time of night, was busy with traffic, as the roads surrounding the hospital were never quiet except during the dead of night. Lots of cars headed their direction, running south toward downtown, but she couldn't see the widely spaced headlights, large lit front windshield, or the brightly illuminated orange-on-black display overhead with the large number 3 and *Downtown via Fourth Ave* that said the bus was coming. She checked the time. "Bus should be coming along shortly."

"We have time." Viv turned back toward Quinn. "And that gives us time to talk about why you aren't going after a thing with Will. He's single, you know."

A truck drove past, creating enough wind to whip Quinn's hair, loose on her shoulders tonight, into the air before settling again. "Good to know, since I didn't remember that little tidbit, if I ever knew it in the first place. How do you even know that?"

"I asked him." Viv's tone was matter-of-fact, with no embarrassment about possibly pushing personal boundaries.

Quinn stared blankly at her for a moment. Even before the attack, she'd never have had the courage to ask a man in a professional setting if he was single. "You're kidding me."

"Nope." Viv shrugged carelessly, a graceful movement

Quinn would never be able to emulate even if she spent hours practicing in front of the mirror. "I learned long ago if I wanted to know something to just ask. Beating around the bush leads to not getting an answer or misunderstandings."

"Did you ask him out once you knew he was single?"

"No. I was just curious if it was a possibility." She waggled her eyebrows. "Possibilities are always good to keep in mind. But no, if you're asking if I'm interested so you shouldn't be, I decided he's not my type." She grinned and tossed her head, forgetting she had her hair up in a loose knot, which downplayed the effect. "I like them bold and adventurous. He's great. Smart and intuitive, but a little too quiet for me. You, on the other hand . . ." She let the sentence dangle, her point clear in the silence.

"Are you just focused on my nonexistent love life because you don't want to talk about yours?" Quinn countered. "How is your love life, anyway? Are you dripping with bold, adventurous men? Have we ever discussed it?"

"I told you about a disastrous blind date I had on our ride home a few weeks ago. It made you laugh." She chuckled quietly. "Looking back a few weeks later, it makes me laugh, too. So ridiculous. Definitely *not* bold or adventurous."

"I'm sorry I don't remember the story. On the other hand, you can tell it to me again. It'll be all new and I'll enjoy it like I've never heard it before. You know, that's the one positive about this brain of mine in its current state. Ever seen a movie or read a book and loved it so much you've been sorry you'd never be able to experience it all new again? Experience the rush of discovery of something new to love? That any other time you see it or read it, you'll always know what comes next? I used to have that problem, but don't now. It's fresh every time. How's that for a bright side?"

"That would definitely be a bright side for some things."

The sound of an engine racing drew Quinn's eyes over Viv's shoulder to the street, but all she could see in the fading light was spotty traffic moving toward her in glowing lights. *Must be someone showing off on the next street.*

Except the sound got louder instead of fading. Suddenly a speeding vehicle came out of the shadows in the right-hand lane, a dark SUV with no illumination of any kind. Worse, it was picking up speed as it got closer and was entirely too close to them in the near lane of traffic. Quinn took a step back from the street, then realized Viv stood with her back to the flow of traffic and couldn't see the danger coming. She reached out to grab Viv, but even as her fingers closed over Viv's forearm, the SUV shot forward with a squeal of tires.

It was swerving right for them.

"Get back!" Quinn lurched away from the edge of the road, but her hand slipped on the light knit of Viv's three-quarter sleeve, her fingers sliding free.

Viv's head jerked around to see the car barreling toward them. She tried to turn and sidestep, but the spastic stiffness of her post-TBI muscles impeded her leg movement, and she stumbled. Quinn crashed into the shallow bus shelter, her back slamming against the rear wall at the same moment the car popped over the curb at high speed.

And barreled right into Viv.

"*VIV!*" Quinn's scream echoed inside the shelter, tearing at her throat, as she watched in horror as her friend was thrown up and over the hood of the SUV. Viv smashed into the windshield before being tossed like a rag doll over the roof and tumbling to the road to lie broken and bleeding against the curb.

The SUV bounced back into the right-hand lane, and,

tires screaming, sped off into the night, disappearing into the dark.

"No, no, *no*!" Quinn scrambled forward, not gaining her balance, but stumbling to the road to where Viv lay, dropping to her hands and knees beside her.

Immediately, several drivers who witnessed the event stopped and ran to help, one already calling 911, and two more kneeling down next to Quinn to surround Viv.

But Quinn had no eyes for anyone but Viv. She lay at an angle not possible without a plethora of broken bones, possibly a broken spine. Her stylish capris and summer boat-neck top were filthy and torn, and one of her espadrille sandals lay ten feet away on its side in the middle of the lane. Her gorgeous red hair was tangled around her colorless face, while a vicious scrape scored her right cheek, and a trickle of blood ran from her nose. Her blue eyes were open and staring at the stars just coming into view.

"Viv! Vivian!" Quinn held both hands just above Viv's shoulders, wanting to shake her, wanting to bring her out of whatever stupor she was locked in, but part of her knew never to move someone with potential back and neck problems. Her hands paused, useless, wanting to touch, or comfort, to help, but unable to do any of it. "Viv, can you hear me? It's Quinn, I'm here." Deciding she could at least do this, she brushed a hand over Viv's forehead, pushing the hair back from her face, her skin warm and damp under Quinn's touch.

Quinn pulled her hand away, only to find blood smeared on her fingertips from an unseen head wound.

So much damage. Too much damage?

"You know her?" the man beside her asked.

"Yes, I just came out of a meeting with her. She's Vivian . . ." Quinn's voice trailed off as she realized she didn't remember Viv's last name.

In the distance a siren wailed, coming from the direction of downtown.

Quinn craned her neck to look down the street. They were so close to the hospital—she could see it *right there*—what would it take to get help? Part of her knew EMS services originated from outside the hospital and they'd need to wait for an ambulance and paramedics, but part of her wanted to scream until someone with medical knowledge came running.

She bent over her friend so Viv couldn't help but see her and be comforted by her presence. A chill ran through her when Viv's eyes didn't focus on her. "Viv, it's Quinn, I'm here. Can you hear me? Blink if you can hear me."

Viv remained motionless, and a moan built in Quinn's chest.

"Quinn? Quinn! Vivian! My God, what happened?"

Quinn raised dull eyes toward the new voice, one she felt she should know, then recognition belatedly kicked in as Will knelt beside her, his hands on her shoulders to push her back, push her out of the way so he could get closer.

"SUV rammed her on the sidewalk," one of the two men said. "We saw the whole thing. They were standing there waiting for the bus and this SUV came roaring down the street, went over the curb, and hit this woman. The other one managed to get back, get out of the way. Then the SUV drove off."

Will slid two fingers against Viv's throat. "Did anyone get the license plate?"

The two men exchanged a look before the second one said, "I'm not sure it had one."

Will looked up sharply, then shifted his fingers to another spot on Viv's throat. "What do you mean?"

"No plate, no lights; it just came out of the dark."

Quinn was barely listening to the men. She knew all this, she'd lived it. Will needed to help Viv, not chat. Her heart still pounding, a pressure building in her head she wasn't sure how to vent, Quinn crouched, needing to do something, *anything*, able to do nothing.

Fear swelled as Will bent to press his ear to Viv's chest, holding still for more than ten seconds as everyone around him went silent. Straightening, he looked deep into Viv's sightless eyes before closing his own for a moment, as if steeling himself. Then he turned to meet Quinn's gaze. "Quinn . . ."

The softness in his tone and the pity in his eyes telegraphed what he was going to say, and Quinn scrambled backward over the curb, trying to climb to her feet. If she walked away, ran away, and didn't allow him to say it, it couldn't be real. This was all part of her broken brain. False memories, false visions, false reality. Viv—smart, sassy, vivacious Viv—was just fine.

She, on the other hand, needed to be locked away because she clearly wasn't well.

None of this was real. None of it could be, because if it was, she wasn't sure she could survive it.

"Quinn! Wait!"

Will stepped onto the curb as Quinn scrabbled backward, then tried to struggle to her feet. She lost her balance, started to fall, but caught herself on the side wall of the bus shelter. Before she could straighten, Will was beside her, his hands on her upper arms, helping her upright. But Quinn couldn't take her eyes off Viv, broken and bleeding in the road.

Dead.

Will hadn't said it, but she'd seen it in his eyes. She was already gone.

It couldn't be real. Was she losing her mind?

She looked into Will's face. "You have to help me. Something's wrong. I'm hallucinating."

"No, you're not. Viv's gone."

The word made no sense to her as her heart struggled to comprehend what her brain was telling her. It was why her heart was telling her she didn't understand the world around her. "Gone?"

"She's dead." Will put his arm around her shoulders, drawing her away, but some of the words of the people around her penetrated as disjointed bits of information.

Poor girl, never had a chance.

That car had no lights on and no plates.

It's like it meant to hit her.

Will led her to the bench in the bus shelter, holding her shoulders as he lowered her down. Her knees buckled, taking her down the last foot in a rush, and she moaned softly. He sat beside her, taking both her hands in his. "It was fast. I doubt she felt anything after the initial collision."

A siren screamed as an ambulance roared down the street, stopping parallel to the crowd. Two paramedics got out, ran to the back, opened the doors to pull out two large packs and the gurney, and ran over.

"Stay here." When Quinn tried to rise, Will pushed her down. "There's nothing more you can do for her. Stay here. I'll be right back."

Will joined the crowd that had grown when Quinn wasn't looking. Dully, she studied the scene as if it were a tragedy in a movie-of-the-week—the crowd of people, some horrified, some morbidly curious, the witnesses hanging back to give the statements they knew would be required, the body lying in the gutter, the effervescent spirit it used to hold, gone forever, all washed in flashing red and white lights. When the paramedics only stayed bent over Viv for a few minutes, and then stood and backed away, she knew the truth.

Gone forever.

A sob built in her chest, and she brutally battled it back. She knew better than to expose her weaknesses to those around her. That's what her apartment was for. That was the place where she could fall apart for however long she needed.

The first police car arrived, followed shortly after by a second and third. Quinn watched, a silent, stiff specter set apart from the emotion of the scene, as Will talked to the police, no doubt supplying Viv's full name and information, then waiting as the witnesses gave their accounts, his already somber face taking on an unusually stiff cast.

When he returned to Quinn, his strides were long and quick. "Where's your phone?"

Quinn looked up at him, trying to make his request compute in her short-circuiting brain. "You need my phone?"

"Yes."

"You need to make a call?"

"Yes."

She didn't have the energy to question further, just opened the cross-body bag she still wore and pulled out her cell phone to hand it to him. He held it up to her face—she had a brief view of the waterfall landscape on her lock screen before the phone opened to her home screen. He pulled up her contacts list, searched for a moment, selected a name, and placed the call. Then he put the call on speaker so Quinn was included and took her hand in his.

"Quinn? Is anything wrong?" Concern was clear in Reyes's tone.

"Detective Reyes?"

"Yes." The voice was instantly all business with an unfamiliar male voice.

"My name is Will Dawsey. I'm a friend of Quinn Fleming's."

"She's mentioned you. You're the TBI expert."

"Yes. We need you up at UC San Diego Medical. At the Front and Arbor intersection."

"*We?* Did something happen to Quinn?"

"Nearly. Quinn and Vivian Gibson were leaving tonight's TBI group therapy session when an SUV jumped the curb where they were standing waiting for the bus. Quinn managed to get out of the way. Ms. Gibson was hit and killed."

"Did they stop the vehicle?"

"No. Hit-and-run."

"How is Quinn?"

"Badly shaken." Will paused and looked her over. "She's right here listening because I have you on speaker so she stays involved. She's shocky, so I'm going to get a blanket for her as soon as I hang up. It may have been presumptuous of me, but I took her phone because I knew she had your number, and she needs you looped in. She might not be thinking that right now—as I said, she's in shock—so I'm doing it for her. This wasn't an accident. Witnesses saw it happen."

"You?"

"No, unfortunately, I missed it by only moments. I was coming out to my car when I spotted the gathering crowd and came over. But several drivers witnessed it and pulled over to help. The cops are talking to them now and they're describing a speeding SUV running with no lights or plates who purposely aimed for two women standing out in front of the bus stop on Front Street just south of Arbor Avenue." Will looked down at Quinn, who stared at him silently, her face frozen. "Quinn has shared with me the story about what happened that night in the alley. I know at the time she was concerned she was somehow seen, though I find it hard to fathom how if she was that far into the shadows. But if you assume she was seen, or if they somehow found out who she was, this looks more like a targeted hit following a scheduled meeting she attends weekly."

For the first time since Viv's death, the fog parted as fear sliced deep. *Not an accident? Not just a drunk driver or someone losing control of their car and then running in shame and alarm for what they'd done? They'd meant to kill me, and Viv died in my place?*

The cry that broke from Quinn echoed inside the shelter, a knife stab of grief and agony. She tried to pull her hand away from Will's, tried to rise, but he held on, so she dragged him up with her when she surged to her feet and staggered several steps, her eyes scanning for any place of safety. Anywhere to run. She was exposed here, as exposed as Viv was as the vehicle barreled toward them. And look how that turned out.

"Quinn, hang on. Detective Reyes is coming. We need you to stay here." Will's voice seemed to come from the end of a long tunnel.

"Front and Arbor?" asked Reyes.

"Yes. I asked the cops if I could move Quinn, but they want her to stay handy for questioning, so we're here on-site."

"Don't let them question her. I'll do it. I'm on my way."

The line went dead.

Will jammed the phone in his pocket and then wrapped his arms around Quinn and held on even when she tried to push away. "I have you. Just hang on, help is coming."

All Quinn could think about was escape. If someone was trying to kill her, she needed to run. Maybe they didn't know where she lived and she could hide out there. She'd take some vacation, or tell Jacinta she had the flu and needed a week or two off. Or maybe she'd take a train trip.

If she left herself notes, she could keep herself on track as to why she was on the run. Until the coast was clear. Or maybe—

She started to shake, wracking tremors that quaked through her. Then her knees gave out.

Will's arms locked around her, keeping her upright, then he half walked, half carried her to the bench and sat her down again. "Don't move. I mean it, Quinn. We need to wait for Detective Reyes." He stepped back, made sure she wasn't going to face-plant onto the concrete, and jogged off, returning a minute later with a thick gray blanket, which he wrapped around her. Then he put his arm around her and drew her head onto his shoulder.

They waited in silence for Reyes to arrive. There was nothing else to say. Quinn couldn't stand to stare at Viv's body, still lying in the gutter, though now covered with a yellow tarp to shelter her body from curious bystanders as they waited for the coroner to arrive. She angled her head against Will's shoulder, closed her eyes, and allowed herself to pretend for a few minutes that none of it had happened. If anyone needed her, Will would let her know.

Twenty minutes later, Reyes found them in that same position.

"Quinn."

The voice was close, and when Quinn opened her eyes, Reyes crouched in front of her, her sharp cop eyes searching her face. "I'm sorry we dragged you out here." Quinn's voice was a low rasp.

"You didn't drag me anywhere. And I was still at headquarters, which put me closer to you here than if I'd already gone home." She sat down on Quinn's other side. "Are you okay? Do you need to be checked out? The cops told me the witnesses said you crashed back into the bus shelter pretty hard."

"I'm fine." Quinn's voice was flat as she pulled away from Will to sit upright. Her blanket slipped off one shoulder and Reyes pulled it back into place. "I may be sore tomorrow, but if that's the worst of it, I got off lucky." She couldn't help her gaze shooting to the tarp. She closed her eyes and turned her face away.

"Can we get her out of here?" Will asked. "I didn't want to move her until you got here, but . . ."

"Yeah. Just give me a minute to check in with the officers. I see Detective Purnell, too." Reyes stood and walked away to talk to the three patrol officers and an umberskinned man in a dark suit.

"You should call your boss and tell her you won't be in tomorrow," Will suggested.

"No."

He turned to her with questioning eyes. "You think you'll be fit to work? I sure wouldn't be."

"I won't remember by tomorrow." Quinn's voice was toneless. "If I don't write it down, I won't even know." The smile she gave Will was sad. "That's a handy thing about my broken brain."

"Don't call it that." The words came out with a harsh edge, and Will held up a hand in instant apology. "Sorry. That was uncalled for. But people recovering from a TBI are often too hard on themselves. It's a process, and everyone goes through the process at their own speed. And the last thing you need now is to come down hard on yourself. Let's say your brain is healing."

"Then it's a handy thing about my healing brain."

"Your plan is to leave yourself in the dark about this incident?"

Quinn shook her head. "Not totally. I don't need to torture myself about every detail. I think knowing someone is trying to kill me and that someone else died in my place—"

"Quinn—"

"Is enough," Quinn finished. She paused for a moment and then raised her eyes to Will's. "If I ask you something, will you be totally honest with me?"

"Yes."

"How well did I know Viv? I feel like I was connected to her, but I don't remember the connection. I know most of my friends disappeared from my life after the attack because I couldn't keep up with them socially anymore. I can tell by looking at my email and social accounts. Most contact just dropped off. I guess the term 'friends' may not be accurate. Real friends stick around through the bad times. I don't have any concrete memories to base it on, but Viv felt like a friend."

"How is your love life, anyway? Are you dripping with bold, adventurous men? Have we ever discussed it?"

"I told you about a disastrous blind date I had on our ride home a few weeks ago. It made you laugh. Looking back a few weeks later, it makes me laugh, too. So ridiculous. Definitely not bold or adventurous."

"I'm sorry I don't remember the story. On the other hand, you can tell it to me again. It'll be all new and I'll enjoy it like I've never heard it before."

It felt like friendship. It felt like the kind of conversation familiar women had when they were razzing each other in fun. Because it was.

"She was a new friend," Will said, unconsciously reinforcing her opinion, "but definitely a friend. I don't know if you talked to her outside of the sessions, but you guys were friendly from the first meeting you attended. The two of you seemed like yin and yang from what I could see. She was outgoing and confident. You were quieter and a little less sure of yourself, but her confidence boosted yours. She was happy taking you under her wing from the first meeting. You were about the same age, and you seemed to click."

"I got to the point where I remembered her from one week to the next. She always picked up from the week before as if I remembered all of it. It never bothered her or held her back that I was a blank slate."

"I think she liked you, valued you for who you were, and understood what you were going through because she was going through something herself."

Quinn's throat was tight again, and a single tear slipped down her cheek. She closed her eyes and bore down, burying the emotion deep. *Keep it together.*

It was a relief to see Reyes walking toward them. If there was no more talk about Viv on a personal level, she'd be able to keep her anguish tamped down, where it belonged. For now, at least. Later, she could let it out. Much later, there would be no memory and no anguish with it.

Reyes sat beside Quinn again. "I'm sorry about your friend. If it's any comfort at all, they think it was quick. She didn't suffer."

"It shouldn't be her under the tarp. It should be me."

"It should be neither of you," Reyes said in a no-nonsense tone. "Look, normally, I'd put this off to tomorrow if I could, but I need to ask you questions tonight. I know by tomorrow you won't have a good recollection of it. The witnesses have filled in a pretty complete picture of what happened, but I'd like to hear your version of it. Starting with earlier in the evening. Did you come to this meeting straight from work?"

Quinn stared at Reyes, searching her memory for a detail that had evaporated. "I don't know."

"I can answer that," Will said, "or I can at least tell you what she told me when she arrived this evening. The shop closed at six PM and she stayed behind to finish a few things, then she grabbed a wrap she could eat on the bus from one of the local restaurants, and came up."

"Helpful, thanks. Did anything out of the ordinary happen at the session?"

"No."

Reyes turned back to Quinn. "Start at the end of the session. What happened as soon as it was over?"

"Viv and I grabbed our things. She was taking the same bus as me to go back downtown, so we walked out together."

"Do you know where she lived?"

"No, sorry. I don't know if she ever shared that with me."

"That's fine. We'll get all that. Run through it for me, from the moment you left the church. How long has it been? Can you still remember what happened?"

Will glanced at his watch. "It's been about fifty minutes." He bent his head to look into Quinn's eyes. "Quinn, do you remember everything still?"

"Yes." Quinn took Reyes through everything that had happened from the time they left the session, describing the vehicle as best as she could, how it had appeared out of the darkness, destroyed anything in its path, and disappeared into the night. She described Will's arrival and Reyes switched the questioning to him and his role in the evening.

By the time Will was finished, Quinn was exhausted and visibly drooping.

"Is that all you need, Detective?" Will asked. "I'd like to get Quinn home. It's been a hard evening for her, and she's determined to go to work tomorrow morning."

Reyes looked like she was going to question that decision, but changed her mind. "Yes, that's all, but I'm going to take her home. I'd like to check out her security at home, windows, doors, that kind of thing. It would make me feel better." She turned to Quinn. "First, though, I know you say you're fine, but I want the EMTs to check you out to confirm you're okay. Are you ready to go?"

Quinn nodded, too exhausted to speak, her gaze locked on the police cruisers still filling the intersection, blue, red, and white lights flashing.

Was the driver of the vehicle really after her?

If so, when would they be back to try again?

CHAPTER 24

"My place is up here. You can park on the street."
Reyes took her eyes off the road long enough to give Quinn a quick glance where she sat in the passenger seat. Those were the first words she'd spoken to Reyes since they'd reached the car. Reyes had Quinn's address in her Uber app, so she hadn't even needed that information from her. Reyes was content with silence; Quinn had been through enough tonight. Now she just needed to get her home, make sure she was safe.

Then she needed to figure out what the hell was going on. Just seconds after the nerds' email had come through, Will Dawsey had called and she'd run out the door, leaving Cervelló to clean up the mess and carry it all to her desk so she could hit the ground running tomorrow morning.

But the revelation that Alf Williams was David Soto, or vice versa, could be the tipping point. Who was Alf Williams and why had Soto felt the need to bury him so deep? Would he put someone else six feet under to keep Alf there as well? If he would, had he done the hit personally? She needed to see more of Soto than his smiling mug on a campaign headshot. What was his alibi for the night of the murder? More than that, what was his alibi for tonight?

Alf Williams was a problem for tomorrow. Right now, Quinn needed one hundred percent of her attention.

The beginning of which was going to be putting a car outside the house for the rest of the night so Quinn could feel safe enough to sleep. There was likely little budget for having someone follow her around, though they could do more frequent pass-bys, but, for tonight, she'd make sure Quinn was watched.

Reyes had spent the quiet ride considering the night's incident. Running on the assumption that Quinn was right and the killer did know someone had seen him, and assuming he'd seen her in return and had come back to the Gaslamp to find her, it was plausible in the weeks since the murder that he'd identified her. The number of people with legitimate access to the alley was limited to employees on that block. Each store had a rear entrance that doubled as an emergency exit, and each business would create the kind of refuse that would need disposal in the bins at the back of the alley. That meant it wouldn't necessarily need to be one of the shops or restaurants at that end of the alley only; the end-of-the-day timing could have brought anyone from that block back there. Exactly as it had for Quinn.

The killer could have been watching the area since the attack. Quinn worked full-time in the shop, coming in five days a week, walking in from Seventh Avenue to Gaslamp Blooms so she was visible to the public multiple times a week. While it would have been less likely, she worked behind the counter at the shop, and the killer could have walked in and ordered flowers just to see if she recognized him. The killer would have no idea Quinn suffered from a memory deficit and therefore was less of a danger to him than a typical witness. If he'd actually talked to her, he'd have thought she didn't recognize him because she hadn't gotten a good look at him, not because she might have had a better look than anyone thought, but that memory was gone, possibly permanently.

The hit following the session tonight made Reyes believe the killer didn't know where Quinn lived. It would have been easier to have broken into the apartment at night while she slept and quietly killed her than to make a failed attempt on a public street, albeit under the cover of oncoming night. At the very least, the driver of the vehicle had been successful in remaining unseen until the last few seconds, and then had disappeared into the night. The front end and windshield would be badly damaged, and in the morning, they'd alert local repair shops to watch out for that particular damage on incoming vehicles, but she doubted that was going to happen. In a scenario like this, it was much more likely the vehicle would be driven off a cliff into the ocean, or end up in a crusher in a junkyard. Still, they'd get the word out.

The attempt to kill Quinn tonight showed a ratcheting up of the stakes and of the desperation of the killer. They weren't willing to wait until they could track her home; they felt forced to attempt the hit in public. And, in doing so, had killed an innocent bystander.

To dot every i, Purnell would work the Gibson homicide, looking into anyone in Ms. Gibson's life who might have wanted to harm her, but Reyes knew that wasn't it. Could feel it. Vivian Gibson was nothing more to the killer than an inconvenient footnote. The young woman deserved better than that, and Reyes would make sure she got it.

She found a spot about a half block short of Quinn's address, pulled over, and parked. Wordlessly, Quinn opened her door, so Reyes got out, locked up, and circled the hood to fall into step with her.

Reyes wore her Glock 19 service weapon in a holster on her right hip under her blazer; she hoped she wouldn't need it, but all bets were off after tonight. She scanned the street and the neighboring yards as they passed driveway after driveway. Oceanview was a fairly busy west-to-east through street with multiple lanes of traffic—parking on each side at the curb, a driving lane on each side and a center turning lane. Many of the residents had created a barrier between their houses and the road, so the sidewalks were lined by long runs of bushes, palm trees, concrete or wood fences, and iron gates. The multiplex that housed Quinn's apartment was separated from the road by a line of large agave plants, their stiff, dusty-green, sword-shaped leaves making a formidable border.

There was no driveway, just the concrete walk on the far side of the agaves that led to the entrances on the east side of the building.

Reyes kept her eyes moving, looking for anything out of place—someone sitting in a car, keeping an eye on the building, people on foot where they didn't belong—but the few people she saw sat on their own balconies, enjoying the calm and quiet evening.

Calm and quiet for some.

She stayed only a half pace behind Quinn as she climbed the stairs to the second level, stopping at the first door on their right. Quinn dug into her bag, pulled out a key, and unlocked the door. When she moved to open the door, Reyes put an arm out to block her. "Let me go first."

Fear crept into Quinn's eyes. "You think someone is in there?"

"No. But I'm not taking any chances." Reyes crowded her back a little and opened the door, quickly finding the light switch by the doorjamb, which lit the living room and gave enough light to see the dining and kitchen areas. She scanned the open living space quickly, then moved to the rear of the apartment and checked it as well.

It was a small apartment, sufficient for a single woman

living alone, with a bedroom and bathroom at the back and a few tiny closets. It was neat, cozily decorated with natural woods and bright colors. She didn't know Quinn well, but it felt like her.

She came down the narrow hallway to find Quinn standing stiffly inside the closed door. "All clear. Thanks for humoring me. I just wanted to be sure."

"Of course." Quinn crossed to the kitchen area and flipped on a few more lights, brightening the whole front of the apartment, giving Reyes her first real look at how Quinn lived her life at home.

Color popped from every surface. A rainbow of sticky notes on drawers, cupboard doors, and tables. A large sign hanging above the oven with DON'T WALK AWAY in block letters. A massive desk calendar, covered in multicolored ink and a few more bright sticky notes.

Her gaze shot to Quinn, who stood silently by the stove. She didn't need to speak; the misery was carved into her expression. Along with embarrassment.

On a night where so much had gone so tragically wrong, Reyes had it in her power to do a little bit of good. She grabbed for the chance. "This is how you taught yourself to get by."

Quinn gave a single nod as her eyes dropped to the floor.

"You're incredible."

Quinn's gaze shot up, confusion in her eyes as well as in the open mouth that tried to form words, but couldn't.

"Absolutely incredible," Reyes repeated, walking into the kitchen. "You made sure you knew where everything was. You probably already knew, unless you moved something after the assault, but you didn't want to give yourself even a moment of panic that you might not know, so you made it obvious where everything was." She studied the calendar on the counter, running an index finger down the weeks. "You set yourself up for success from the beginning when you had no idea how long any of this would last, and you had to assume it might be forever."

All Quinn could do was nod.

"Very smart. I assume you don't really need all of this anymore, now we know repetition is working to build your permanent memories."

"No."

"Makes sense to leave it for now. You don't need a bad moment while you have so many other things going on." Reyes spun around, her gaze going over the living room and onward. "Playing it safe is a good idea. And then when things are—"

Reyes froze, the words crumbling to dust on her tongue at she stared at the corner behind the door.

Because the sketches were pencil and somewhat in the gloom away from any ceiling light fixtures, she hadn't spotted them at first. But now she couldn't take her eyes off them. Pages and pages of sketches, some zoomed out, some zoomed in. Without another word, she strode to the corner to stand behind a drafting table where another sketch—this one of a jungle of plants and a divided window, behind which stood a van—lay incomplete, four pencils and an eraser lined up neatly beside it. On the walls, what had begun as a neat grid of pages was now a mad collage with some sketches nearly obscured behind others. She flipped up one sheet to look behind it, and then the next to find the one originally taped to the wall. A similar investigation of a few other spots told her how the wall had been built—like a photographer with a lens, starting with a wide-angle shot and zooming closer and closer.

The detail on the top layer of sketches was amazing. She saw DeWitt—as he had been in life, she assumed—and another man standing behind him, one hand clawed around his jaw, ready to jerk. Reyes could practically hear the snap of bone that followed. In another, the two stood in a shaft of light coming from out of frame to the left, the dead man on his knees on the ground, his arms dangling loose— she could sense them still swaying—his head tipped over the killer's forearm. The killer's face was partly in shadow, but menace flowed off it in waves. The next sketch was a further zoom in of the previous. Here the face was at the same angle but sketched in detail: It was hard and fierce, all harsh angles, with a wide forehead and protruding brow, his gritted teeth showing from within a close-cropped goatee. Harsh lines cut into the skin around the eyes and wrinkled the forehead. It was a face old before its time, aged by rage and violence.

It was the kind of detail Reyes could feed into facial recognition to see if anything clicked.

She turned to Quinn, who had drawn farther back into the kitchen, her eyes wary. She'd seen defiance in Quinn before, seen spirit and confidence, the kind that offered to look at a dead man in case there was any way she could help. The shock and agony of the evening had beaten it all out of her—for now, anyway.

Reyes took the time for a deep inhale and exhale and then extended a hand to Quinn. "Come here. Please." When Quinn didn't budge, she said, "I'd like you to walk me through this. I think we have some details here that might be helpful."

A dim flame of hope flickered in Quinn's eyes. It reminded Reyes that perhaps the best motivation for a young woman so beaten down by the last few months was the action of turning outward. When circumstance dragged one's life down, sometimes satisfaction could be found in raising up someone else's. The fact someone had died before her eyes definitely made it more challenging, but it was something they could both latch onto.

Reyes turned back to a wall of sketches and selected one

of the wide-angle shots. "Tell me about this one. This is the actual alley, is it not?"

"Yes." Quinn drew breath to speak again, then stopped. "I'll talk about this with you as much as you want, but can I take a minute?" She frowned down at her clothes. "I'd like to change out of the clothes I knelt in the street in, and get something to drink. Is that okay? Can you stay that long?"

Reyes wanted to kick herself. She was in cop mode and was so surprised by the emotional blow of the sketches she hadn't given Quinn a second to breathe. "Oh, God, I'm sorry. Of course you need a minute. Or ten. Take what you need. Is it okay if I wait here for you?"

"Sure. Do you want something to drink?"

"Don't go to any trouble for me."

"Go ahead and help yourself, then. Honestly, I'm not sure what's in the fridge, because that's always changing depending on what I buy. You shouldn't have any trouble finding the glasses." She tossed Reyes a crooked smile and headed toward her bedroom. A moment later came the click of the latch as the door closed.

Reyes spent five minutes looking over the sketches and building a list of questions in her mind. And she had questions. The alley sketches she understood, but why the garden center, and who was the hard-eyed man on the bus?

After that, she wandered into the kitchen, opened the fridge as Quinn had offered, pulled out a carton of strawberry orange banana juice, found the clearly labeled glasses cupboard, and poured herself a drink. She was leaning against the counter, studying the calendar when Quinn returned.

"Sorry that took so long. I just needed a minute."

"Totally get it. I hope it's okay, I grabbed a glass of juice."

"What do I have?"

This was a first for Reyes, telling someone else what was in their own fridge, but she understood why Quinn didn't know the information. "Strawberry orange banana juice, milk, Diet Coke, filtered water."

"The juice sounds good."

"I'll get it for you." After Reyes poured a second juice, they went back to the corner, glasses in hand. "You've spent a lot of time doing this."

"Yes, especially on Sunday and Monday. I was off work and . . ." Quinn ground to a halt, stopped, her mouth pursed tight, and her eyebrows snapped together as she stared at the hard-eyed man.

"And . . . ?" Reyes prompted.

"I didn't want to bring you in on something until I had some proof." Quinn eyed the sketches. "Not that this is actual 'proof.'"

"Let's back up a bit. What is this?" With one hand, Reyes indicated the sketches as a whole.

"I've been using my art to push my memory. I sat in the alley on my lunch hour, drawing it in reality and then adding in the men as I saw them in my imagination based on what I noted. For me though, my question was what was I drawing. Was it pure imagination or was it fueled by actual buried memories? I started out with a wide focus and gradually narrowed in, increasing the detail. I thought it might all be hooey, but Will saw these last week and said I was trying to build recollection. Bringing out a memory based on logical cues. So there might be some truth in these."

"What I can tell you is there's enough detail in some of these top sketches to run against the database."

"You can run a sketch and come back with an actual name?"

"There are some decided challenges when a sketch is compared to a photograph versus when two photographs are compared. The computer nerds tell me they have to compare facial components between the sketch and multiple actual images, and some components are better than others and it depends on how accurate that component is in the sketch. And because of the complexity, it can take considerably more time, et cetera, et cetera. But it's amazing what the nerds can do. I love them, and they love me because I bribe them with fresh baked goods to bump my stuff up to the top of their list. Can I take some of these?"

"Take as many as you want. I did them so they'd be useful to you, not to plaster my walls. I can't wait until they're all gone."

"I can imagine. I'll take a bunch with me tonight, the ones that'll be best for the facial recognition software, and will show up tomorrow with something to grease the nerds' wheels. It could take them at least a few days, so best to get them started on it." Reyes walked away from the sketches, stopping in the kitchen to turn off the light, leaving the sketches in shadow, and then headed for the couch. "Stop looking at those and come sit down. I feel like there's something else you need to tell me." She sat down on one end of the couch, took a sip of her juice, and set the glass down on the table. She waited until Quinn took the other end of the couch. "What happened?"

"I don't know if any of it is real." Quinn stared down into her glass, still clasped in both hands.

"It looks like it was real to you. And it sounds like you remember it happening."

"That it happened, but the details are fuzzy. I've reviewed it enough to know it happened, but not all the finer points are sticking yet."

"That's okay, because we know where to look. Can I read it?"

"Yes." Quinn put down the glass and pulled her notebook out of her pocket. "I know the general concept of what happened. I had a flashback one morning walking to work. From that, I thought I'd seen a Carmelite belfry the night of the murder."

"Where? There isn't anything that looks like that in that area of the Gaslamp."

"Not an actual belfry; a logo of one. I did a little research and found three places in town that had a logo with that same kind of image on it. I checked them out."

Suspicion and foreboding wound down Reyes's spine. "What do you mean 'checked them out'?"

"I rented a car and went to the three locations." Reyes was about to jump in, but Quinn cut her off. "I know, it was stupid, and it could have been dangerous." She gnawed on her lower lip. "I think it might have been. I may have seen someone." She met Reyes's gaze. "I should have told you, but, honestly, I don't trust myself. I had what could have been a memory flashback or a hallucination for all I knew. I could tell you the wrong thing and send you off on a wild-goose chase, and then the killer would get away, not because I didn't remember him, but because I dreamed up something totally false. Do you know what a confabulation is?"

"No."

"I didn't either until Will explained it to me, but now it's my number one concern. When he told me about it, I wrote down the term and what it meant, and I keep coming back to it. It's a false memory. It can happen to people suffering from traumatic brain injury and it seems as real to them as an actual memory. I'm terrified that's what this is." Quinn threw her hand out toward the sketches. "What if there's no truth in any of it and I've made it all up?"

"That one's simple. It won't match any real person." When Quinn blinked at her blankly, she said, "It really could be that straightforward. Also, I'm not going to grab some guy who looks like anyone you've drawn, read him his

Miranda rights, and toss him in jail. It's the beginning of a new phase of the investigation, Quinn. It's not the end of it."

The breath Quinn released and the way her body went from stiff to relaxed told Reyes how much this had been a concern for her.

"Also, it sounds to me like your flashback isn't that different from your dreams about the murder, just in a different state of mind. It could be your brain is trying to get information out to you in any way it can. And you took those hints and then used your own natural skills to finesse it even more. So, was that all you didn't tell me?"

Quinn's cheeks went bright red.

"Clearly not." Reyes reached for her glass, took a calming sip, then set it back down. "Tell me now so we can clear the slate, then I'll read the details and we'll figure out where to go from there."

"Right." Quinn paused, took a breath, then it all came out in a rush. "I think I was followed home from work on the bus on Saturday. I could just feel it, you know, that someone was watching. But every time I looked, I couldn't see anyone. I didn't want to let anyone follow me to here, so I ditched the bus, squeezing out last minute between the doors before they closed at Twenty-Fifth and Imperial. Then I sat on the SDPD Central Division steps until an Uber came to pick me up. I spent the next two days trying to squeeze as much out of the art as I could so I had something for you. I was going to call you about it yesterday, but I think I was stalling, because I knew I should have called you about it long before then and didn't know how to admit I'd screwed up, so I told myself we were too busy in the shop yesterday and today. Then I had group therapy and then . . ." Color drained from her face as she thought about what came next.

"It's okay. I'm in the loop now. But no more going off by yourself anymore. You're not the cop; that's my job. Got it?"

"Yes."

"And I think we need to give some serious thought to your security in the next little while. Let me read the details of what happened so I'm up to speed, then I'm going to grab some of those sketches and get out of your hair. You need some rest and quiet."

She held out her hand, and Quinn laid her notebook in it. Flipping until she got to the more recent entries, Reyes settled in to read the details.

Twenty minutes later, Reyes waited at the door until she heard Quinn shoot the deadbolt home, then was on the way to her car with a dozen sketches in a file folder under her arm. She was going to need a lot of baked goods, preferably many different kinds, to bribe the nerds for this one. She was up to the challenge, because, at this point, one thing was very clear.

Quinn *was* a threat to the killer, especially now she could produce potential detailed images that could lead to his identification. Where that information fit in with what Reyes was learning about DeWitt's work, she wasn't quite sure, but she was going to put the pieces together as soon as possible.

Before someone took another crack at Quinn, and was possibly successful the next time around.

CHAPTER 25

R eyes was in an hour before the official start of her shift. She had the bit between her teeth now and she wanted answers.

She worked for an hour at her desk, then left the paperwork spread wide to have a discussion with her lieutenant about protection for Quinn now that the patrol officer she'd called in for overnight had gone home. That hadn't gone nearly as well as she'd hoped, as every argument she had about risks were met with practical statements of budget. In the end, as their raised voices had died down, her lieutenant had promised to work the numbers to have something in place for tomorrow at the latest. They wouldn't be able to manage it for weeks on end, but they could do something. Reyes made it clear they were making headway and she didn't think weeks would be needed.

The bottom line was that solving the murder was one aspect of the case. If the killer got through to Quinn, no one would need protection anymore, but their case might evaporate.

As for tonight, Reyes herself would go there after her shift ended if that's what was needed. She'd owe Frank for backing out of yet another late dinner, but she'd make it up to him. They just needed to get through today, then she could take a breath. She'd call Quinn and ask her to avoid the bus and to Uber home. She wasn't comfortable with how long Quinn was exposed during the MTS ride, and, clearly, they'd identified her bus stop, even if they may not know her specific workplace. Ride-sharing home a block away from the bus stop would offer some safety.

More safety would come if Reyes could figure out what DeWitt knew that was so dangerous it got him killed. Starting with why exactly Alf Williams became David Soto. And when. Breaking the case wide open would go a long way to taking the pressure off.

Here she was, this time sitting at her desk, trying to ignore the normal day-to-day noise of the bullpen as detectives came in and out, dealing with their caseloads for the day, and being called out to new ones. She was hoping another one wouldn't fall in her lap, because she needed a good few hours to concentrate on this. If she got it, she might be able to come out the other side, since she had resources DeWitt didn't.

Cervelló had already stopped by her desk to see if she needed a hand; she'd thanked him but said she'd manage. Last night had been free time for both of them; today they were back on the clock, so she would be working solo. But she appreciated the offer; appreciated him even more when he said he'd try to keep things clear for her to keep working. He then made sure everyone knew Reyes had a hot one and could use a hand staying clear of interruptions, receiving nods all around.

Some days her colleagues drove her crazy. Some days she loved her job and every officer in the bullpen with her. Today was one of those days.

She began a deep dive on Alf Williams. The first bell rang when she found out he was born in Chicago, cementing that connection. The second rang when she discovered the name on his birth certificate was Alfred David Williams. Sometime after high school he'd ditched a first name he didn't like—keeping in mind that back in his high school days, that name was also claimed by a stuffed alien in a sitcom on network TV—and started to go by his middle name. She followed David Williams as he left Illinois and came to California for law at Stanford. And that's where he met the woman who would become his future wife—Jaclyn Soto.

Reyes wondered if a giant light bulb had appeared above her head the moment she made that connection. Suddenly so many things clarified in her mind, but she still needed to back it up with actual details.

The details around his identity started to click rapidly from that point on as, the closer and closer she came to current times, the more information she could easily find without having to depend on government records. But the most important government record was the one filed just after their marriage—Jaclyn didn't change her surname, David did—when David Soto was born.

If it was any other surname, she might have wondered why he'd done it, and maybe there was more to it than she initially surmised, but the Soto name itself pretty much said it all. The Sotos were well known in California and beyond. Darren Soto, the family patriarch, began as a small-time real estate agent, but had found his knack with big-name clients and moved up in the world. Now he owned huge chunks of real estate and left the selling to the little guys. There was power in the Soto name, prestige, and, maybe as importantly, a unique quality. Williamses were a dime a dozen, found in every corner of America. But David didn't need any corner; he needed California. And in California, the Soto name carried a whiff of privilege, wealth, and—deserved or not—class.

So . . . why had Alf Williams legally changed his name to David Soto? Even then, did he have ambitions to become *someone*? If so, he'd married into enough money to take him anywhere he wanted to go. He'd been San Diego County's district attorney for the past seven years, having won two consecutive elections. Now, instead of running for a third term, he was taking a left turn into big-city municipal politics. Was that the end goal? Or did he have bigger dreams? Perhaps governor? Or higher still?

Or had something else prompted him to leave Alf Williams behind? She had to think DeWitt must have thought so. Otherwise, why the concentration on Chicago? Armed with this new information, Reyes was going to find out.

One thing she did know, however, was Soto wasn't the killer, if Quinn's description, and now sketches, were to be believed. Reyes had arrived home the night before in time for the 11:00 PM news, and made a point of catching the election coverage. David Soto had spoken at a fundraising dinner, appearing onstage with his beautifully dressed, perfectly made-up and coiffed wife, their arms around each other as they waved to those who had paid likely way too much for the dinner they were about to be served. He was a nice-looking man, in good physical condition, but he was too short and not muscular enough to be able to get the jump on a man as tall as DeWitt. To have used brutal force to end DeWitt's life. That had been a disappointment, but Reyes knew this was a one-step-at-a-time kind of thing.

Today's step was about whether or not Chicago was the key to the motive in the death of Jack DeWitt.

And that meant tracing every move DeWitt had made before his death.

Back to the call logs. There was one number DeWitt had called multiple times over the days leading up to his death. Most of the calls were less than a minute—the kind of call where you'd get voice mail and either leave a message or not, if you'd previously done so, but weren't having your calls returned. The day before he died, there was one longer call of over ten minutes followed by two shorter calls immediately after. Like what might happen if someone hung up on you and you then tried to get them back, but they wouldn't accept your call.

The day of his death, calls to that same number were the last he made, but, from the length, went unanswered.

The name of the recipient was Taylor Richards.

She reached for the 1987 yearbook, turning it to the section that held each year of students' photos, and flipped to the final year. The students were in alphabetical order, and she flipped a few more pages to get to the *R*s, then ran her index finger down the list until she found Richards. So, Williams and Richards had gone to the same high school at the same time. That didn't mean they were friends, but it at least placed them together at that point in their lives.

Fortunately for Reyes, she had DeWitt's backups from the *Union-Tribune*. She'd printed much of it for easy organizing—and which in the end made for easy shared research—but it was also on her desktop PC. And that meant she could do a keyword search for Richards's name. She started the search, and the file on David Soto instantly popped as the result. Opening the file in Word, she searched again, finding his name mentioned eleven times.

They hadn't just graduated at the same time; they appeared to have been long-time friends. They'd played soccer together for four years. They'd medaled in track and field. They had been on the backstage crew for several high school productions. And that was only the documented connections. Kids who went to school together had so much more in common than official school activities showed.

Reyes selected the 1984 yearbook, finding the sports teams and their associated images. There was the entire soccer team, Richards kneeling in the front row, Williams standing in the back. Then a candid of the boys following a track meet, grinning, shoulder to shoulder, both holding out their medals, Richards taking first, Williams second in the four-hundred-meter run.

She studied the young faces—Williams already suffering from the acne he'd hide behind a beard sometime in the next three years; Richards looking like a smooth-skinned golden boy next to him. So young, so happy.

Then there was a wedding picture from years later, with a young David and Jaclyn surrounded by six attendants on either side, arranged down a sweep of white marble steps. The note under the image marked Richards as the best man. Dressed in a classic black tux with a red rose as his boutonniere, he stood one step below Williams, now blessedly acne-free. Williams and Richards, still together years later, still connected. No, more than connected, if Richards was his best man. Separated by distance, if Richards was still in Illinois, but still close enough that Williams—soon to be Soto—asked him to be his best man.

That was the thing about best friends. A best friend not only knew where you buried the body—metaphorical or otherwise—he often helped you bury it.

What were they hiding?

Time to give Mr. Richards a call and see if she could find out.

Reyes dialed the number, tapping the end of her pen in a rapid staccato against the papers strewn in front of her as the call rang in her ear. Four rings, then straight to voice mail. "Mr. Richards, this is Detective Nura Reyes of the San Diego Police Department's Homicide Unit. I'd like to ask you a few questions about a current case, if you could please return my call." She rattled off her number, then hung up, and went back to skimming through DeWitt's electronic file backup from the *Union-Tribune*.

She was still staring at the wedding picture when the phone rang only a minute later. Her hand on the handset, she checked the caller ID. *Well, well . . . Mr. Richards already. Call screening an unfamiliar number, were you?* She answered the call. "San Diego Police Department. Detective Reyes, Homicide Unit." She didn't normally announce her division's title when she answered the phone, but this time, she thought it would be good to remind Richards. This wasn't the lost and found, this was serious business. Serious death business.

"Detective, this is Taylor Richards returning your call."

"Thank you very much, Mr. Richards."

"I'm a little confused as to why a murder cop from California would call me in Illinois. I haven't been to California in years. It's been decades since I've been in San Diego."

"But it's only been weeks since you talked to Jack DeWitt of the *San Diego Union-Tribune*."

Dead silence met that statement.

"Are you there, Mr. Richards?"

"I'm here." The voice was detached now.

"You did talk to Mr. DeWitt?"

"I'm not sure how who I talk to is relevant—"

"Mr. DeWitt was brutally murdered the day after your conversation." The only indication Richards had heard her was the tiny intake of breath. *Time to give him a little incentive.* "I know he was on the trail of something big. You do, too. Lives are being lost over this, Mr. Richards. Now is the time for transparency, so what happened to Mr. DeWitt doesn't happen to anyone else."

Richards paused for a moment before speaking. "How was he killed?"

"He was attacked on the street the evening after you spoke on the phone. There was a struggle and his neck was broken. He died instantly."

"*Jesus Christ.*"

Reyes stayed quiet for a good ten seconds, letting the

shock of the slaying sink in. "Talking to me will help the case, and it will help you. Someone is willing to kill to keep certain information quiet. If you also know this information, you may be a target. Whatever it is, no matter how much someone wants to keep it buried in the past, it's clearly coming to light. If you know something that will put your life in danger, you can help us both by talking to me now."

More silence.

Time for a bigger push. "Or, if you'd rather talk to someone in person, I can bring one of my colleagues at the Chicago Police Department in on this and they could bring you down to talk there. Would that be preferable?"

"No!" The word came out too fast and too emphatically for Richards to claim he was staying calm, but he took a breath and tried again. "No. What do you need to know?"

"You discussed Alf Williams. Tell me specifically what you talked about."

"What do you know about Alf?"

This was the real test and the detail that could open the door. "You mean in his current persona as David Soto? Who is so far the front-runner in the San Diego mayoral election? That Alf?"

A sigh carried down the line. "DeWitt knew we had a history."

"A history is putting it lightly. You were buddies as teenagers, maybe even before that. You were his best man."

"Yeah, we were close. Are close. David would make a great mayor."

Would make a great mayor. Unless something gets in his way?

"What happened, Mr. Richards?"

"It's not my story to tell. I didn't tell it to DeWitt. Wouldn't."

"But you know what he's digging for?"

Another sigh. "Look, this was laid to rest decades ago."

"Laid to rest? Someone died?"

Richards muttered a curse. "That's not what I meant. It's an expression. The case was closed. No, I mean, the issue was settled. That's what I meant."

"Case, as in police case?"

"I didn't say that."

"But you're not denying it."

"I have to go. I don't have anything to share with you."

"You've shared more than enough, Mr. Richards. Thank you. If I have any further questions, I'll be in touch."

The line went dead.

Reyes smiled as she lay the handset down. Richards was rattled over DeWitt's death. So very rattled, in fact, he slipped several times. What had Williams done before he moved out west that had required police intervention? And had someone actually died? Was "laid to rest" a Freudian slip or simply a bad choice of words? She didn't know, but had to keep all possibilities open.

She ran Soto's records but only found a parking ticket and a speeding ticket, both paid immediately. And who hadn't been nailed occasionally for either of those? Then she ran Williams, looking specifically for charges in Illinois, and came up empty.

Is this the wrong track?

She didn't think so. If Williams had a sealed juvenile record, she'd be able to find it. However, if the record was expunged, and many states were expunging old juvenile criminal records, it could be entirely removed. It could also have been expunged years ago—a good lawyer and a lot of money could do that. And Reyes knew from reading through the notes yesterday, money wasn't an issue for the Williams family in their fancy Forest Glen home, with their fancy country club memberships. They were local high society back in the 1980s. If their precious child had gotten into trouble, they'd have been able to erase any trace of it.

Unless it had already been reported. That was the thing about newspapers—the good ones were building and maintaining their archives. She opened the Web-based archives for the *Chicago Sun-Times*, which went back to 1986, and had to hope nothing had happened in 1985, dooming her before she even began. But what to search for? If Williams was a minor at the time, his name wouldn't have been released, so it was going to be a slow process of tracking juvenile crime reporting.

This called for coffee. Reyes sent a long sideways look at the coffeepot. As much as she loved good coffee, she hated the tar that came out of that pot. Maybe if she tossed the quarter pot that had been cooking there for at least an hour and made a fresh pot, it would be better. She knew how to make coffee, made it at home all the time, but somehow the coffee here was always terrible. Whether it was the coffee itself, the water, or the machine's bad juju, it was always awful. But she needed to fuel up; awful was better than nonexistent, and she didn't have the time or money to have decent coffee delivered every time she wanted it.

She made a fresh pot and started her searches while it brewed. Pouring a cup as soon as it was ready, she went back and waded into years of stories.

It was hours later when she finally came up for air. She had a queasy stomach from too much coffee, but also had a solid possibility. She sat back in her chair and looked at the article on-screen from January 1987: SUSPECT IN UNDER-AGE RAPE DETAINED. It outlined the story of an unnamed fifteen-year-old minor female who had been raped by an unnamed minor seventeen-year-old male. As expected for a case that involved so many minors, the details were sketchy at best. But the key for Reyes was the tiny detail that said the unnamed suspect had turned himself in, with his father and their lawyer in tow, to the Chicago Police Department District 16 station on North Milwaukee Avenue—the station that serviced the Forest Glen neighborhood and was located less than two miles from where the Williams family home overlooked Edgebrook Woods.

The cop sense she'd relied on for years told her it was Williams, even though all she had right now was speculation. A rich kid used to getting his way, who took what he wanted, even when it wasn't freely offered. She'd seen the type all too often in her career in the SDPD, and was willing to bet Richards knew all about it, but wasn't talking. Since the charges had been expunged, maybe he felt he could also pretend it hadn't happened. An expungement legally meant the charge hadn't happened. It didn't mean the crime hadn't happened, just that it couldn't be proved that one particular suspect was guilty.

There was going to be very little trace left of a case that old that no longer had documentation. But she knew from her own career those were the cases that stuck with you. The ones you knew down to your bones you had cold, but couldn't prove, so the whole thing fell apart.

Time to go where Jack DeWitt couldn't. With a crime as old as this, she might not have a real chance. Nevertheless, she needed to try.

She began with the main line for the Chicago Police Department, explaining who she was and what she wanted. She was shuffled through divisions, finally landing in the right place, only to find the officer in the unit with the most seniority had started in 1995. Cursing quietly in her head, she asked to be passed to him, and was fortunate enough to find him at his desk.

"Detective Barnes."

"I'm Detective Reyes from the San Diego Police Department. I'm trying to find some information about an arrest from January 1987. The rape of a fifteen-year-old girl by a seventeen-year-old boy. The record has been expunged, but I think it might be related to one of my current homicides."

"Unfortunately, everyone from the department from that time is gone. Many dead, a few retired."

"The last officer I spoke with implied that, but said you were the longest-standing detective."

"Only for the next month, then I'm joining the ranks of the retired. But I can't help you. Anything I remember about a case that early would have been passed down second- or thirdhand."

Reyes couldn't help the sigh of frustration. "I figured as much, but had to give it a shot. I appreciate your time, Detective Barnes."

"You haven't used much of it." Barnes paused for long seconds, then, "Tell you what. Give me your contact info. If I come up with something, you'll hear from us."

Reyes gave him both her phone number and email address. "Thanks, I appreciate that."

She ended the call and pulled the yearbook over again to look at the face of the bearded boy from 1987. "You did this. I can't prove it, but the ramifications of this coming out would be devastating. Yes, we live in a world where shame apparently doesn't exist anymore in many of our leaders who are just grubbing for power, but an underage rape should turn at least fifty percent of the population against you. And you can't win a runoff without that fifty percent."

Reyes had suspicions San Diego was only a stepping stone for Soto. Watching him last night on TV, he seemed like too bright a light, too big a personality to be satisfied with the second biggest city in California. She could see him with his eye on the governor's mansion, or past, to the White House. He was only in his mid-fifties; he could work his way up to it.

Cynically, she had to wonder if he'd had to wait, had to time his climb to make sure the family fortune was under his control when he needed it. Darren Soto was in his late seventies now, and while he seemed to be in good health, no one lived forever. And once he died, his money would go to his only daughter. Reyes mused as well if it was joint ambition, and if a woman like Jaclyn Soto would like the trappings of First Lady. She flipped back to the wedding photo, this time studying the bride. How much of this was coerced by Jaclyn? A run for the White House took two willing participants to pull off spectacularly.

On that note, did she know about the potential little incident in her husband's youth that could scuttle their attempt at glory?

Her phone rang and Reyes answered after noting the unfamiliar number with a Chicago exchange. "San Diego Police Department, Detective Reyes."

"Detective, my name is Robert Cox. Detective Barnes gave me a call. Said you're looking for some information from the department."

"I am, yes."

"Barnes suggested I reach out to you. I was on the force at the time of the case you were asking about."

He had Reyes's undivided attention. "You were Detective Cox?"

"I was. Now I'm just Rob."

"Once a detective, always a detective. Did Detective Barnes tell you which case I was asking about?"

"He did."

Reyes found herself actually leaning forward in anticipation, waiting for his response. Finally prodding when he didn't continue. "And?"

"I think it was one of mine. If so, it's not a case I've been able to forget. You know how some of them stick with you?"

"Especially the ones you can't close? Oh yeah."

"Precisely. And this one stuck in spades, right down to the details, partly because of how it turned out."

"How did it turn out?"

Cox drew breath to speak, then paused for a moment. "You understand my reluctance to bring this up with someone who hasn't proven to me she's a police officer. When a case is expunged, legally the charges never happened."

"But we know that's garbage for some cases." Reyes reached for her personal phone. "Are you talking to me on your cell phone?"

"Yes."

"I'm going to send you a picture. Hold on a second." Reyes pulled out her flip case, the one with her badge and photo ID, and then snapped a picture of her holding it up to her face, the chaos of the bullpen in clear view behind her. She texted the photo to the number displayed on her desk phone. "Detective Cox—"

"Just Rob is fine."

"Rob, take a look at the photo I just sent you."

The pause drew out for over a half a minute before Cox came back on the line. "Thank you. And I'd recognize a bullpen anywhere. Coffee bad?"

"The worst."

"That's a bullpen."

"Rob, let me hopefully make this easier for you, so you don't feel like I'm fishing. I'm looking for information on a crime for which Alfred David Williams was charged, and for which the record has been expunged. I think the January 1987 rape was the case, and that Williams, his father, and a fancy lawyer showed up at District Sixteen, and he turned himself in. Do I have it correct?"

"You do."

The relief surged through her like a wave, taking the brutal weight of stress with it, leaving her exhausted in its wake.

You hear that, Jack? We just broke your case wide open.

"There are a few reasons the case still sticks with me," Cox was saying. "Yes, Williams was an entitled jackass, and his father was even worse. But that's not why it haunts me."

"Why?"

"Because the girl, Cassie Hopkins, got pregnant following the rape. And when she couldn't take the shame, couldn't take carrying a child she hadn't asked for, and was underage with religious parents who wouldn't allow an abortion, she killed herself. Took her mother's sleeping pills. Took the whole damned bottle. Never woke up. Mother and child, gone, just like that."

For a moment, Reyes simply sat, stunned.

"She was fifteen years old," Cox continued. "Had her whole life in front of her, but there were no witnesses. It was his word against hers, and he had some buddy of his giving him an alibi. Didn't believe it for a heartbeat."

"Let me guess, Taylor Richards?"

"I'll be damned. Yeah, that's him. Cassie was brave enough to report the rape, but we didn't have DNA back then. Williams turned himself in, and both his story and Richards's never budged an inch. The fancy lawyer made sure it didn't. Cassie was humiliated and embarrassed and depressed . . . and then she found out she was pregnant. She was dead only weeks later."

"And the case was dismissed due to lack of evidence."

"Yes."

"Do you think Williams did it?"

"That entitled fucker?" It was the first time Cox had sworn, and the banked fury behind the single word told

Reyes the rage had been simmering for decades. "No doubt in my mind."

"It's my understanding Illinois doesn't have a statute of limitations for prosecuting sex crimes."

"No, ma'am, we don't. Not since 2019."

"I may be able to close this one for you. Do you remember the details of the case, and would you be comfortable sharing them with me?"

"I may not remember what I had for dinner two nights ago, but I'll never forget the details of that case. I'd be happy to take you through it."

As Cox talked, Reyes made notes. But as Cox wound down, she pulled the 1987 yearbook toward her again, flipping to the front of the book until she found the single page *In Memoriam* for the only student lost that year. She stared down into the shy, smiling face of a girl, just on the cusp of becoming a woman, her blue eyes bright and full of hope. A pretty girl with wavy blond hair and a slender figure, she must have been an instant attraction for someone like Williams. She might have looked at the older Williams, with his dark beard and pockmarked skin, as frighteningly mature for her. But Williams apparently wouldn't take no for an answer.

I'm so sorry, Cassie. But you're mine now, too. When I bring him down for Jack, he'll fall for you as well.

CHAPTER 26

Quinn did as Reyes had asked when she called earlier in the day—she booked an Uber to pick her up from Gaslamp Blooms at the end of her shift to take her home. Reyes had been insistent, but Quinn hadn't needed much convincing. She knew from her constant reviewing of her notes that she thought someone had attempted to follow her home. It was a comfort that Reyes believed her and took it seriously enough she wanted to ensure Quinn's safety. Quinn might have doubted herself if it hadn't been for the night before.

The night she couldn't forget.

Quinn knew from her notes that after viewing the dead murder victim with Reyes, those images had stayed with her hours longer than she expected, but had been gone by the next morning.

She wasn't so lucky this time. Especially at a time when forgetting would be the only thing to soothe her, she remembered every moment of the night before. Was it her brain healing and her memory improving? Possibly. Were the severe emotional shock, terror, and anguish all combining to burn the memory into place? Her money was on that.

It was all still so vivid in her mind, which was a shock to

her system after months in the fog. The SUV coming out of the dark, the squeal of tires on asphalt as it sped up, the roar of the engine as it headed directly for them, the scream coming from her own mouth, a warning for Viv. The slip of the fabric of Viv's sleeve as it slid from under her fingers when she leapt back, trying to pull her friend with her. The pain of slamming into the bus shelter, the air whooshing from her lungs, seeing stars as her head crashed back against the side wall.

The look of terror of Viv's face just before she was struck.

The limpness of her body as she flew through the air.

In the back of the Uber, Quinn covered her face with both hands, her fingernails biting deep into her hairline.

She'd hardly slept the night before, seeing the crash over and over in her head, interspersed with bouts of weeping. The kind of rehearsal that cemented the details in place, even though it was the last thing she wanted. She wished she could let it go, but this was out of her control. Her brain couldn't disengage from it, only letting her sleep for brief snatches, waking her frequently to find her cheeks wet again.

Finally, just after 5:00 AM, she'd given up trying to sleep and got out of bed. She'd showered, checked the calendar for her start time at the shop, took one look at the sketches in the corner, and turned away from them. She didn't have the heart to keep trying. The tragedy of Jack DeWitt was overshadowed by the loss of Viv.

For now, anyway. Maybe she'd find the strength in a day or two.

She wished she could remember Viv better. Whereas Viv's death seemed burned into her memory, the woman herself was not. And that felt like a loss. She should have memories to fall back on—conversations, the shared experience of bus rides home, moments she shared in sessions—

but it was a blank. *She* was a blank. Maybe, if she was really lucky, it might come back someday. She'd known how to coax her memory in that direction for the murder; she could do it here, too.

She'd retrieved her sketchbook from her drafting table, purposely keeping her eyes off the sketches tacked to the wall, and, while morning TV shows had played in the background for company, she'd drawn Viv as best she could from memory. Not the terror she could remember so vividly, but the less clear moments from just before, imbuing the sketch with vivaciousness, with laughter and joy. Maybe if she did this enough, concentrated on this kind of rehearsal, *this* would be how she'd remember her friend.

She'd caught the bus to work that morning, standing room only, surrounded by people who chatted, or listened to music, or babies who fretted as her body swayed over every bump, her eyes watchful in case of any threat. But nothing notable stood out. No one watched her, or, really, even noticed her.

Work had kept her distracted as she and Jacinta started prepping for two Saturday wedding orders. It was too early to put together the bouquets, boutonnieres, aisle and altar arrangements, and corsages for the mothers and grandmothers, but they set aside the flowers in their own containers of water in the cold room so the work of arranging them the next day would go smoothly. Added to that, the casket spray and altar arrangements for the Herrera funeral that needed to be created for Jacinta to drop off at 1:00 PM, as well as the usual walk-in purchases, and it was a busy day. It was exactly what she needed.

But now, in the Uber on the way home, she had nothing to occupy her mind, so last night came flooding back again.

Next time you feel sorry for yourself because your memories don't stay, try to remember the fresh hell of this memory never going away.

She concentrated on looking around her for distraction as they left the Gaslamp and headed east on Market Street. Just to be sure she wasn't being followed, she did a quick glance behind her. Market Street was two lanes in each direction, but the right lane was partly filled with metered parking, so it was slow going in mostly single file for those moving straight through, waiting at almost every light, and then proceeding.

But it gave her time to check out the traffic behind her. White Hyundai sedan, red hatchback, black pickup, with a silver sedan in behind. Nothing that gave her a bad vibe.

No black SUV with a shattered windshield.

Calm down. You're already wound tight enough without convincing yourself someone is following you. And that vehicle won't be on the road until it looks like brand new. Whoever did that won't advertise it.

Into the Sherman Heights neighborhood, the driver took the right-hand turn onto 21st Street. There was still only one lane in each direction, but the traffic instantly quieted somewhat. Another look behind her showed her a navy Subaru SUV, a black pickup, and a silver sedan. They'd lost some of the traffic, but others were following the same route in an attempt to get out of heavy downtown traffic.

Her phone signaled and she pulled it out to find a text from Reyes. **Did you get that Uber?**

Yes.

Still at headquarters. Made some breakthroughs today on the case. Let me know when you're home and safely locked in.

Will do.

She slid her phone away as they made the turn onto Commercial and back into steadier main thoroughfare traffic. For a while she just watched the world go by. Then came the turn onto Oceanview Boulevard as they made their way through Logan Heights and headed for Mountain View. Headed for home.

A quick look behind—charcoal Toyota sedan, white hatchback . . . black pickup.

Her heart started to race. Was that the same pickup truck who'd been with them all the way since Fourth?

Black, white, and silver seem to be the base colors these days. Black pickups could be a dime a dozen.

Still, her nerves pushed her to take a better look. But she didn't want to look obvious doing it, so she pulled out her phone, opened the camera app, and then switched it to the front-facing lens. Positioning the phone so the camera shot over her shoulder and out the rear window, she waited, her eyes on the screen. Glancing forward a few times, she realized she had the attention of the driver of the car, who watched her repeatedly in the rearview mirror, but didn't comment.

Quinn's chance came when the car between them turned right onto 30th Street, and for a moment they were only a few car lengths apart with nothing between them. She shot several photos and then the pickup fell back, putting more room between them. Dropping the phone into her lap, she blew up the first photo, the one taken when the pickup was closest, before it started to coast to slow, she surmised, based on how smoothly it lost ground behind them.

It was a Ford, not too big, so it didn't stand out as being out of place on city streets, but that didn't tell her much, because she didn't know trucks. Someone else might be able to ballpark the model from the front grille, but she wasn't one of them. The front window was tinted, Quinn suspected illegally, and the occupant—occupants?—were obscured.

"Everything okay?"

Quinn's gaze rose to meet the driver's eyes in the rearview mirror. She pasted on a smile she didn't feel. "All good, thanks."

"Have you home soon."

"Thank you."

It was another seven or eight minutes home, and she took occasional photos over her shoulder. Several cars were between them, and the truck fell farther and farther behind. Then it disappeared. Oceanview at this location was a straight run to her house, so there was no curve to see if it was hiding behind the white cube van about five cars back, but for the first time in ten minutes, she relaxed slightly.

Was she getting paranoid? It could easily have been someone on their way home who'd cut left or right at one of the many side streets. Oceanview was a common artery between downtown, I-5 S, CA-15, and I-805 S. It was entirely reasonable for someone to be on the same route for a good part of the journey.

Minutes later, they pulled up in front of her building. After thanking the driver, Quinn slid out of the car, walked up the front walk, then took the stairs at a jog, digging in her bag for her keys. Reaching her front door, she flipped them over in her hand, searching for the correct key, but she fumbled them, and they fell to the balcony. Rolling her eyes at her clumsiness, she bent to retrieve them. As she straightened, keys in hand, she glanced back at the street.

A black pickup truck with darkly tinted side windows cruised by slowly.

Quinn nearly dropped the keys again from fingers gone numb with shock, but she clutched them tight at the last moment. She opened the door, stepped in, and slammed it shut behind her, then locked the handle and slid the deadbolt home.

She stood there, panting, her heart rapping a staccato

beat against her breastbone. Had she been followed home? Could someone have trailed her all the way from Gaslamp Blooms? If so, they'd spotted her when she'd dropped her keys, to the extent they'd know which unit she lived in.

Once again, she had no proof she was followed, only her intuition, and the swamping wave of fear that put her on alert.

Screw paranoia—she'd take the chance she was crying wolf. She pulled out her phone and bypassed a text to call Reyes directly. She didn't even give Reyes time for a salutation. "It's Quinn, I may have a problem."

"What problem?" Reyes's voice was sharp. "You're at home?"

"Yes. But I may have been followed." She quickly outlined her concerns. "I'm going to text you a picture of the vehicle in question. Keep in mind, I may be blowing this out of proportion."

"Or you may not be. Stay locked in. I'll try to get a patrol car there first, but there's a mass incident in Balboa Park and most available units are already there and occupied. Still, help is coming. If you're scared, grab whatever defensive weapon you have, even if it's only a carving knife. I'm on my way." The line went dead.

Quinn sent the photo of the truck with the clearest image of the front license plate.

Grab whatever defensive weapon you have, even if it's only a carving knife.

She didn't own a gun, but she had kitchen knives. And she might only have a few minutes, less time than it would take for Reyes or a patrol officer to get here—with lights and sirens and taking I-5 S, Reyes would easily still be six or seven minutes. She might not have that long.

What to do?

Running to the kitchen, she pulled out her only truly big knife—a butcher knife—and then scanned the space, strategically considering the exits. California bylaws said only one entrance was required for a unit with fewer than ten occupants, so while there was a front door, there was no back door to the unit. The windows on either side of her front door led out to the balcony, but that was a no-go if an intruder was coming in that way. Which left the rear-facing window in the bedroom. They were two stories up, but there was a shed on the back wall between her unit and the next, so if she was careful about jumping out, she could land on the shed roof—hopefully it would take the impact and her weight without collapsing—and then jump to the ground and run.

Should she try to get away now? The problem was, she didn't know how many were coming—she could run out the front or jump out the back, right into the arms of someone approaching or scoping out the building. They might be checking out the back of the building to see if she could get away, but would find a two-story drop that, even with the shed, you'd only attempt if you were desperate. If they were coming up the front steps, they'd have to pick the locks to get in, but they had a few aspects in their favor there. She'd locked the handle and the deadbolt, but they were run-of-the-mill, hardware store locks. Anyone with a set of lockpicks and some underworld knowledge would likely handle them in under a minute or two. And the fact that the building's unit entrances ran along the side, facing the solid wall of the adjacent building, meant they could do their job unobstructed unless someone looked at them directly from the street—in which case they'd likely just look like they were struggling to get their key in the lock—or unless someone exited one of the other two units on this level and saw them. That would be a matter of bad timing for them, and good luck for her. She wasn't sure that kind of luck was on her side.

Get the screen out of the bedroom window in case you need to get out fast.

Taking the time to draw the drapes in the front of the apartment—it didn't block all of the evening light, but it did make it considerably gloomier—she ran back to her bedroom. Setting the knife on her dresser, she made quick work of removing the window screen, then sliding it into the narrow gap behind the dresser so as not to telegraph an escape route. She left the window open so it was a clear path for an escape where seconds could save her life, hoping an intruder wouldn't realize the screen wasn't in place. There was a slight risk someone from below would try to scale the wall and enter that way, but there was no way to do it quietly, and would allow her to escape through her own front door.

Unless there was two of them.

She couldn't think about that right now. That way led to terrified immobility.

Turning back to the bedroom, she scanned the space, looking for any other potential weapons. Her gaze landed on the combination linen and storage closet across the hall, and it came to her—her palette knives. She had a set of palette knives for her oil painting in various shapes— oval, triangular, flared, trapezoid, rectangular. But it was the sharp, pointed knives of various sizes she was thinking of, the ones she used to scrape off excess paint or when she wanted a truly clean line. They weren't as sturdy as she'd like, but she needed a secondary option and they'd be better than nothing.

She strode to the closet, yanked it open, and was reaching for her knife case when her gaze fell on her oil paints, and then dropped below to the floor, where she kept a box of empty oil paint tubes and cans until they could be taken away for proper hazardous waste disposal.

And realized she had a much better tool in her arsenal.

She had all the makings of an incendiary device . . . so reactive it was essentially an explosive. It wouldn't be a big explosive—which was fine as she didn't want to lose her home, just buy time for an escape—but it would be big enough to damage anyone close to it.

Dropping to her knees, she pawed through the box, pushing tubes out of her way and sorting through the cans. Some projects only needed limited amounts of paint, but for a larger project, she sometimes bought small cans of paint to make sure there was no deviation of color between containers.

She'd bought a small can of silver paint to mix with various shades of blues and grays to give the background of her peony painting a slightly metallic shimmer. She'd used all the silver paint during that process. Now if she could only find the empty can . . .

"There you are." She pulled an eight-ounce can of silver oil paint from the box. Grabbing the box of palette knives and picking a short, sturdy knife, she pried off the lid and stared down into dried silver paint on every surface.

Bingo.

All oil paints were considered hazardous. Linseed oil was the oil of choice in most fine art oil paints, and was a natural oil used for cooking and consumption. However, it was the compounds mixed with the oil that gave the paints their vibrant hues that were the toxic components, many of them heavy metals requiring specific disposal. And in the case of silver paint, it was the aluminum powder mixed with the linseed oil that gave it that metallic shine.

Dried aluminum powder was explosive. At the very least, it was highly reactive and extremely flammable if quantities were small. As well, any oil residue left in the paint would only make it more flammable.

She was going to set a booby trap. If a male assailant came through her door, her chances of overpowering him likely approached zero. She needed to get the drop on him, and the element of surprise was the only thing that would allow her that advantage.

She could do this, but she needed to work fast.

She grabbed the can of silver paint and a rake-shaped palette knife. Opening her bedroom door wide, she used the tines of the palette knife to shave off thin flakes of dried silver paint from the walls of the can, scraping up and down as quickly as she could, dumping the shavings onto the carpet in the path of the door so the door could be open about a foot while the pile would remain hidden right behind it. When she considered the can clean, she went to work on the lid, adding to the pile and spreading it a little wider to increase her bull's-eye. The last thing she needed was matches, and she ran into the bathroom where a box of wooden matches sat beside the trio of candles on the short windowsill that she often lit when she used to treat herself to a glass of wine, a good book, and a long soak in the tub. She closed the door behind her, giving the intruder another location to search to slow them down.

She retreated to the bedroom and partially closed the door, the bottom of the door narrowly clearing the pile of aluminum shavings to swing shut, leaving it open about six inches. Grabbing the butcher knife, she crouched down behind the side of the tall dresser. Anyone coming in would presume that with the door closed that far, someone was likely hiding behind it and might not be looking the other direction. All she needed to do was light and toss a match into the pile; the shavings would react with the heat and oxygen in the air and instantaneously turn into a fireball, burning anyone nearby. She needed to make sure she was close enough to hit the target and not blow out the match throwing it from a distance, but far enough away that, in the second it would take her to pull back, she wasn't in danger of being caught in her own trap.

Her hands were shaking as she pulled out a match and arranged the matchbox so she could hold both it and the knife in her left hand with the striker of the matchbox facing out, as she held the match in her right hand. Then she held still, closing her eyes and listening.

All she could hear was her heart pounding in her own ears. No sirens, no intruder.

If this wasn't real, how many times could she pull this kind of stunt with Reyes before the detective wouldn't believe her anymore? Once? Twice? Reyes's trust and belief was a currency she simply couldn't afford to squander. As the seconds of silence ticked by, the heat of embarrassment built, shame at what was looking like an overreaction rising.

Her eyes flew open as, with a faint click, the front door opened, light flooding briefly down the hallway toward the bedroom before it closed again, leaving Quinn in the gloom.

If it was Reyes, she'd have called out for Quinn, let her know she'd arrived and Quinn had her protection. But the silence meant only one thing.

She was trapped in her apartment with an intruder.

CHAPTER 27

Quinn fought to keep her breathing quiet and steady, clamping down on her lungs' apparent need to saw air in and out as her pulse skyrocketed.

Any satisfaction that she wasn't paranoid was swamped by the terror of facing an unknown intruder alone. If it was the man from the alley, this was an act-first-don't-bother-with-questions kind of killer, who would end a human life as carelessly as if he was swatting a fly. There wouldn't be time to hold him off using conversation until Reyes got here. This was the kind of killer who got in, did the job, and got out. The only way to beat a man like this was to best him. If she couldn't, Reyes would find her body when she arrived.

Quinn *really* didn't want to die. She'd do what was necessary to survive.

The muscles in her thighs were burning from crouching behind the dresser, but she didn't dare drop to her knees. When the time came to move, when the intruder walked through the door, she needed to spring forward, then back. The only way to do that was if she was already on her feet.

She closed her eyes again, not being able to see down

the hallway and into the living room, using her ears to track the intruder instead. She heard footsteps moving through her space, and then heard the slightest rattle of curtain rings on the rod. She stiffened as she realized what was happening.

He'd found the sketches and had allowed in a little more light to see better.

If he was one of the faces on the wall, she was the walking dead. He'd kill her and take the sketches with him as he strolled away from her cooling corpse.

She was in greater danger than she'd anticipated. Truly a fight for her life.

She was ready for it. She had to be.

She silently adjusted her stance slightly, keeping her body behind the bulk of the dresser, but making sure she could see the top of the door move. She knew how far open the door would have to be to clear the paint shavings for the trap to be effective. With the bedroom window open and the curtains drawn back, evening light flowed in, washing the room in soft, golden glow. She'd have no trouble seeing the door move.

Ten feet down the hallway, the bathroom door gave a quiet squeak, and Quinn thanked her faulty brain for never remembering to oil the hinges.

Won't take him long. Nearly here. Be ready. She stared at the door, her body tense, ready to go.

The door swung open slowly and silently. Twelve inches, eighteen . . . she saw the top of a dark head.

And sprang.

It all happened at once as she leaped forward. She ran the wooden match over the strike plate and it burst into flame, then, with a flick of her wrist, she tossed it into the pile of paint shavings, stumbling backward even as the man turned on her, a black pistol in his gloved right hand, his dark eyes glinting with malice and intent. She had a brief flash of dark hair, sharply angled features, and the shadow of a goatee.

She had no doubt—it was the killer from the alley. And he'd just seen her sketches of him, so he knew she could identify him.

She had one chance. If she didn't get free of him in the next minute, chances of her surviving the night were miniscule.

With a whoosh, the pile of shavings caught fire, then flashed brilliantly bright a millisecond later, flames shooting high, along and inside the man's pant leg. Knowing what was coming, Quinn instinctively threw up her arm to shield her face from the writhing flames, flare of searing white light, and wave of burning heat that rolled over her. The man screamed in agony, and, now off balance, lurched farther into the room.

Quinn moved again, transferring the knife to her right hand, dropping the matches on the floor. Clenching her fist around the handle, she didn't allow herself to think or measure the consequences when the only relevant issue was survival, and drove the butcher knife into his side while he was still half-blind. The knife stabbed deep, but met resistance halfway in. Gritting her teeth and bearing down, Quinn gave it everything she had. With a groan from deep in her chest, the knife slid home as the man screamed and a wet warmth flowed over her fingers. The explosion of a single shot boomed through the room, but the fiery agony Quinn expected as he took her life never struck.

Not wanting to wait around to see the results of her attack or if the man could aim better a second time, Quinn yanked the knife free, turned, and bolted for the open window, throwing first one leg, then the second over the sill. She only took the time to throw the knife to the ground below so she wouldn't impale herself on the way down, and pushed off, leaping in the direction of the shed off to her left and about eight or nine feet below. She hit with both feet, but then started to slide, scrabbling with both hands at the rusted roof, but she couldn't catch an edge. It slowed her speed, but she still slid off to land on her back in the dirt behind the house.

For a moment she lay there, wheezing, the wind partly knocked out of her, her ears still ringing from the gunshot, but then she rolled over, struggled to her hands and knees, staggered to her feet, grabbed the bloody knife, and stumbled toward the front of the house.

She broke from behind the house just as Reyes was sprinting up the front steps. "Detective . . ." she wheezed. Then stopped and pulled in as big a breath as she could manage. "Detective!"

Reyes stopped at the bottom of the stairs. "Quinn!" She redirected. "Are you okay?" She eyed the knife. "What happened?"

"Man . . . inside." Quinn had to stop to pull in a breath. "Gun . . . stabbed him in my bedroom, jumped out the window. There may be . . . fire. Extinguisher under kitchen . . . sink."

Reyes pulled her weapon and looked past Quinn to where a patrol officer was running up the front walk. "Get her in your vehicle and keep her safe. Call in more backup and send them in as soon as they arrive. Bag the knife as evidence." Reyes turned and ran up the stairs, staying low at the top of the stairs so she was under the window. She tested the door, found it was unlocked, threw it open, and went in low, leading with her firearm. "SDPD! Get on the ground!"

"Come on, ma'am." The officer grabbed Quinn's arm and jogged her down to the street where a patrol car blocked traffic behind Reyes's car—she hadn't taken the time for a parking spot; she'd just double-parked and left the car right there. "Hang on a moment, ma'am." He opened the front door of the car and came out with a large plastic evidence bag. "Put it in carefully, please."

Quinn slowly lowered the knife into the bag, then retracted her hand.

"Thank you." The officer opened the back door of the cruiser. "Get in, please. I'm going to close you in for your protection until we know what's going on."

Still breathless, Quinn nodded her assent and slid into the back seat as he held the door open for her. Then he slammed it closed, intercepted more officers arriving, and sent them into her apartment while he stood guard outside the cruiser.

Exhausted, Quinn tipped her head back to stare at the ceiling and spent the next few minutes getting her breath back. Not just from the fall, but from the moment the intruder had stepped into her home, she hadn't truly been able to catch her breath. Now she could.

As her heart slowed and her breath stabilized, she became cognizant of other things—the wail of incoming sirens, the footfalls of more officers running inside, the rattle of a gurney as it bumped up the front walk, the eyes of onlookers on the street and farther down the balcony. Then she noticed the stickiness of her right hand. Tipping her head up, she gazed in horror at the blood splattered over the backs of her fingers and oozing onto her palm.

Had she killed him? She hadn't cared where she'd sunk the blade, she just needed to give herself time to get away before he put a bullet in her brain. She had literal blood on her hands . . . did she have his life as well?

Reyes opened the door at that moment and took in Quinn's hand and expression. As Quinn turned horrified eyes up to hers, Reyes cut off the question she knew was coming. "He's alive."

Quinn sagged back in relief. "Thank God."

"You would have been within your rights had you killed him. You were defending yourself against an armed attacker who illegally entered your home with a deadly weapon." She stepped back a pace. "Come on out here. Just keep that hand free. We'll need to photograph it and sample the blood, then you can clean up."

"Can I go back in?"

"Not tonight. I can pull out a few things for you, but you need to stay somewhere else while the crime scene techs come in. Is there someone you can stay with tonight?"

"I can call Jacinta. Actually, if I don't call her, I think she'd be hurt. She'll be more than happy to take me in tonight."

"Good. She seemed like a nice lady when I met her."

"She's been my substitute mom since my assault. I'll call her in a bit. What happened inside?"

"You didn't leave me much to do." Reyes's smile softened her words. "I'm glad I'd been here before, because it was an advantage to know the layout of the place, so I could clear it quickly. When I got to your bedroom, he was attempting to bleed out on your carpet, which, by the way, was burning from whatever it was you did in there. I got the fire out before it caught the bedding, so thanks for the tip about the extinguisher. But our perp has some pretty severe burns. You got him but good, especially considering the scorching up the bedroom door. How did you manage it all?"

"Kitchen knife, like you suggested. And I made a little homemade incendiary device using dried silver paint, which is a mixture of linseed oil and aluminum powder. *Extremely* flammable, would have been truly explosive if I'd had more dried paint on hand. I didn't have much, but apparently it was enough."

"I'll say. He's going to have some gnarly scarring while

he's serving his time. But, for now, paramedics are getting him stabilized and have already started an IV to keep his volume up after that kind of blood loss. He's going to the hospital under police guard and will stay that way. He's going away, Quinn. He won't be able to get to you again."

"He's the one who killed Mr. DeWitt. As soon as I saw him, I knew his face matched my sketches."

"To an almost scary degree. He won't be up to it tonight, but I'll interview him tomorrow and we'll figure out what's going on. How he found you, and how he's connected to David Soto. I know he is; I just haven't connected those last few dots."

Quinn stared at her, confused. "David Soto. You mean the man running for mayor?"

"That's the one. You and I have some catching up to do. But not tonight. Tonight, I want you to call Jacinta, then we'll get you cleaned up. After that, I want you to go home with her and get a good night's sleep. Be proud of yourself, Quinn. You worked hard to figure this out, and you managed a perilous situation using your wits and courage. And you came out the other side."

As Reyes grinned and rubbed a hand up and down Quinn's back, Quinn felt the enormous weight that had essentially become a part of her fall from her shoulders. Immensely lighter, she grinned back for the first time that night.

She'd done it.

There would be justice for Jack DeWitt after all.

CHAPTER 28

"You're sure we're clear to go in?" Will's head bobbed as he peered in through the gap between the drawn curtains adjacent to her drafting table.

"Nura said we're clear to enter."

"It's Nura now?"

Quinn chuckled. "I guess I *Detective Reyes*ed her once too often and she told me to call her by her first name, especially now the case is over. She's been great. She got me settled with Jacinta on Thursday night, and then made sure the crime techs wrapped up early enough yesterday that the trauma scene waste management practitioner—"

"The what?"

"That's the official term for the person or team who come in to clean up biohazardous waste following a death or serious injury. It's California law—you have to have a professional licensed in body fluid containment come in to take care of it."

"I had no idea."

"Me neither, let me assure you. They came in yesterday and did their thing, so now I'm free to come home." Quinn slid her key into her front door lock, but then paused and met his eyes. "Thank you again for coming with me this morning."

"You're very welcome."

"I appreciate you taking time out of your Saturday morning. Jacinta wanted to come with me, but one of us needed to open the shop and finish off the flowers for the Montgomery wedding this afternoon. I promised her I'd be in by one o'clock so she can drop them off in plenty of time for the four o'clock ceremony."

"Happy to do it. And this isn't something you should do on your own the first time. You want to claim the space back as yours, but considering what happened here . . ."

"Yeah. And I'm not going to let what happened here color my love of this place. It's home," she said simply. "Even if it's full of accommodations that now everyone and his cousin has seen."

"You're embarrassed by that."

"No one wants to look weak."

"No," Will agreed. "Maybe today's the day you take some of it down."

Quinn had just shot back the lock, but stopped to look up at him. "Take it down?"

"You told me the night I was here that a lot of the apartment hadn't changed from before the attack, but you labeled everything to make sure there were no slipups. Maybe it's time to take down the security blanket on the stuff you know, and the stuff you've learned because now you know what works for you. Maybe you'll never recover some of the memories, but you'll build new ones. And with those new ones, you won't need the same supports."

"You really think I can do it?"

"I think you've already shown both of us you can. But until you let yourself stop depending on the crutches you no longer need, you won't know you not only can walk, but you can run. You need to trust yourself. You may fall down a few times, but you'll dust yourself off and try again because that's who you are. And if you'll let me, I'd like to help."

Quinn could hear everything behind the simple statement. He was offering so much more than just an expert's knowledge of brain function and recovery. Her answering smile was shy. "I think I'd like that." She opened the door and stepped in, then went to the east-facing window in the living room and pulled the curtains wide, letting morning sun stream in. She turned around to study her space. "That's not as bad as I thought it would be."

Will pulled aside the curtains by the drafting table. "You said he was wearing gloves. They could have dusted the entire apartment and they'd only find you. Not him."

"And you, if prints last that long. And Nura from the night before. Nura said they wouldn't have to cover the scene the same way as an unattended death. With a witness to attest to what happened and a suspect wearing gloves and not leaving fingerprints behind, they didn't have to cover the whole apartment with fingerprint dust." She joined him at the drafting table, and paused to study the sketches. "He'd stopped here to look. I realized as I was hiding in the bedroom that if he saw these sketches, he'd only be more determined to kill me because it was clear I was able to identify him. Nura figures that, had he killed me, he'd have taken the sketches with him. He wouldn't have known she already had some of the sketches to take a run at facial recognition. Which they just started yesterday. She thinks it will be at least a few days until they have an answer."

"If they have his face in the database in the first place, or else they'll turn up nothing. But I agree, your intruder wouldn't have known about your memory challenges or about the process you were using to draw them out. All he'd know is you could identify him. And, for that, his plan was to get in, kill you, and get out, probably as quickly and quietly as possible, but he carried a gun as backup. And to get you to comply. He picked your front door lock, so from the outside, it didn't look like forced entry. I've heard these kinds of locks aren't much of a challenge for an experienced lockpick with the right tools. All he probably needed was about thirty seconds of no one watching to get in." Will turned and looked down the hallway. "He went after you down there?"

"Yeah. Let's go see how much carpet I have to replace."

"You have to replace it?"

"Well, no, my landlord. He's already been in touch. The charges from all of this—the biohazard remediator, several necessary repairs—will be covered by his property insurance. I won't have to cover it."

"That's good news, at least."

She led him down the hallway, past the open door of the bathroom and to the door of the bedroom. "It is, because even though they—amazingly—got the blood out, the carpet is still going to need to be replaced because my little incendiary device burned a massive hole in it. Right down to the subfloor, which may also need repairing."

"Going to need a new bedroom door, too." Will studied the pattern of scorching up the wooden panel. "That is some impressive height you got out of that silver paint. He must have been concerned about the family jewels."

"It's very reactive, which is why artists know to take care around it and to dispose of the empty containers properly. And I'd be fine with him being a Darwin Award winner if torching the family jewels knocked him out of the gene pool."

Will's bark of laughter filled the room, but then died as his gaze settled on the single hole in the ceiling. "That's the bullet hole?"

"Yes. I didn't know what he'd shot, I just knew it wasn't me and that was enough in that moment. That's going to have to be fixed, too."

Will scanned the rest of the room, his gaze lingering on the spot where she'd described hiding, waiting to launch her counterattack in an effort to save her own life. "Considering how this could have gone down, him in the hospital and these few repairs seems like small potatoes compared to what it could have been."

"That's how I look at it, too." A trio of knocks sounded at the front door. "That's probably Nura."

They returned to the living room, where Quinn checked the peephole and opened the door for Reyes. "Good morning."

"It is a good morning." Reyes came in with a folded newspaper under her arm. "Following a good day yesterday. Have you seen the news? Read a paper?"

Will shook his head, and Quinn said, "I didn't really want to see if I was making headlines."

"You did, but you kind of ended up being a footnote. I bought this on my way here because I like to keep souvenirs from the cases that go particularly well. The ones where you know you made a difference. This is what you did." She unfolded the paper and handed it to Quinn.

Quinn looked down at the Saturday copy of the *San Diego Union-Tribune* and its screaming headline: SOTO ARRESTED ON CONSPIRACY TO COMMIT MURDER and then in smaller print underneath it: DROPS OUT OF MAYORAL RACE.

"Soto was behind it all?" Will asked, stunned. "Where did that come from?"

"Let me lay it out for you. It's quite a story." Reyes pointed to the living room. "Can we sit?"

"Absolutely." Quinn led the way, sitting on the couch, Will taking the spot beside her and Reyes sitting in the chair. She pushed the African violet to one side of the coffee table to make room for the paper.

"You named your plant Paula?"

Quinn looked up in confusion, then followed Reyes's gaze to the purple flowers and its bright label. "Yes. According to my notes, I bought her at the garden center when I was snooping around."

Reyes shook her head, but a smile curved her lips. "A souvenir of an adventure you'll hopefully never have again."

"Amen to that." Quinn laid the paper face up on the coffee table to stare at it in wonder. The picture under the bold headline showed Reyes walking a handcuffed Soto out of his house. "How did the press know this was going down to catch it in progress?"

"Something may have been leaked to the *Union-Tribune*," Reyes said, her gaze innocently fixed on the ceiling before dropping down to Quinn and Will. "They lost one of their own in this scheme. It seemed fitting to me they got the scoop on it. Anyway, I had a busy day yesterday, as you can see. I spent a good part of the afternoon at UC San Diego Medical Center, the trauma center where they took Curt Probst—the gentlemen you helped put there on Thursday night. By that point, he was out of surgery. While in some pain because I asked the medical staff not to let him get so drugged he couldn't be interviewed, he was more than ready to talk. He knows his ship is going down and he's determined to take the captain with him. Especially when I could assure him the deputy district attorney was willing to make a deal with him because he has a much bigger target to take down."

"Soto. His boss."

"Right. It turned out that while Jack DeWitt was doing the usual, run-of-the-mill backgrounds on all the mayoral candidates as part of his beat as the *Union-Tribune* political reporter, he stumbled on something unexpected. And then kept investigating. It appears David Soto, as we know him now, was known in his youth as Alfred Williams."

"He changed his name?" Will asked.

"Partly, yes. His full name was Alfred David Williams, and after he left Chicago to come to Stanford for law, he started going by David Williams. He officially changed his name when he married Jaclyn Soto. Decided her last name had more clout than his. He wasn't wrong."

"Her last name carried the air of wealth and the notoriety of Darren Soto, assuming Jaclyn is related to Darren."

"His daughter. David used that air of wealth and notoriety to work his way up. The few people I talked to yesterday confirmed what I suspected—David has his eye on the governor's mansion or the White House, or both, depending on how things went. The problem was, while the name change helped, David had a secret. From all the way back in Chicago when he was Alf Williams."

"DeWitt discovered the secret?"

"Soto's not talking, but Probst says yes, which is why he had to die. We don't have proof of that, because so much of DeWitt's research was on his phone and we're still waiting for access to any data he backed up from his phone to the cloud. Probst confirmed DeWitt had his phone on him when he was killed, and they smashed it and then dropped it into the ocean when they took DeWitt's body out in Probst's boat. On Soto's orders."

"What does Soto have on Probst to force him to do all of this?"

"Just large amounts of cash. Mr. Probst is a businessman."

"*Was* a businessman," Will interjected.

"Was. Correct, his business days are over. We'll never know what was on the phone if that data wasn't ever backed up to the cloud. It was secured, not by biometrics, but by a password they couldn't brute-force and couldn't get out of a dead man, so they had to trust DeWitt didn't have backups on the *Union-Tribune* server or any personal cloud backups. They were wrong on both accounts, by the way. Anyway, they crushed it and tossed it where no one would recover it, just to be safe. They thought if they snipped this string, they'd be home free."

"That's insane thinking," Will said. "If one reporter could uncover something, another could. And, if Soto decided to reach for the gold ring, anyone running for president would be under the biggest magnifying glass possible."

"True. But with the amount of money Soto would have at his disposal by then, assuming the death of his father-in-law and his wife inheriting an absolute fortune, he thought he'd be able to bury it for good. Whether that's actually true or not is a different story. Anyway, it seems when Alf Williams was a young, rich teenager, he got an underage girl named Cassie Hopkins drunk and then raped her. Cassie had the courage to report it, something he didn't think would happen, but he denied the incident occurred. And had a rock-solid alibi for where he was at the time of the assault. The problem is the buddy who gave him the alibi was lying."

"Did they have a way to prove that?"

"That I don't know. If DeWitt knew information to definitively prove it, it died with him. But even not having that piece of information, this was a scandal Soto couldn't afford to come out, because Cassie found out she was pregnant with his baby. Keep in mind that back then, in early 1987, it was just before genetic fingerprinting was available and years before PCR perfected the process, so a lot of it was based on blood types and something called HLA typing. It was *not* the exact science it is today. Cassie was pregnant, Williams denied being responsible, the science couldn't definitively prove it was Williams's baby, she was underage, and her parents wouldn't give consent for an abortion . . . so she killed herself."

Quinn gasped, the horror of such a loss stabbing deep. To be so young, sexually assaulted, carrying your rapist's baby, and no doubt with a rich family ready to humiliate and denigrate you to avoid any kind of blame. She probably felt she had few options available to her and none that she could live with. "She and the baby both died. What a tragedy."

"Absolutely. But the situation was handy as far as Williams was concerned, because now it would go away and no one else would try to pry apart his alibi. A few months later, he graduated high school, set out for Stanford as David Williams, met Jaclyn Soto, wooed and married her, and David Soto left Alf Williams behind forever."

"Until he decided to follow his ambitions and run for office," said Will.

"If he'd stayed under the radar, no one would have looked at him again. He could have lived as a very rich man people respected. Now he's going to jail for conspiracy to commit murder. Oh, and since Illinois has no statute of limitation on rape, he's also looking at a criminal sexual assault charge there, which could net him up to fifteen years in jail, so Cassie will get her shot at justice, as well. Though, I admit it's too little, too late in the eyes of her family. It may not stick due to lack of evidence, but I have Taylor Richards in my sights. Everything rested on the alibi he gave Williams. I'm going to work with the Chicago Police Department, including the retired detective who originally had the case, and we're going to go after Richards with everything we have. He may decide that if we're determined to go into every corner of his life, past and present, it may just be easier for him to admit he lied thirty-plus years ago. Sadly, Soto's aggravated assault charge would have lapsed years ago, but we'll take what we can get. If Soto gets there at all, I guess, as conspiracy to commit murder can carry a life sentence."

"Surely, his high-priced lawyers will get him out of that." Disgust was heavy in Will's tone.

"They'll try. Whether they succeed remains to be seen. DeWitt was onto something so definitive it got him killed. I'm hopeful that once we have his cloud backup data, it'll be enough to put the final nail in Soto's legal coffin. If so, with the combined charges between California and Illinois, if he gets out, he'll be an old man."

"What about Probst?"

"I assume you mean Curt."

"Could I mean anyone else?"

"Well, there's his cousin, Guy Probst." Reyes turned to Quinn. "That's who you saw at the garden center standing beside the van and who you later sketched. Which reminds me, I need more of those sketches for evidence." Reyes rose and walked to them. "I only took the ones enlarged enough to try for facial recognition last time."

Quinn joined her. "Take them all, if you want them."

"I don't need them all, just the ones which are clearly identifiable as our perps. And maybe a few long shots to illustrate the process."

"Help yourself."

Reyes picked through the sketches, taking the ones she thought were useful, then stood back and looked at the remainders. "What do you want to do with the rest of them?"

"Get rid of them. They've served their purpose, and I'd really rather never see them again." Quinn started to pull them off the walls, continuing until nothing was left but a few smudges of tape adhesive and builder's beige paint. She neatly lined up the sheets of paper, dropped them into the paper recycling can she kept beside her drafting table, and turned her back on them to walk back to Will.

Reyes smiled her approval as she sat down again. "So, back to the van at the garden center. Yes, that was the van they used the night of the murder. Curt killed DeWitt, but Guy drove the van. Curt needed someone he trusted to help him with the body, so Guy got a cut of the fee for his part in the hit."

"Curt sold his cousin down the river?" Quinn asked.

"No, your quick thinking did that. The picture you snapped of the truck following your Uber, the license plate led us to Guy. Let me back up a bit, back to the night of DeWitt's murder. You were right, Curt Probst was concerned someone had witnessed the murder in the alley. In fact, he thought he might have seen someone in the shadows, so he and his cousin started watching the block, looking to see if anyone stood out. They suspected it had to be an employee of one of the stores, so they went into the shops and restaurants, and watched from the street, but no one popped out."

"They came into Gaslamp Blooms?"

"Guy did. In fact, you helped him buy a mixed bouquet for his 'mother.'"

"I don't remember that."

"You wouldn't," Will stated. "One visit only? It wouldn't stay with you."

"But then you went to the greenhouse, which happens to be where Guy works in their receiving department. Bringing in stock, making deliveries in the van."

"He had access to the van when they needed it."

"All he had to do was remove the magnetic sign on the outside and stash it inside to make the van anonymous. Problem was, Quinn got a look at part of the logo the night of the murder, which led her to the greenhouse. You saw Guy there, and he recognized you from the flower shop. He told Curt, and Curt followed you home on the bus that day. But you bailed, and headed for a police station, so he let you go and never found out where you lived. However, on Thursday, Curt and Guy double-teamed with

Curt watching the shop from the street and Guy a block away in his truck. You caught an Uber, Curt had Guy pick him up, and they tailed you. You snapped a photo of the truck the one time it got close to you, and that gave us Guy. Guy dropped Curt off, Curt doubled back to the unit he'd seen you go into, and you know the rest from there."

"Handy having Guy as his driver all the time," Will said.

"Well, there was a reason for it the second time." Reyes met Quinn's eyes. "Curt's SUV was in the shop. Busted front fender, crumpled hood, smashed windshield."

"Viv," Quinn breathed.

"Yes. We have him on first-degree murder there as well. The killing was deliberate and premeditated, even if, in the end, the wrong woman died." Reyes relaxed into her chair and stared at the photo on the front of the newspaper. "That's everything we know for now. Once we have De-Witt's cloud backups, I'm hopeful we'll find out more details, but the bones of what happened are there."

"And they seem solid," Will said.

"I think so. Both Probst cousins and Soto will go away for a long time." She grasped Quinn's hand and gave it a squeeze. "You won't ever have to worry about them again."

Quinn squeezed back, the relief so all-encompassing she couldn't speak.

Reyes seemed to understand and let go of her hand to pick up the paper, folding it inward so Soto no longer looked out at them, and then she tucked the sketches inside, as well. "Next thing I need to update you on. I leaned on the crime lab nerds and had the DNA from the samples found under your fingernails after your assault run against the sample from the man you identified from your dream." Her grin was a mile wide. "They're a match. You did it, Quinn. You found the man who attacked you. And now he'll have that charge added to his rap sheet. Let me assure you, you won't have to worry about him anymore either. He won't be getting out for a long, long time."

Quinn wasn't sure how to handle the tangled feelings that rose to clog her throat and moisten her eyes—elation, validation, satisfaction, and, overwhelmingly, relief. "I don't know how to thank you." Her voice was thick with emotion.

"You don't need to thank me. You did all the hard work. But I'm not done yet. I have one last piece of fabulous news." She slid a hand into the pocket of her pants and pulled out a small plastic evidence bag. "I believe this belongs to you." She extended the bag to Quinn, the item inside it still hidden under her curled fingers.

Confused, Quinn held out her palm and Reyes dropped the bag into it.

Quinn gasped in shock at the sight of a gold ring lying under the plastic. "Is that my mother's ring?"

Nura sat back, crossing her ankle over her opposite knee, her relaxed posture clearly conveying how much she was enjoying herself. "It sure is. We can thank Detective Ketty in the Robbery Unit. She took the pictures you sent me and tracked it down. It was in a pawn shop down on Imperial. Lucky for us the guy priced it so high it never sold. Unlucky for him, of course, because he's now out a lovely sapphire ring."

Quinn opened the bag and tipped the ring out onto her palm. Then she slid it onto the ring finger on her right hand, cradling it in her left hand as she gazed down at the long-lost piece of jewelry. "I love this ring. I was devastated when I realized it was gone, that one of the last pieces of my mother was lost. I wrote about it in my notebook. I was sure I'd never see it again."

Will slipped his hand under hers, angling the ring toward him, taking in the oval center sapphire surrounded by a trio of smaller diamonds on both sides. "It's lovely. Is this the ring you lost in the attack?"

"Yes. Nura said she'd try to track it down. And she did." The ring started to waver before Quinn's eyes as tears blinded her, and she hurriedly wiped at the dampness that threatened to overflow. "Now I really don't know how to thank you."

"And again, you don't. You've given me something, and that's more than enough."

"What could I have given you? Besides a ton of work and a bunch of phone calls in the middle of the night that interrupted your sleep."

"You reminded me why I got into police work. Sometimes, crimes are never solved and it's hard knowing you put your heart and soul into something for absolutely nothing, and that all too often, crime does pay. But sometimes, if you're lucky, the stars align, a case gets solved, some scumbags who really deserve it go to jail, and the arc of the moral universe continues to bend toward justice. That's why I became a cop. Thank you for the reminder." Reyes slapped her hands down on her thighs. "Now, enough of this serious stuff. Does anyone want to get out of here and grab a coffee?" Reyes asked. "Fancy coffee is a weakness for me. I could really go for a caffè mocha right about now. It's been a hell of a week."

"How do you feel about small-batch gourmet donuts?" Will winked at Quinn. "We know just the place. And they do a killer mocha. My treat."

"I'm not going to say no to that. Quinn?"

"I'm in. Let me grab my bag."

As she grasped the door handle to pull it shut behind them, Quinn's gaze fell on the garbage can beside her drafting table, where she could just see the edges of the pages holding sketches she never wanted to look at again. Then her gaze slid up the empty walls that now struck her as more of a blank canvas.

She'd sketch some new character studies, put up new faces to cleanse the space. Maybe she'd draw the warriors she already knew—the men and women at Will's TBI sessions who fought every day to get back the lives they'd lost, or to create satisfying new ones.

She'd start with the sketch she'd already completed of Viv. She'd be the first on her new wall of heroes and would forever hold a place of honor there.

Turning away from the discarded sketches and all they represented—violence, fear, loss, and chaos—she firmly closed the door, locked it, and followed Will and Reyes down the steps.

That was the past.

A new chapter started now.

ACKNOWLEDGMENTS

An author's name may be highlighted on the cover of a book, but producing a novel is never a one-person job. I'm so very grateful for all the smart, talented people who contributed to making *Echoes of Memory* the book it is today:

Shane Vandevalk for his ongoing creativity in title brainstorming. This one we came up with together, so, Shane, as far as I'm concerned, that's a point for both of us! Thank you for always being so enthusiastic in your willingness to contribute to all my books in so many different ways.

Jessica Newton, Rick Newton, and Sharon Taylor, for all your work on this manuscript, right from the very beginning. Your comments at the proposal stage helped produce a successful package, and then your critical analysis of the full manuscript helped shape the final product. So many thanks for always being willing to share your time and talents on each project.

My agent, Nicole Resciniti, for all the extra help in dealing with recent contract shenanigans, and, as always, for going the extra mile so that every project finds a home. As well, thanks to the Seymour Agency team of Marisa Cleveland and Lesley Sabga for communications and promotion support.

My editor, James Abbate, for having the faith to take on the Driscoll standalones, a new angle on the brand, as well as for his assistance in managing a very busy writing and publishing schedule. Your flexibility and camaraderie are endlessly appreciated.

Louis Malcangi and the Kensington art department for creating such an amazing cover. They took a challenging concept and embodied it in a really eye-catching and intriguing image that not only captured the main theme of the novel, but also subtly worked in aspects of Quinn's characteristics.

Lauren Jernigan, for stepping outside her official role at Kensington to share her personal experience with individuals suffering from traumatic brain injury. It was gratifying to hear that aspect of the book was on point. Thank you for sharing your real-world take on it.

The greater Kensington team, including Jesse Cruz, Larissa Ackerman, Lauren Jernigan, Robin Cook, Susanna Gruninger, Vida Engstrand, Kait Johnson, Alexandra Nicolajsen, Kristin McLaughlin, and Sarah Beck. It's always a pleasure to work with all of you and to know that you're working behind the scenes to support your authors in every way possible.

—Jen J. Danna, writing as Sara Driscoll